Lindworm

Jenny Prater

Lindworm

ISBN 978-1-952185-18-2
Printed in the United States of America
Published by Wax Heart Press, 2025
First published in 2021
www.waxheartpress.com

For my grandparents,
Lynn and Lowell Nystrom.

This story began with afternoons spent reading fairy tales in your basement, and continued when you took me to Norway, and later when you sent me to Denmark. So many details of this story come from little things you've taught me, Christmas traditions and picture books and things I'll forever associate with you.

Table of Contents:

Author's Note:

It has been four years since I published *Lindworm*, eight since I shared an earlier draft on Patreon, and eleven since I first started writing it. This was my debut novel, my biggest project in university, and the culmination of so, so much work over so many years. It's based on the fairy tale that made me first start not just reading fairy tales, but critically analyzing their sources and the process of recording them. I learned so much from not just the story, but the research I had to do to make sense of it, and track down its poorly documented origins. And of course, it provided my username for countless websites.

I hope that my writing has improved in the last four years, and that it will continue to improve for many more. I hope that all of the books I have published and will publish after *Lindworm* are better than *Lindworm*. But even if they are, I suspect Lindworm will always be my favorite.

This special edition includes five short essays and seven deleted scenes of various length, as well as the same original translation of the original fairy tale included in the first edition. You may notice that this book is not much bigger than the previous version; it certainly doesn't look big enough to include sixty pages of bonus content. The reason for this is that I have updated my formatting to both look more professional and take up less space.

This project has meant a lot to me for a very long time. I'm so glad for it to have been my first published novel, and now my first hardcover/special edition, and I hope you'll enjoy reading it as much as I've enjoyed writing it.

Chapter One

"Thank you so much for thinking of me," Marit said, "but really I would rather not marry a monster."

Marit would not have thought herself the sort of person to talk back to kings, had she ever had cause to contemplate such matters. But then she never would have thought the king the sort of person to sacrifice a girl to a lindworm, and yet here she was, the third victim.

She was only seventeen, and this wedding was a death sentence.

Six months ago, Prince Harald had set out to find a bride, and had been stopped by a great serpent in the road. Since then, the serpent—the lindworm—had eaten two foreign princesses, both after a sham of a wedding. Both women had thought they were coming to marry Prince Harald.

Here, in the forest outside the capital city, rumors had flown. Rumors that they would shortly be at war with both kingdoms that had lost a princess, and rumors, more interesting to their small family with no members likely to be sent to the battlefield, of the lindworm, of why a man-eating dragon would be welcomed to the palace and fed. Rumors that said the lindworm was Prince Harald's brother, that the king humored it instead of killing it because the monster was family.

Marit didn't know how much truth there might be to such rumors. She didn't know how a queen could bear and birth a serpent, but she did know the world was full of strange, incomprehensible things.

The king stared at her, his men standing stiffly by. It had not, of course, been thoughtfulness that led him to her cottage in the woods. Marit knew this, and knew that the marriage was not optional, and that one could not speak to a king in this manner and expect to keep one's head. But when one has already been sentenced to death, such things as respect for royalty matter very little.

"It is not an offer," the king informed her when he found his voice. "It is a command, and you may choose to obey or not, but willing or unwilling, you will find yourself before a priest in my great hall one week from now."

One week, she thought. One week to live the rest of her life. She could run—could she run?

No, if the king was leaving her a few days to say her goodbyes, it was only because he knew she could not run. There would be guards posted. She would be caught and brought back. She would still end the week dead, and likely her father and sister, too, if the king suspected they had helped her. As they certainly would.

Her family—they were away from the house now, deeper into the woods, scavenging. There was little left to eat, their winter stores almost empty by March, and the ground still too frozen to begin the year's planting. She had stayed behind to tend to the animals, too likely to slow them down after twisting her ankle yesterday, falling from a tree; it had barely hurt, and would be healed by tomorrow. The king would be long gone before they returned, and it would fall to her to explain her upcoming death.

"There will be a bride price, of course," said the king.

Marit wasn't quite sure what a bride price was, thought it may be like a dowry—she'd sewn items, slowly, over the last several years for her dowry, but doubted the lindworm would demand her linens as well as her life.

The king went on to explain the bride price, the amount of money her father would be given for this farce of a marriage—the opposite of a dowry, then, and a staggering amount.

It had been a long, brutal winter following a short, dry summer, and for that price Marit may have volunteered herself. Any number of young women may have; it was enough to save not only their own small farm, but those of a few near neighbors. Enough to buy a second goat, a few more chickens, enough to pay all of their debts in the city and have their broken tools repaired.

For such a sum, she would have volunteered. She would have gladly given her life to so dramatically improve the lives of her father and younger sister.

But the king had not asked. The king had demanded, and Marit knew she would resent him for however many days she had left to do so.

He left her, as she'd expected, with guards posted nearby, and she led the animals back to their shed and let herself back into the cottage, not wanting to look at them, their clean uniforms with shiny brass buttons, their polished boots slowly gathering mud, their faces as they avoided her eyes, because they knew, must know, that this was wrong, and yet they were loyal to their king, and would not let her run.

♛

Marit watched through the back window, working idly on her knitting, unable to stay focused on the difficult stitch she'd meant to master this week, until she saw her sister and her father coming out from the woods. She ran to meet them, and hurried them inside before they could ask about the soldiers scattered about. And then she told them.

"Why you?" Greta cried. "Why you?"

She hadn't asked how he'd chosen her, out of all the unwed maids within walking distance of the palace. She didn't think she wanted to know why it was her that must die, and not Annette, who had no father to protect her, or Martine, who was more beautiful, or Signe or Gretchen or any of the other girls she knew.

She didn't want to die. She didn't want to be the kind of person who wished death on her friends, either.

Besides, the lindworm had already eaten two women, and there was no reason to expect he might stop at a third. They may all be dead before this ended, Gretchen and Signe and Annette and Martine, and the younger girls, Greta and her friends, all the forest, all the city, someday all the kingdom sacrificed to satisfy the appetite of a monster that should have been killed the moment it showed itself to Prince Harald.

She could only hope that the fathers of the dead princesses would declare war, that they would kill her king and his lindworm with him before the whole country was devoured.

King Olaf had always been known as a kind and noble king. He'd lowered taxes and held festivals and been much loved, before these last six months, and Marit didn't understand. She didn't understand how a good king could become a bad one overnight because of one monster.

Maybe it was his son. Marit would throw the whole world over for Greta, she knew, but she'd been at Greta's side since she'd emerged from their mother's stomach, been the first to hold the new baby, tiny and wrinkled and red, getting blood all over her vest, as their father had said his goodbyes to Mama, only turning his attention to Marit and the new baby when his wife was gone.

For Greta, for her father, for Mama if she'd lived, Marit would do anything. But if a boar walked out of the woods and claimed to be her long lost brother, she wouldn't take him at his word, wouldn't escort him into the city to trample the blacksmith just because he asked her.

She didn't think the king could hide a paternal relationship with a lindworm for several years. They must have met only when he stopped the prince on the road. And Marit didn't understand.

She gathered Greta in her arms and listened to the younger girl cry, unable to shed any tears for herself, unsure why. She looked over Greta's head at her father, and saw the same desperate sadness in his eyes that she had seen when she was five years old, and her mother was dying in childbirth. Her father loved her, but he could do nothing to save her, and they all knew it. He could not defy the king; to try would only make him angry, would likely risk Greta's life too.

He came and wrapped himself around them both, and Marit thought, but was not quite sure, that he wept too. She sat, dry-eyed, between them, for long hours, until it was time for dinner and bed.

They watched out the window as a new group of soldiers marched in, and the first group left. At least they weren't expected to feed and board their prison guards.

In the morning they found that the soldiers would let Marit go where she pleased, but one or two would always follow, from a respectful distance. No one followed her sister or father, so they went in three different directions, to the neighbors and to the city, Marit to make her farewells, and all of them to give warning. The king is feeding maidens to his lindworm. Marit is the first; she will not likely be the last. Send your daughters quietly to family in other cities, if you can. Marry them quickly to boys in the village, if you can. We do not know why the lindworm wants weddings, but he does, so make your daughters unweddable.

Gretchen, when Marit told her, said it probably had to do with a dragon's fondness for virgins. She then said that if the king came to her, she would rid herself of virginity with the first man she could find before she would go to the lindworm, with the whole town to watch as proof, if necessary.

Gretchen's older brother, the only other person there save the guards, too far away to overhear, made a sound of disapproval in the back of his throat, but said nothing.

Marit wondered if it was too late to try Gretchen's plan for herself, and concluded it probably was—if the lindworm demanded a virgin, then the soldiers would not let her cease to be one. The small chance of success wasn't worth giving herself to a man she didn't want and wouldn't be allowed to keep. And the kind of man who might cooperate with such a plan would likely not make it a happy experience to cherish in her final days. She reminded

Gretchen of the soldiers before moving on to the next neighbors.

Marit spent her days wandering, mostly. There was work to be done, and she helped, or tried to—her father said not to trouble herself with anything in these last few days, and when she insisted, she often found herself too distracted to finish, or at least to finish well, haunted constantly by imaginings of what the lindworm might be like, how it might feel to be eaten. She remembered breaking a finger in a slamming door as a child, the sharp crack of it, the pain. She imagined the pain and the cracking both amplified as an enormous snake swallowed her whole, as snakes will do, and then, bizarrely, imagined cowering on a banquet table as the lindworm sliced her to pieces with a knife held in its tail, popping each slice into its mouth one at a time, sometimes dipping a slice in a butter-sauce first.

She still had not cried, though she had found herself several times laughing hysterically at humorless jokes she couldn't explain. Greta didn't need to know about the butter sauce.

When there were two days left before the wedding, she went out intending to collect eggs from the chickens, and her feet carried her, instead, deeper into the woods.

The guards followed at a distance.

Marit stopped when she saw an old woman ahead. She was short, with white hair spilling from her cap, bright and cheerful in a blue skirt and red vest, and she smiled like an old friend at Marit, and asked why she was so sad.

Marit wasn't a fool. She knew how it was with mysterious old women in forests, knew they were to be respected. Knew how often they carried magic within themselves. Knew that to cross them was idiocy, and that to be kind and respectful could change the course of one's life.

So Marit told the woman her troubles, and the woman smiled again. "It will be all right," she said. "If you obey me, it will be all right. Now, here is what you must do."

Marit wasn't foolish enough to think she might live through

this, but she wasn't foolish enough to ignore the gift of a wise woman in the wood, either, even when that gift was the strangest advice she'd ever been given. Wear ten shifts beneath your dress, have milk and lye and whips waiting in your bedchamber.

She was already going to die; what did it matter if the king's servants thought her a madwoman?

Ten shifts, though, would not be an easy thing to manage. Marit had two shifts, and two night shifts, which were wool instead of linen, with sleeves too wide to be hidden beneath her dress. She would have to rip them off. Greta owned the same, not much smaller as she was tall for her age, but Marit could not deprive her sister of all her undergarments, so only took one day shift and one night shift from her. That brought her to six, and four more yet to find. She couldn't buy them; the king's money wouldn't come to her father until the day after the wedding. She had her dowry linens, unneeded now, and could use the fabric to make more shifts. But she had two days left to live, and wasn't willing to spend her last precious moments sewing. With Greta's help she converted one white bedsheet into a shift, but would sacrifice no more time when she had so many goodbyes to say—to friends, to livestock, to trees and streams and every future she had ever imagined for herself.

She begged one more shift from Olga, whose family was wealthier and who had one to spare for an acquaintance going to her death. Eight shifts, eight, two short, and no time to find more. It would have to be enough.

♛

The morning she was to be taken away, Marit's father pulled out her mother's wedding dress and offered it to her.

Marit shook her head. "It should go to Greta. To a real wedding."

"You shouldn't be alone," her father said. "Take it, so your mother can be with you, as Greta and I cannot."

So Marit put on her eight shifts, and she put on the dress. She was a bit smaller than her mother had been when she married, and it still fit despite the extra layers. Greta had wanted to make her a crown of flowers to match, but there were still few flowers in bloom, so she wove the crown from evergreen branches instead, coating her hands in sap, and placed it carefully on her sister's head.

The three of them waited, solemnly, for Marit to be taken away. There was nothing left to say. All of the goodbyes were finished, all of the plans made. The next morning someone would come from the palace with the bride price and whatever was left of Marit to be buried. Her father would sell the animals and the house, give them away if he couldn't sell them fast enough, and he would hire a wagon to take them far, far from the capital, to start a new life where the lindworm would never touch Greta. They'd gone over the details last night. Greta had cried again.

Marit still hadn't cried, and thought she might be able to, now, but would not let herself; she didn't want her tears seen by whoever took her away. She found she was more angry than sad. She felt a sharpness growing within her. Her life was forfeit, and so too was her sense of obligation to respect, to loyalty. The king, the queen, the prince, the priests who'd performed the weddings and the soldiers and couriers who'd stood by—damn them, she thought, damn them all, and damn the idea she owed them the barest amount of anything.

The king came to fetch her himself, and she refrained from spitting in his face only because of the guards that surrounded him, the fear they might kill her where she stood and cost her father the bride price.

The king was different, not angry and demanding as he had been a week ago, but stiff with an awkwardness that might almost be shame. Marit hugged her father and Greta one last time, and followed him back toward the city, his guards forming a circle around them. She didn't care that he may feel shame; she had enough anger by now for the both of them.

He was quiet, and Marit didn't want quiet. Not quite understanding the compulsion, she found herself goading him.

"What will happen after this?" she asked, and the king looked at her, then quickly away again. It was a long walk on foot, and she didn't know why a king wouldn't take a carriage, but she didn't mind the extra time in her forest.

"You will be prepared for the wedding by lady's maids. The wedding will be in the great hall, and after that we will have a banquet."

"Not tonight," Marit said, spurred by the thought of Annette being sent hundreds of miles away to an uncle she'd never met, of Gretchen searching for a man to defile her rather than be eaten. "Not to me. What will happen to your kingdom? After me, you'll kill off every maid in the country, and then I suppose you'll have to go to war, and find slaves to feed his appetite? Discipline is important for growing boys, Your Majesty. Learn to say no to your son."

He raised a hand as if to slap her, and she tilted her chin forward, daring him—let him hit her, here surrounded by a small army, let all these soldiers, already uneasy with their roles, go home and report to their friends and families that their king was a man who struck defenseless maidens.

He lowered his hand, leaving Marit oddly disappointed. It would have been another reason to be angry, and her anger was protecting her from her fear.

The king sighed heavily. "We all do foolish things for our children."

She wondered if he meant the lindworm, or only Prince Harald, who could not be married until it was satisfied. It didn't matter—the result was the same for her.

"Yes, Your Majesty," she said, suddenly exhausted. Maybe a king could afford to do foolish things for his children. Her own father had to be sensible—foolishness would only have hurt Greta. She felt the anger draining away, the fear rising up again. She didn't want to die.

♛

They arrived at the palace from a side gate, not taking the wide, paved road beneath the cherry trees, where any number of people might have seen their arrival. The king and his soldiers handed her off to a large group of women, some more elegant than others, and she asked him, before he left, what time the wedding would be.

"At eight o'clock," he said. "Will that give you enough time to prepare?" One of the more elegant women assured him it would, and he told her, "Give the girl whatever she wants. It's her wedding day, after all." He laughed, unamused, more bitter than cruel, and then he was gone.

"Is there anything special we can do for you, miss?" asked one of the plainer women, who was likely a maid.

Marit thought of the old woman in the forest. "This is going to sound a little strange."

All of the more plainly dressed women left to carry out her last request, leaving Marit with a flock of beautiful women whose most simple everyday clothes were likely ten times more expensive than her mother's wedding dress. They tried to have her out of it, into borrowed silks instead, but she refused. It was the last gift from her father, the only familiar thing in this place. She kept her evergreen crown as well, but let them take it away long enough to clean away the sap, rubbing it from the branches and brushing it out of her hair.

They re-braided her hair into a more elaborate style, stringing in gemstones to match her dress, and applied powders and creams to her face, which itched and made her sneeze. She watched them carefully, picking out one who seemed both kind and fancy enough to know little of a peasant's daily life. She drew her away from the crowd and explained, in a whisper, "I haven't any underthings. I only own the one shift, and I left it for my sister, so she would have one to wear on laundry day. I didn't think it would matter, when I'm only to die tonight, but I'm—I'm embarrassed to have all these fine people watching me, thinking that if the light hits just so they'll see I'm not dressed properly."

The woman believed, somehow, that a peasant girl might have come to a royal wedding with no undergarments, and offered to find a spare shift.

"Could I have two, please?" The woman raised her eyebrows, and Marit ducked her head. "It's a tradition—I know it shan't be a real wedding night, but it's a tradition to make the groom work a little harder the first time."

The woman believed the tradition she'd never heard of, as well, and came back shortly with two more shifts, beautiful, silken things, bringing Marit to the required ten.

The next problem came when she realized the women had no intention of leaving her alone while she took off her wedding dress and put on the shifts, which was awkward for more reasons than the eight shifts she already wore. She explained that she was not accustomed to being seen undressed by strangers, and finally they left her, for the first moment of privacy she'd had in hours, and the last she expected to have in her life.

She took off the dress and put on the shifts. She paused to look in the mirror—a thing she'd heard of but never before seen—and wondered if that was what she truly looked like, or only the effect of the powders and creams. She pulled the dress back on, took a few deep breaths—she had not cried yet, she would not cry now—and reopened the door so that the women could help re-fasten the dress in the back.

They set the evergreen crown back on her head, and took her to the priest that would read her last rites.

The hall where they held the wedding was gorgeous, with shining wood floors and dark walls covered in rosemåling, blue and gold and red. All the court was seated when she arrived, dressed in their finest clothes, looking horrified. She recognized the king and the queen and the prince, familiar from a dozen parades, sitting in the front row. The rest were strangers.

And then she saw the lindworm.

It was the height of six or seven men, white like a maggot, or the mold on stale bread. It had dark wings on its back, too small to hold its weight in flight, and shiny white fangs quite visible even when its mouth was shut. It had no legs. There was a crown balanced at the top of its head, the size a man would wear, which might have been funny if it hadn't planned to eat her.

It was staring at her with an expression of mild curiosity, recognizable because its eyes were the eyes of a man, over-large, but still small in its serpent head, the same shade of blue as a dozen young men she'd seen in the city.

Marit recoiled, and the priest escorting her to the altar gave her a moment before pulling her forward again.

He left her there beside the lindworm—another priest was performing the ceremony.

♛

The priest spoke, repeating himself two or three times whenever he reached a line that required her response. Her eyes were locked on the lindworm; she was unable to think of anything else. She had never seen a monster, not even a picture of a monster, but there had been stories enough. She had thought she knew what to expect, but nothing could have prepared her for those human eyes.

The lindworm watched her, too, maintaining eye contact, his tongue flicking occasionally past his fangs. He did not miss his lines.

It was a short ceremony, and when it was finished, the lindworm slithered down the hall away from her. Prince Harald stepped forward to offer his arm, and Marit took it, not knowing what else to do.

He was very handsome, their prince—well, the whole kingdom knew that. But he was also rumored to be funny, and kind, and very charming. If she had any hope of rescue outside the old woman, it lay with him. But he had already failed to save two girls more important than her.

The natural response, she thought, to meeting a monster on the road was to chop it into small pieces, not bring it home to meet the family. (The natural response, at least, for a prince, who even now wore a sword on his belt.)

She wouldn't allow herself to beg for a rescue she knew he would not perform.

"It will be over soon," Prince Harald told her, in a voice she thought was meant to be soothing.

She was not soothed, and found herself scolding instead of begging. "You're the prince. You're supposed to be a hero. It's your job to kill him and save me. How can you let him do this?"

He had the grace to look uncomfortable, at least. "So I should chop off my brother's head to save a stranger? I'm sorry. I am. I hate him. I hate all of this. But there are bigger things in this world than a farmer's daughter, or even two princesses and a war, and I will not live with his blood on my hands."

"But you'll live with mine."

"I'm sorry," he said again, sounding as if he meant it. And then they were in the banquet hall, and she walked unaccompanied to the lindworm's table. He looked up with interest as she sat, then ignored her as the food was served.

A short blonde girl caught the prince's arm as he walked away. "This is dreadful. Harry, please."

He shook her off. "Don't call me that."

Marit did not see the prince again. She watched as the wedding cake was cut, a golden tower of ever-narrower rings, white icing dripping down the sides.

A little boy, six or seven, charming with curly copper hair, ran forward to whisper, "If I were bigger I'd kill him for you," and his mother dragged him away. The lindworm stared down at his plate and said nothing. He must have heard.

They were served, finer foods than she'd ever seen before, but she had no appetite. She moved things slowly across the plate and back with her fork.

The lindworm had been given a slice of cake, and was flicking his tongue at it. He must have felt her eyes on him, because he swiveled his head to stare at her, blue eyes dropping down to her full plate then up to her face again.

"Not hungry?" he asked, and she flinched. She'd known from the rumors that he could speak like a man, had even heard him during the ceremony, but she'd been distracted then, and this was the first time he'd spoken directly to her.

"Not particularly," she answered.

"Me neither."

Marit laughed—she thought it was probably a bitter sound. "Well, they haven't catered this event for you, have they? You'll have dinner later."

His eyes met hers again. He held her gaze, and she shuddered.

"Marit," he said, and it was the first time anyone but the priest had used her name. "Marit, I am sorry. If it is my choice, you will live through the night."

She looked away. "And who else's choice would it be?"

The lindworm didn't answer. Instead he said, "If you are not hungry, and I am not hungry, shall we be done with this joke of a wedding?"

"Yes, please," she said. Better to have this all over with than to be surrounded for hours by people determined to pretend it was a happy occasion.

He was low to the ground then, head nearly level with hers, and yards and yards of body spread out across the floor. He rose, looming above the crowd as he announced, "Princess Marit has had a long day. We will retire to our room for the night."

A small part of her had wished that someone, when it finally came time, would object, but that was a fool's hope. There was a grand procession up several flights of stairs to their wedding bed. Marit noticed that none of the children who had been at the banquet followed them up the stairs, nor did many of the people who had looked the most uncomfortable. They were joined by a large group of soldiers, likely to ensure she would not embarrass herself by trying to run at the last moment.

She wondered how a lindworm would manage stairs, but most of them were no longer than he was, and he ascended with ease. A few times, on the longest staircases, she saw his small, useless wings flutter a little.

Finally, the stairs ended, and they went down a long hallway to a single door, which a maid stepped forward to open. Everyone but the maids and the soldiers peeled away then, the royal family each bowing to her as they left, which would have been an honor if they hadn't been feeding her to a dragon.

♛

The lindworm lowered his great head, and a maid, shaking, stepped forward to lift off the crown. He slithered into the room. Marit stood frozen in the doorway for several minutes before a soldier nudged her. She took a few reluctant steps forward, then, remembering, turned to catch the sleeve of the last of the rapidly departing maids.

"Wait, please. I just—the buttons, on my dress. Will you help me unfasten them? It was my mother's, and I don't want it to be ruined when—could it be sent back home, please? After I—to my little sister. Tell her it doesn't—I mean, she should still wear it. She'd look beautiful in it." The girl nodded and stepped into the room after Marit to undo the buttons, glancing nervously over at the lindworm as she worked.

"Good night, princess," she whispered, just as if Marit were a real princess. And then she fled.

Marit glanced around the room as she stepped out of the dress. It was a large, open space with high ceilings. There was a bed, larger than any she'd seen, but certainly not large enough to accommodate the lindworm. There was a large fireplace burning merrily, a window with clear glass panes, and an enormous pile of furs which she suspected was where the lindworm slept. In the far corner of the room was a wardrobe, and beside it small doors which must lead to a closet. That, she hoped, was where her requested supplies had been left.

She crossed the room, carefully folding her dress, and stood on her toes to place it on top of the wardrobe. Then she turned to face the lindworm.

"That is my mother's wedding dress, and it's not to be damaged. It's to be left alone so it can be returned to my family. Do you understand?"

The lindworm nodded. "You may return it to them in the

morning."

"That's just cruel," Marit said. She would not cry, not now, not in front of the monster.

He stared at her for a long moment. He didn't blink—well, snakes didn't, did they? Finally, unsettled, Marit turned away.

"I'm a monster," the lindworm said. "I know I'm a monster. I'm a lindworm, with the needs and the urges of a lindworm, but I don't mean to be cruel."

"Then don't be," Marit snapped. "We both know you'll eat me. Let's not pretend."

"I'm not hungry tonight," he said. "The other girls—if you run now I'll let you."

"They locked the door before they left." She'd heard the bolt slide into place.

"The window—"

"We're several stories up. The drop would kill me."

"Oh."

"You'll eat me, yes? If not tonight another night, when you're hungrier?"

"Yes," he admitted.

"Then let's have it over with. I don't want to wait on your hunger. I don't want hope to build." There would be false hope not just for her, who had at least been told it was false, but for her family, for the whole kingdom. The lindworm had eaten both princesses on the wedding night.

Unless he had let them escape and then lied, but she did not think he had. She thought he had eaten them.

"All right," he said, and he drew himself up to so great a height his head nearly brushed the ceiling, suddenly remote and frightening, a monster again. "Please take off your shift," he hissed.

"Don't like the taste of fabric?" she asked acidly. Their strange moment of camaraderie was past. She didn't allow herself, as she had been since meeting the old woman not allowing herself, to think on why else a monster might want his bride naked on their wedding night.

"Take it off, please," the lindworm repeated.

"You first," Marit said, remembering her script. He drew back a little—she thought he was confused.

"I'm not wearing a shift," he said after a moment, and it was so absurd she nearly laughed, but she knew that if she allowed herself to laugh she would soon be crying instead.

"Your skin. You shed your skin, and I'll shed my shift."

"Oh." He hesitated. "I'm not due a molt for months yet."

"I don't care about your schedule. Skin, shift."

A look she couldn't name came into his human eyes, and she was sure for a moment that he would abandon all this talking and eat her as she was, shifts and all. But he just began to wriggle, squirming out of his skin.

Marit stood and watched. She was standing too near the fireplace, overly hot in her ten layers, but she didn't want to move. There was a comfort to the heat. She suspected fireplaces were the only thing the palace had in common with her cottage. The wise woman's first step had played out as promised, but there were still many steps to go.

It took him a long time to shed the first skin, but when it lay on the floor, he was bigger than when he'd started.

She should have expected this—it was the nature of snakes, and what was he but a great, winged snake?—but she hadn't, and was alarmed.

There was nothing to be done now, nothing to be done except hope the plan would keep working. It wasn't as if a slightly larger lindworm could make the situation worse than it already was.

She slid off her first shift and laid it over the discarded skin, and the lindworm stared, dismayed, at her still-clothed body.

"I'll need that shift off too, please," he said. At least he was a well-mannered monster.

"Shed another skin, and I'll shed another shift."

"I'm really not supposed to do that."

Marit crossed her arms and waited; after a moment he began to wriggle again.

By the fourth skin he had stopped growing bigger, and had begun to grown translucent instead. By the fifth skin the fire had begun to die, and Marit felt safe enough to turn her back on the lindworm and tend it. Each skin took longer, and each skin seemed to cause him more pain. He seemed determined, though, to have her out of her shifts, and she was frightened anew of his intentions when he had her undressed.

It didn't matter; he wouldn't be in a state to do anything to her. When he had finished shedding his tenth skin, and Marit was still wearing her tenth shift, she thought it wouldn't matter if she followed the rest of the wise woman's instructions; the lindworm would surely be dead by morning.

She would still follow them—she didn't want to take chances. But the final skin was slimy with blood, and the lindworm was all muscles and veins barely held together into a serpent shape. She thought for a moment she saw his blue eyes leaking, but talked herself out of it quickly. Reptiles couldn't shed tears.

He was gasping and panting, his distress obvious, and she couldn't imagine what had compelled him to keep going. Surely he must have felt how he was hurting himself.

She had gone while he shed the last skin to check the closet, and found all as she'd asked. There was a tub of lye, a tub of milk, a handful of whips. She'd been viciously glad when the woman told her the next step, thought she would enjoy it. But looking at the writhing mass of lindworm that had suggested she run, she felt almost sorry.

Still, she would do as she was told. She dragged both tubs out into the room, as she doubted the lindworm could drag himself, in his current state, any closer to the closet. And she dipped the whips into the tub of lye.

"What are you doing?" the lindworm asked, and his voice was high and frightened and young. She hadn't thought, before—she didn't know how dragons aged, but if he was the prince's brother, he couldn't be very old. Prince Harald was twenty.

"I'm sorry," she told him. "I don't know. I'm sorry." And she lifted the whips.

If anyone heard screaming, they would assume it came from her.

He screamed, and sobbed, begged for someone called Ida to help him. Marit wanted to stop. She didn't. When mysterious women in the woods gave instructions, you obeyed them. And the lindworm would have eaten her. Maybe not tonight, but someday he would have.

She was glad to be done, to toss the whips aside, but not to carry out the next step, which required touching him. She dragged the tub of milk to him and dunked him once, or as much of him as she could manage, reminded absurdly of a baptismal service she'd seen last spring. Then the milk turned red with blood, and she dropped him whimpering to the floor, and found her hands and arms still streaked in it.

He didn't look like a lindworm anymore. He didn't look like anything, really, except maybe a creature near death. He'd been helpless, or near enough, since the eighth or ninth skin. She could have cast him into the fireplace and been done with it. All these extra steps—either she'd been made the instrument of a revenge scheme from someone the lindworm badly hurt, or this was all about something much more complex than her surviving the night.

She suspected the latter.

Her final step was to get him to the bed, and then she was to embrace him, which had sounded disgusting before, but she'd already dragged the remains of him in and out of the tub.

She lifted him again, a quivering mass of blood and twitching muscle, and pulled him to the bed, where he fit from head to small, bedraggled wings, the rest of his tail in a heap on the floor.

She hugged him quickly, getting it over with, and then carefully tucked the blankets in around him; if he was to die in the next few hours, he should do so in comfort.

She looked into his eyes, the blue even more startling now against the red of his damaged head.

"Is it over?" he asked.

"I'm sorry. I don't know."

Her task was finished. She didn't know what would come next for him. The sun was rising now, she could see it in the window, and it would not be long before someone came to check on them. She didn't know how she would explain the mess they would find. She could explain killing the lindworm, she was sure, but not torturing him. She didn't want to be the sort of person who tortured anyone, even monsters, and if she lived to see strangers in the woods again, she would run in the opposite direction.

She reached up to catch a trickle of blood before it dripped into his eye, and slowly lowered her hand.

The blast threw her across the room.

When she sat up, she was half convinced she'd been knocked out, and woken in some dream world.

Instead of the bedraggled lindworm, there was a young man sitting in the mess of bloody sheets, pale and thin and crying, naked and covered in long red welts.

Marit stood and approached slowly, touching his shoulder when he didn't seem to notice her. The boy leapt up explosively, then slumped down again. She backed away.

"Oh, gods," he said.

Chapter Two

"Hello," she said. She understood what had happened, a little, understood that there was magic here and she'd been involved in a sort of transformation spell, understood that this was the lindworm. But she didn't know what to do about it.

"Hello," he said.

She took a step forward, and he flinched away; she thought it was a reaction to the fact she'd just tortured him, until he said, "I wouldn't come any closer. I might eat you."

"I don't think you can," she said carefully.

"Yes, I seem to have—I've never had arms. How does one use them?"

It didn't seem to be a genuine question; he lifted up a hand to examine it, then burst suddenly into a hysterical laughter that turned quickly to crying. Marit sat gingerly on the edge of the bed, reaching out to pat him on the back, in one of the few places she could find unbroken skin.

"It's over now. Everything will be all right." If this was too obviously a lie, he didn't bother calling her on it, just continued to cry. When she was sure he was paying no attention to her, Marit returned to the pile of skins and shifts, quickly removing her final, bloodstained layer and dipping one of the other shifts in the lye to rub herself clean before pulling on another.

It was all the cleaning she could manage for now. She'd been up nearly the whole night, and had not been sleeping well for the last week. She added a few more logs to the fire, and went to study the door, relieved to find it had a second bolt on the inside. She locked it, then went to lay in the lindworm's pile of furs, which was cleaner, at least, than the bed. In the morning she would hand off this mess to the king, and then she would take her mother's wedding dress home to Greta, just as the lindworm had said she would.

Chapter Three

Marit was woken in the morning by a sharp knock on the door. She glanced over at the bed—the boy who had been the lindworm was still lying in the bloody sheets, staring blankly into the distance. She went to the door, but did not unlock it.

"Good morning," she called, as cheerfully as she could manage.

There was a long pause, and then the king's voice, shocked, asking, "Marit?"

"That's me."

"Where is the lindworm?"

"I've handled it," she told him. She meant to explain, or perhaps to open the door and let him see for himself, but was stopped by the boy on the bed, frantically whispering her name.

She stepped away from the door, and whispered back, "What is it?"

"Ask him to send for Ida. Ida will fix everything. He's not alone at the door, and they shouldn't all see this."

He was right; she didn't care much by now about upsetting the king, but if he was accompanied by servants and soldiers, the city would soon be filled with rumors that she had been involved in something dark and strange. She went back to the door, trying to stir up more confidence than she felt. She was sure the door could be broken down without much difficulty.

"I've handled it," she repeated, "which none of you could manage, and now I'm not opening the door for anyone but a woman named Ida."

She caught snatches of a whispered conversation, and then the king said, more loudly, "She'll be here within the hour."

Marit waited until the sound of footsteps faded to approach the bed again. "Stand up," she told the lindworm. "I need to strip the sheets, and then we'll see about getting you cleaned up."

"I don't know how," he said.

"What?"

"This isn't—this isn't my body. I don't know how to—legs, arms, all these extra bits. I only know how to work a spine."

Marit sighed. She didn't really want to carry or drag him away from the bed, and was relieved to have a good excuse not to try—injured as he was, she would likely only hurt him further in the attempt. She sat down on the floor in front of the bed, not sure how to interact with a former lindworm. He'd led the conversation, before.

"Do you have a name?" she asked him, finally.

"Yes."

When no more information was forthcoming, she added, "What is your name?"

He looked a bit surprised. Well, they'd all called him the lindworm; no one at the palace must have thought to ask a monster his name.

She hadn't thought of it, either.

"David," he said.

"I'm sorry," she said, "about..." Trailing off, she gestured toward the mess at the center of the room.

"I'm sure it wasn't your idea."

"You were going to eat me," she said, not quite sure why she felt the need to defend herself.

"I know," he said. And then he began crying again.

Marit didn't attempt to comfort him. She turned away, staring into the fire while she waited. It was more than an hour.

Finally, there was a soft knock on the door.

"Marit?" a familiar voice called.

She went to open the door, and was not surprised to find her wise woman on the other side.

"Hello, Ida."

But Ida ignored her entirely, rushing to the bed and gathering David up into her arms. Marit collected the large basket she'd left in the hallway, then closed and relocked the door.

After a few minutes, Ida released him and began pulling at the sheets. "All right, sweetheart. Let's see how bad the damage is."

She produced, from her basket, ointments, bandages, trousers, and a shirt. Marit gave them space, as much as she was able in the large, open room. There would be time later for questions about why a wise woman had let her pet dragon terrorize the kingdom.

When David and his wounds were both dressed, Ida lifted him easily and deposited him in the pile of furs.

"Marit," she said, "come help me strip the bed."

"Maybe you should clean up your own messes," Marit said, knowing it was foolish to antagonize her.

"And who bloodied him?"

"Who told me to?" Marit retorted.

Ida glanced over at David, but if he was surprised to hear she'd ordered his torture, he didn't show it. He was lying on his stomach, eyes closed, and occasionally a shudder went through his entire body.

"I'll handle the sheets," Ida said after a moment. "Dump the milk and the lye out the window, and hide the tubs."

Marit did, checking first that the ground below was clear. She dragged them back into the closet, along with the whips, and came out to find Ida shoving the lindworm's discarded skins under the bed.

"I'll take care of the sheets later," she said. "Now we need breakfast and a bath for you both, and to get our stories straight. Davey, sweetheart, what would you like to eat?"

"Nothing," he said, voice muffled by his face pressed into the fur. "I shall never eat again."

"Nonsense," Ida said briskly. "Porridge, perhaps."

He sat up a little, bracing himself on his elbows. "I ate them," he said, almost a wail. "I remember how they tasted. How it felt when the bones—I swallowed them whole. Why did I do that? Why did I do that?"

"Because you were a lindworm."

"And what am I now?"

"A man."

David, apparently unconvinced, collapsed back into the fur pile.

"I'll be back shortly," Ida told Marit. "Open the door for no one but me."

She took her basket, full of the soiled sheets, and Marit locked the door behind her. She had not asked what Marit might like for breakfast, and she had not brought her clothes, either—David was dressed, and she was still in her shift.

Ida returned after some time, leading two maids, neither of whom she let through the door. One carried a tray with two bowls of porridge, two slices of toast, and two cups of milk, which Ida took from her, leaving Marit to collect the bedsheets from the other maid.

"Might I borrow a dress from someone?" Marit asked. "I've only my mother's wedding dress here, and I don't want it dirty or damaged."

"Of course." The maid bobbed a curtsey before she left—Marit didn't know why. Last night she had been a pretend princess, for a few short hours; now she was only herself again.

She dropped the sheets in a heap on the bed, then turned to watch Ida explain to David that he would have to chew the bread before he swallowed it. He was still refusing to eat at all, and Marit thought Ida was trying to draw him out with a new experience.

She was wary—a little of David, who might have eaten her, but more of Ida, who had likely orchestrated all this, who had at least known what David was and where he was, and hadn't stopped him from eating the princesses. She stayed on the far end of the room, not claiming her own breakfast, until there was another knock on the door.

The maid had returned with a beautiful dress, and with two young men bearing a large tub with steam rising from the top. "I thought you might like to be clean before dressing. If we may bring the water in?"

"You may not," Ida said, appearing suddenly behind Marit's shoulder. "We'll bring it ourselves."

They dragged it into the room and locked the door again. Ida let Marit have the first bath, still trying to coax David into eating something.

She didn't want to be completely undressed in front of two near strangers, one of them a man. She didn't think they were paying her much attention, but still bathed too quickly to enjoy it. The dress she'd been given was brightly colored and very soft, much finer than anything she'd ever owned. It had laces up the back, which she left undone, slipping on her own shoes and collecting the wedding dress from the top of the wardrobe.

"I'll be going home now," she said. "Thank you for not eating me."

Ida stood up. "You can't leave."

"Why not?"

"You married Davey. You're a princess now."

"That wasn't a real wedding, he's not a real prince, and I'm certainly not a princess. I did what you asked. My family needs to know I'm still alive."

"They'll be told when the bride price is delivered. I need you here, Marit."

"For what?"

"To protect Davey. I need you here as his wife, to make it a fairy story."

"A fairy story? People are dead, Ida. He ate them."

"I tried to speak to the princesses," Ida said, "but they were foolish and proud."

"They were frightened! And you offered them lunacy with no explanation. Did they even understand?" Marit had grown up in the forest, knowing the legends of the forest and the role a woman like Ida played. These girls, from lands far away, could not be expected to have such knowledge. "Are you the kind of witch who turns half-starved boys to frogs when they refuse to give the last food they have to a stranger in the woods?"

Davey's sharp stare burned into her, and she shifted a little so that she couldn't see him from where she stood. The correct term was wise woman, and witch was horribly insulting—well, maybe she wanted to insult someone.

"Kindness is a virtue, Marit," Ida said, which was practically a confession to the frog-turning.

"Kindness is good. But a moment of selfish desperation is not worth a lifetime of misery. And now you've shackled me to a monster—where's the kindness in that?"

"Davey is a good boy," she said, with the conviction of the deeply insane.

"Davey is a bloodthirsty dragon who's eaten two women already, and perhaps they've the better end of things—better a dead maiden than the wife of the snake prince."

Ida frowned for a moment, and then her face cleared, and she offered cheerfully, as if holding the solution to all life's problems, "You need not assume all wifely duties if you feel unready. I doubt the king and queen are eager for Davey to produce an heir."

Marit laughed, feeling decidedly hysterical. "Well, it's all fine then, isn't it? I'm to give up everything I've known, to dedicate my life to babysitting a monster, cooped up in the room where he nearly ate me, but as long as I don't allow him to get me with child, I'm sure we'll have no problems!"

"Davey is not a monster," Ida said, indignant.

"Call him what you like; he's certainly not a man. And I—I shan't be a wife to him, and I shan't be a mother, either, teaching him to walk and to chew his food."

"Perhaps you could be a friend."

"He tried to eat me," Marit said, because if anyone could forget that small detail, it would be Ida.

She scoffed. "Hardly an attempt. He was thirty feet long to your five, and venomous, and yet here you are, unharmed."

"This is lunacy! I shan't stand for it. I shan't allow it to continue."

"And what will you do about it?" Ida asked.

Marit took a moment to consider this. "I'll tell the pope. I'll tell him everything. I'll make the priest tell the bishop, and the archbishop, and he'll go to the pope and he'll excommunicate the lot of you."

"And what will become of the kingdom, Marit? When the papal orders throw the palace into disarray, and the fathers of the dead princesses take advantage of the chaos to attack? How many people will die in a war you've denied us the chance to prepare for?"

She'd thought, earlier this week, that war would be preferable to all the kingdom's maidens sacrificed one by one to the lindworm. But the lindworm had become a pathetic boy, unlikely to devour anyone, and she knew a war would be devastating, knew foreign soldiers would sweep through, eating their crops and burning their forests, as had happened in her grandfather's time, knew how many would die not just in battle, but of starvation and illness and wounds going septic. If going to the pope would worsen their chances in a war—and she thought that Ida was right, that it would—then she could not go to the pope.

"And what about you?" Ida continued. "What will happen when they press you for details? Will you tell them the dark magic you performed?"

"Dark magic?"

"How did you think the spell was broken? Nothing with that much blood in it can be pure."

Marit gave in—she had known she would give in before Ida had all but threatened her. "So I'll stay. And how will you make it a fairy story?"

"They need not know he was the lindworm. We'll tell them he was kidnapped as a child. By the lindworm. You learned his location and slew the lindworm, then went to rescue him."

"And you think anyone will believe that?"

"They'll believe it because it is better than the alternative, than the truth, that the queen birthed a serpent that came back to haunt her twenty years later. It will save them from asking why the queen would birth a serpent, and it will let them trust their king again—we'll say Davey was a hostage for their cooperation with the lindworm. They will believe it because it is what they want to believe. And you will be the hero of the story."

"I don't want to be the hero. I just want to go home."

"You'll be able to visit your family in time. Now help me make the bed."

It wasn't until later, when Marit was eating her cold porridge, and David was bathed and asleep, that she thought to ask, "Why did the queen birth a serpent?"

"Because she did not follow my instructions as well as you did."

"The queen will know your story is just a story. And the king as well. What will you tell them?"

"The truth, with less blood in it."

The day passed slowly. David slept in the newly made bed. Marit and Ida dumped the bath water out the window, then left all three tubs in the hall to be taken away. The whips were moved under the bed with the skins. Marit stood at the window for a long time, watching people going about their business below. She hoped that her father had believed it when he was told she lived, hoped he was not even now selling their belongings and preparing to leave.

Ida left again. When she came back it was evening, and she had the king and queen with her, Prince Harald trailing behind. Marit looked at the queen, who was frowning, and saw that she had the same bone structure as David, although he had his father's coloring. Prince Harald was the opposite.

Marit was sitting at the fire, and she did not stand to curtsey. They had sentenced her to death—that she had lived despite them did not make them worthy again of her respect.

It didn't matter; they all ignored her. David was still asleep, and Ida shook him gently.

"Darling, your family is here to see you." She maneuvered him into a sitting position. He said nothing.

"So this is the lindworm," the queen said.

"Please, Your Majesty," said Ida. "He doesn't remember a thing."

"How convenient." She stared at Davey, and for a moment he stared steadily back. Then he turned to the king.

"I remember threatening you, and I remember you caving. I remember two innocent girls dying because you—" He looked back at Ida; Marit saw his face, and thought he was going to cry again. "Because you—why didn't you stop me? Why did you let me do that? Why didn't you just kill me? Why don't you just kill me? Why did—why did—why—"

"He doesn't remember anything?" the queen asked.

"I remember everything."

"I can see that," she said. "What is your name?"

"David."

"David. And how do you propose we explain this to the rest of the country, David?"

"I propose you have me quietly executed, and tell everyone that Marit killed the lindworm."

"Don't be ridiculous," said the king. "Ida, tell me you have a plan."

"I have a plan. If we could discuss it in private—Marit, watch Davey."

He was crying again by the time they left.

"At least you didn't eat me," Marit said. He did not seem comforted by this, and unsure what other comfort to offer, she left him there, returning to the fire.

Some accord must have been reached, eventually. Ida

returned, and brought with her a small troupe of maids who swept the floor, took the furs away, and brought in a thick rug, three large, stuffed chairs, a small table, and more firewood. There was a chamber pot which they placed behind a folding wooden partition for privacy. They brought a cot into the room, too, ostensibly for Ida. Marit claimed it as soon as the room was clear, and left Ida to the bridal bed with her monster.

She put the cot beside the fireplace, and silently assigned herself the task of keeping it lit, as they wanted no servants coming and going. She watched Ida, wrapped protectively around Davey even in her sleep, and thought longingly of long winter nights, huddled for warmth in one small bed with Greta and her father, and she wept for the first time since the king stepped into her garden.

She was prepared to die, whatever strange stories a woman in the woods had to tell. Death was simple. She didn't know how to live the rest of a long life like this, alone.

♛

Marit woke in the morning to Ida lecturing David, or trying to. It didn't seem to be taking.

"We cannot have a repeat of yesterday. I did not sacrifice lives and morals and the last sway I held over Olaf and his wife for you to throw it all away over a sense of misplaced guilt."

"Misplaced? I ate two women."

"You were becoming every day less yourself and more the lindworm. If they had done as I said, the spell would have been broken long ago and they would have been safe."

"I was born a lindworm."

"You were born in the body of a lindworm, but you were always meant to be a man. Listen to me, Davey, and I will make everything right."

"Listening to you is what got me into this mess. I should never have come to the palace, where they would serve up innocents for me to eat. I would have lost myself, eventually, and Harald or one of his friends would have slain me. He would never have had to know I was his brother."

"And you would have been dead."

"Better dead than this," he said. "I never asked you to make me a man."

Marit made some noise getting out of bed, and they both fell silent. Ida left to speak again with the king, and shortly after she was gone there was a knock on the door.

It was a maid, holding a small bowl of oranges. "A treat from the kitchen," she said, "for the new prince and princess."

Marit took the bowl carefully. Her father had brought home an orange once, at Christmas time, the year after a particularly good harvest. The three of them had shared it. It had been wonderful.

She sat on the edge of the bed and set the bowl down beside David, who was leaning against the headboard, staring into the distance. He didn't take one, and she realized he wouldn't be able to peel it with his unfamiliar fingers. He didn't ask her for help, and she didn't offer it.

Instead she asked, after carefully peeling her own orange and eating the first segment, "How many people have you eaten?" She needed to know. If she was going to be tied to him for the rest of her life, she needed to know.

"Only the two princesses," he said. "When I was smaller, I didn't have the—even if I'd been large enough to do it, I didn't have the urge. And then Ida was always there to stop me. Asking for the brides—that was her idea. I didn't know I would eat them until I had."

"Oh." Marit offered him a segment of her orange—a small one, remembering how Ida had needed to explain about chewing, and not wanting him to choke. He took it, and it was the first food she'd seen him eat; Ida had had no luck yesterday.

"You should go," he told her. "Now, while Ida is out. Take your wedding dress and go home to your sister. We'll manage without you, or we won't. It doesn't matter to me, and it shouldn't matter to you."

"I think Ida would find me and drag me back."

"I could probably convince her not to."

Ida came back before Marit could answer.

Things were difficult, after that. David fell asleep again in the early afternoon—Marit thought changing form must be very tiring—and woke screaming. He arched his back, and tore open most of his wounds, soaking the sheets in blood again. For days after that he seldom spoke, dividing his time between crying and staring silently at nothing. He ignored Ida when she begged him to eat, but could occasionally be convinced to drink a little water. He slept seldom, and when he did he usually woke screaming. He reopened his wounds several more times, even after Ida began stitching them shut. Ida wanted to teach him to walk, but he wouldn't cooperate, and so spent most of his time lying on his stomach on either the bed or the rug in front of the fire. He couldn't lie in any other position without further aggravating his wounds.

Marit did her best to ignore them without leaving the room. She was afraid to venture out into the palace alone, but didn't know how to help David, and wasn't sure she wanted to help Ida.

She had felt very sorry for him at first, but after nearly a week she was growing annoyed.

She befriended the maid who came most often to their door; her name was Smilla, and when Marit asked, she brought knitting needles and a small ball of yarn. It helped stave off the boredom, a little. Marit had seen the king only once since Ida first brought him to the room. She had asked to go home and assure her family she was safe, and he had forbidden it.

She was not sure if the forbidding was his own idea or Ida's. She was afraid that with no proof she was alive, her father wouldn't believe it, and would move forward with their plan to take Greta somewhere far off and safe.

Prince Harald came by, once, bringing an armload of his old clothing for David. David was on the rug near the fire, then, shirtless since Ida had just re-bandaged him. The prince stared for a long moment, but didn't say anything. He dropped the clothes on one of the chairs and left again. Marit, with little to do to pass the time, busied herself hanging them in the wardrobe, rearranging them a few times until she was satisfied with the pattern.

She had dresses in the wardrobe, too, also hand-me-downs, though she did not know who from. They were all very fancy, and most required Ida's help to button or lace up. They hung beside her wedding dress, which she had decided to return herself, when she was allowed, instead of sending home with a messenger.

The was a mirror inside the wardrobe door, and she stared at it, sometimes, wishing Greta was here to see. Greta would have loved a mirror.

She dragged one of the large, padded chairs to the window, and spent long hours staring out. She had thought she was going to be eaten, not to die of boredom or perhaps loneliness. David and Ida both ignored her, and she didn't understand why she had to be here.

When Marit had been at the palace for a full week, a soldier came to the door and told her that her father and sister had come. They had waited at the gate for hours before anyone would see them. Marit went down to meet them, the first time she'd left her room since the wedding night, and brought them both upstairs where they could have something like privacy; the soldier accompanied her to the gate and back, as she did not yet know the way. Ida left them there, going out into the palace; Davey had fallen finally into a fitful sleep, and Marit spoke quietly, trying not to wake him.

"I'm all right," she told Greta and her father. "I'm all right. He didn't hurt me. They just wouldn't let me go home because I'm a princess now. The lindworm was the king's son, but he's turned into a man, and now they want to keep me here as his wife."

She assured them again and again that she was unharmed, that the lindworm hadn't touched her; her father seemed reluctant to believe it, though she stood whole and healthy before him.

There was a bowl of oranges sitting on their little table; Smilla had learned that Marit loved them, and brought them as often as she could. Marit tried to eat them slowly, not knowing how many even the palace could have. Occasionally David could be convinced to eat a segment or two; it was nearly all he would eat.

She gave Greta and her father each an entire orange, and they all sat down in the large, padded chairs. It was nice, but it wasn't home. Soon they would have to go back, and leave Marit here alone. They'd lost nearly a whole day's work already, waiting at the gate. She thought of asking them to stay, of asking the king to make rooms for them, saying he owed it to her for getting rid of the lindworm. But they wouldn't be happy here; she wasn't.

David woke before they left, more quietly than usual, and Marit went to the bed. "My family is here," she told him. "This is my father and my sister, Greta."

He pulled himself into a sitting position as well as he was able, which was not very well; he still struggled badly with operating his new body. "Hello," he said. "I'm Davey."

"Did you really use to be a lindworm?" Greta asked, because Greta had no tact.

Fortunately, Davey was better composed today than he often was. "I did," he said.

"Do you like it better being a man?"

"No."

"Oh. Are you going to eat anyone else?"

"No," he said again, and Marit decided to send her family home before he became upset. Greta promised to come back soon, and to bring more yarn and a small loom, so Marit would have something else to occupy her time. She forgot the wedding dress.

"I'm sorry about her," Marit said.

Davey shrugged. He'd adjusted much more quickly to his shoulders than to any other new parts. "It doesn't matter. Where's Ida?"

"I think she wanted to give me privacy. I'm sure she'll be back soon. Do you want a bit of orange?"

He shook his head.

"You've not ripped your stitches today."

"No, not yet."

"Are you doing it on purpose?" Marit asked. She'd begun to suspect a few days ago.

"Are you going to tell Ida?"

"Why are you doing it?"

He looked away. "Ida says I shouldn't feel guilty. But I didn't—I didn't just kill two people, I ate them. I ate them. I should have been hung when I changed, if I wasn't beheaded before. I can't do anything to make up for it, but if I—if I can make myself feel a fraction of the pain they felt—"

He stopped abruptly, and Marit didn't press for more. She thought she understood.

"Ida won't give up on you, no matter how many times you rip the stitches, or how long you try to starve yourself. She cares much more about you than about the dead princesses, or anything else; that won't change."

"Are you going to tell her?" he asked again. He was still looking away, staring at the wall.

"I don't know," Marit said.

That night when their food was delivered, Ida manhandled Davey from the bed to a chair in front of the fire, and he let himself be coaxed into eating most of a bowl of soup. A few minutes later he was sick.

Ida frowned. "You've hardly eaten all week. Your stomach has forgotten how to welcome food. What was the last thing you ate before I came?"

"The princess," he said.

"David. That was months ago."

"I don't need to eat often; you know that."

"You didn't need to eat often when you were a lindworm, but even so, that's too long. And humans need to eat every day. More than once every day."

Marit took her own soup to the other end of the room, leaving Ida to clean Davey's mess.

It wasn't what she'd expected from married life. She'd known she would be married in the next few years, but hadn't given it too much thought. She'd known many young men, from the forest or the city, and had known one of them would ask her one day, and she would say yes. She'd thought the blacksmith's son fancied her a little, but they weren't close, and she wasn't expecting anything from him. She hadn't thought, really, that being married would be so different; it would just mean living in a different cottage, seeing her family only once or twice each week. She'd known she would share her bed with her husband, had known there may or may not be other people living with them, perhaps her husband's parents.

She'd never bothered imagining the specifics, but had imagined enough that this was—this was all horribly wrong. She slept alone on a cot by the fire, across the room from her husband, who might have eaten her, who might as well have been a child.

She liked Davey well enough, when she had the chance to talk to him, but more often he was sobbing, or with increasing frequency vomiting, or staring into the distance in that odd, blank way of his. And always, always, there was Ida, caring for Davey and making sure Marit didn't upset him.

The days passed slowly. Davey's stitches ripped less often, and then not at all. He cried less, but still frequently, and woke Marit at least once each night with his screaming. He was sick almost daily.

Marit was sick of being trapped, sick of listening to him cry, of listening to Ida try and fail to console him. She wondered if Ida would ever give up, if she would admit that her attempt to save the monster she loved like a child had failed, and that he would never thank her for it.

Greta came to the palace again, and brought with her the small loom, as promised, and Marit's own clothes, and the sleeves she'd torn off her night shifts. Marit sent her home with all the borrowed shifts that had not got blood on them, and the hat she'd knitted between listening to Davey cry. She forgot, again, to send home the wedding dress.

She knitted, and wove, and stared out the window. She sewed the sleeves back onto her nightshifts and had brief, quiet conversations with Smilla in the hall outside her room—Ida didn't like having extra people in the room when she could help it.

She had her clothes, at least. Dresses that didn't make her feel like an imposter, a peasant trying to be a princess. Dresses she could manage herself, without asking Ida to lace up the back, or going about her day with the dress hanging open in back and the laces hanging down, which she had often done when she couldn't be bothered dragging Ida away from Davey for a few minutes.

March turned to April, which turned to May. Davey learned to manage a spoon and fork for himself, and took his first stumbling steps across the room before collapsing in a heap in front of the fire. They saw no one but servants; the royal family seemed content to leave them be in this small, lonely corner of the palace, and Marit wondered again why she needed to be there.

And then the king came to their door.

Chapter Four

The king let himself in, though Marit had bolted the door herself that morning. Of course, of course the king would have all the keys to his own palace.

Ida was bustling about, straightening the bedsheets and tidying things that didn't really need tidying, when there was never anyone there to see the mess. Davey was sprawled out in front of the fire, as he often was, drawn constantly to the heat like some part of him was still cold-blooded. Marit was sitting at the window. Smilla had found her some colored thread and, with nothing better to do, she was trying to embroider flowers around the collar of her second-best dress.

"Has he learned to walk yet?" the king asked. He addressed Ida, ignoring Marit and Davey both.

"Well enough," Ida said, which was a lie. He could barely make it from one end of the room to the other without support, and he couldn't even stand in one place for more than a few minutes.

"Good," said the king. "He's been only a rumor for too long, and people are growing suspicious. Tomorrow night we'll introduce him to the kingdom and celebrate his safe return."

"Not well enough for a party," Ida admitted.

The king waved away her concerns. "We've been telling them

he was kept by the lindworm in some dark, dank hole for twenty years. Any lingering weakness can be explained by the trauma of his ordeal."

He turned his attention to Marit and Davey, and frowned. "You'll need nicer clothes than that, both of you. Didn't Harald bring anything better?"

Marit was wearing one of her own dresses, and Davey the shirt and trousers that Ida had brought him the day she came. Davey, who'd never worn clothing until a few weeks ago, looked down at his shirt as if he had no idea what might be wrong with it.

"We've better clothes," Marit said. "These are more comfortable."

"Wear the better clothes tomorrow," the king said. "David, you'll do as you're told. You won't say anything inappropriate in front of our guests."

"Inappropriate?" Davey asked.

"I think he means more confessions," Marit said.

"Oh." He looked back up at the king. "I promised Ida I wouldn't."

"Good." He left again, and Ida left with him, probably to learn the details and explain to them later.

Marit cast her embroidery aside and went to sit near Davey and the fire. He hadn't cried or been sick yet today, and was therefore safe to approach; she tried to keep her distance when he was distraught or messy.

"I've never been to a fancy party before," she said.

Davey glanced briefly over at her. "There was our wedding."

"That doesn't count."

"Oh. I haven't either, then."

"Do you think it will be nice?"

"I think it will be awful. I'll spent the whole night trying and failing not to embarrass myself, and you and Ida will spend it trying and failing to keep me from embarrassing myself, and all the people who know the truth and are pretending not to will try to bait us into saying something stupid."

"I'm sure I'll embarrass myself, too."

"Is it more embarrassing to use the wrong fork or address someone with the wrong title, or to collapse on the floor because your legs can't hold your weight? Or to throw up on a duke because your stomach can barely hold food?"

"All right, you'll embarrass yourself more. Will you really not confess everything as soon as someone tries to bait you?"

He shook his head. "We're too far into this now. You and Ida would be punished for helping me. I'll have to find another way to kill myself."

He said it lightly, almost cheerfully, but Marit wasn't sure it was meant to be a joke. Neither of them said anything else until Ida came back.

♛

New clothing was delivered the next day; perhaps the king had not trusted Marit's assessment of their options. Davey's outfit was an old suit of Harald's, as all his clothing was, but this had been taken in so that it nearly fit him. (Harald was strong and healthy; Davey had been too thin when he first changed, and had only become thinner since.) Marit's dress was even fancier than what she'd been given before, and the woman who brought it told her it belonged to the queen.

Ida wore what she always wore. Even the king couldn't tell her what to do.

Prince Harald came into their room not long before they were expected downstairs. He tossed something to Davey, who, standing unsteadily, failed to catch it. It clattered to the ground, and Marit saw it was a crown.

"Remember that, Lindworm? It should fit you now—it's only a spare we took from the treasury."

Marit looked down at it. Gold with red stones. It was the same crown he wore the night they were married.

No one picked it up. Davey walked carefully around it on the floor, and they all followed Prince Harald into the hallway.

Davey couldn't manage all the stairs. It was impossible—he

could barely carry himself down the hall to the first set of stairs. Marit and Ida exchanged glances and silently positioned themselves on either side of Davey, half carrying him. Harald walked quickly, and didn't look back at them, and Marit had to call out once so that he would stop before he was out of sight. She didn't know where they were going—Ida might have, but she wasn't sure.

Harald did look back then, and watched as they struggled to catch up with him. He didn't say anything. By the time they got to the great hall where the wedding had been held, they were late.

"I thought I told you to get him a crown," the king said, meeting them just outside the large double doors.

The prince shrugged. "I did. He didn't want it."

The king signaled a few men standing in the hallway, and they opened the door. Davey had to walk all the way to the opposite end of the room, where a chair was waiting, alone. Marit hovered close behind him, ready to catch him if he fell. He didn't, but he was pale and sweaty and shaking, from the stairs, even before he began, and looked half dead by the time he reached the chair.

Marit had been given no chair, and had to stand beside him. Ida had disappeared—Marit had looked over at her as the doors were opening and found her gone. Hopefully she would come back soon; Marit wasn't sure how long she could manage Davey alone.

The king made a long speech, which was the first time Marit heard how, after slaying the lindworm, she had gone to find Prince Harald, and together they had rescued his twin, Prince David, who had been kidnapped hours after his birth and been held by the lindworm since. David's birth had never been announced to the kingdom, as they had thought he was dead. When the lindworm returned, they had cooperated with its demands in hopes of learning more about their lost son. While the king was overjoyed to have his David back, he was deeply, deeply sorry for the lives lost in the process.

Marit thought it must be true that they were twins, though Davey certainly seemed younger—the queen had only been pregnant once as far as she knew. It was the only thing in the story that was true.

Well, maybe it was true that he was sorry about lost lives, but not sorry enough to have prevented them being lost in the first place.

The king had explained that Prince David was very ill due to his captivity, and he had therefore brought to the palace a wise woman named Ida who would assist in his care. Marit supposed that explained where Ida had gone—she was staff now, and didn't have to stand there and be stared at like the new prince and princess did.

Then the king had announced that Prince David would be married to his savior in one week.

Ida hadn't told them. She must have known.

Of course, Marit should have known there would be another wedding. She had already married Davey, but no one was supposed to know it was Davey she had married. She'd shared a bedroom with him for weeks now; it would be a scandal if she didn't marry him, and probably she would never be able to marry anyone else, either.

But if the marriage was to be her reward for rescuing the prince, couldn't the king have just given her more gold, or maybe a small plot of land somewhere?

Davey stayed in his chair, and Marit beside it, as an endless line of people came to welcome Davey home and to congratulate them both. Marit, out of her depth, tried to say polite things in response. Davey was no help at all. She wasn't sure how aware he was of what was going on by then. He looked increasingly ill and drawn, and Marit thought that if Ida was supposedly here to manage his health, she must be coming back soon.

She didn't.

Finally, the only person standing in front of them was the queen. She did not waste time exchanging pleasantries or displaying affection for her long-lost son.

"You are to be treated as a member of our family now. This means you will act like one. You and Marit will attend church with us every Sunday, and you will join us for breakfast every morning at nine."

"What about Ida?" Davey asked.

The queen sighed. "If she must come. For now you will not be required at dinners, on account of your...ill health, but when you are, Ida will not be welcome. This will do for now; in the future we will work out the details of your place in the court and in the royal family."

She left abruptly. Marit looked around the room, not sure what to do next. They seemed to be done meeting people, but Marit didn't know if they were allowed to leave, or how to get back to their room when they did.

After several minutes, Marit gave up her hope that someone would tell her what to do next, and went to find the king. She didn't want to interrupt his conversation, and stood there waiting until he noticed her.

"We need to leave," she said when she had his attention. "Davey's not well."

The king followed her back to where Davey was sitting. He bent down at the chair, looking, for a moment, fatherly and concerned, then he straightened and nodded brusquely. "Get him out of here."

He left again, and Marit helped Davey to his feet.

"You should have killed me when you had the chance," he murmured as he stood. "It would have been kinder."

Ida met them just outside the doors, and helped Marit to support Davey's weight. Before they reached the first staircase he was sick. They left the mess there and kept going.

He had to stop and rest halfway up the first staircase, and Marit stood on the step below, waiting as he caught his breath.

"We have to do this all again in a week," she said.

Davey shook his head. "It'll be worse. There'll be the ceremony and then the banquet. It'll be much longer, and I'll be expected to stand for some of it."

Ida frowned. "Maybe we can postpone the ceremony."

Davey tried to stand up, and his legs gave out beneath him. Marit started back down the staircase. "I'm getting help."

Ida didn't stop her, which was a sign of how bad things were.

She found the prince before she found anyone else, and decided after a moment of hesitation that if she could insult his father she could make demands of him.

"I need you to carry Davey up the stairs."

"And why would I do that?"

"I noticed you've been cast as another hero in our story—why don't you try and earn it?"

He looked shocked for just a moment before schooling his features. "Marit—"

"My little sister is half in love with you. So are most girls her age. I can't imagine the feeling would stand up to meeting you. You left me and two others to die, for him, and now that he's more vulnerable you're going to throw things at him? Come carry your brother up the stairs."

He did, though he stomped more than necessary as he went up, sullen and silent. By the time he dropped Davey onto the bed and left, slamming the door behind him, Davey was feverish and barely awake. Marit went to her cot and left Ida to fuss over him, worried but aware there was nothing more she could do.

In the morning Davey was still ill, and there was no discussion of going down for breakfast. Marit had forgotten all about it until a messenger came to remind them; Ida told him Davey was ill and sent him away again. She was poking absently at the fire, wondering if she was still going to get breakfast eventually, when there was a knock on the door, and Ida opened it to reveal the queen, looking furious.

Davey was, just then, leaning over the side of the bed to be sick.

"Oh," the queen said. She seemed surprised to see Davey genuinely ill. Of course, she probably didn't know that he was sick almost daily, but he was still suffering from the night before, too.

"I wish you a speedy recovery," she said. "We will see you at nine when you are well."

She turned on her heel and strode away, closing the door with surprising gentleness.

Ida left them, in the early evening. Davey was, by then, much better, sprawled on the rug before the fire, where he usually was when left to his own devices. Marit went to sit beside him when Ida was gone.

"What do you think breakfast will be like?"

Davey shrugged. A minute or two later he said, so quietly she almost missed it, "I'm afraid."

"Of taking all the stairs again?"

"No, that's where Ida went—to tell the king it has to be in a room closer to ours."

Afraid of the breakfast itself, then. "It won't be so bad. They're your family, they must—they must love you?" They'd let girls die because he asked.

He shook his head. "They didn't kill me because it would be wrong to kill their own son. They gave me what I asked for because they thought I might not have the same qualms about killing them."

Marit hesitated, a moment, on the question she wanted to ask, but she knew she wouldn't have a chance to bring it up again when Ida came back. "Why—why did you ask for—that?"

"I was just doing what Ida said. She didn't—she didn't explain anything. I didn't know what was supposed to happen. Just the instructions. Stop Harald from finding a bride. Demand a bride yourself. When you get her alone, make her take off her shift. Keep doing it until it works."

Until it works. "So she knew people would die."

Davey gave one sharp, miserable nod. "She knew."

They sat in silence for a while. The fire started to die down, and Marit put on another log.

"How long have you known Ida?" she asked. "To trust her, even when—even when people started dying?"

Davey looked up at her, a little surprised; maybe he thought she'd already known. "She raised me. Ida told to queen how to conceive. She was worried she'd do it wrong, was expecting something like me. Waiting for it. I slithered out of the queen and out of the palace, and she found me that day." He returned his gaze to the fire. "We used to travel, when I was small enough. But we've been in her cottage in the woods for years now. Until she—until she sent me away."

Neither of them spoke again, and by the time Ida returned, Davey was asleep, there in front of the fire. She'd brought back supper for them, but didn't wake him to eat, just left him there until morning.

♛

Breakfast was in a small sunroom down two hallways and one flight of stairs, much closer than the great hall, but still far for Davey, especially after their trip two days ago. They were late, and the queen glared impressively when they walked in.

"Nine o'clock, David. If you could trouble yourself to remember for tomorrow." He stared at the floor and didn't answer. "David?"

"We'll be on time, Your Majesty," Marit promised.

"David."

He looked up and whispered, "We'll be on time tomorrow."

"Very good. Have a seat, then."

It was a small round table, and the king, queen, and prince sat all in a row. Marit and Ida silently seated themselves on either side of Davey, forming a shield.

It was more food than Marit had ever seen in one place before her wedding banquet. There were only six of them; she knew some of it would go to waste. Food never went to waste in their room, even when Davey would barely eat. Marit wouldn't allow it. She would eat his leftovers, even if she wasn't hungry, to avoid their being wasted, or Ida would set food aside and they would eat it later, cold.

Davey was picking at his food, as he often did, and he'd only taken finger foods. Davey's hands were clumsy, still, and clumsier with utensils. He probably didn't want his family to see him spill a spoonful of porridge on his shirt.

"Have some bacon, David," the prince said.

He shook his head. He never did eat things like that—Marit thought he probably hadn't had meat cooked, as a lindworm, and the bacon was very well done.

"Come on, you're eating like a bird. And I thought you were supposed to be a snake."

"Harald," the queen said.

"You won't eat dead pig—but living girl is fine? Do you want me to go out and find someone for you? I'm sure there are girls in the kitchen."

"Harald," the queen said again.

Marit found Davey's hand under the table and squeezed it. He looked about to cry.

"I apologize," Harald said, not sounding particularly sincere. Ida hurried Davey out of the room, with promises to return the next day, and Marit, who had not finished eating, grabbed a roll before following.

When they were back in their room, Davey collapsed onto the rug. Ida bent over him, fussing like she did, and Marit resisted, narrowly, the urge to kick something.

"Why is he like that?"

"Who, dear?" Ida asked absently, still focused on Davey.

"The prince! He's supposed to be so nice. Even at the wedding, he wouldn't help me, but he was nice about it. Why is he being so awful to Davey now?"

"Because he's a spoiled brat," Ida said dismissively.

Davey shook his head. He looked tired, maybe sad, but not angry as both Marit and Ida were on his behalf. "The things he sat back and allowed to happen—because his parents told him it was the right thing to do, or maybe because he was scared—they must seem ridiculous now. Two nights ago he found me half passed out near a pool of my own vomit and had to carry me up several flights of stairs. I know—I know I'm rather pathetic."

"Davey," Ida said, but he didn't give her a chance to say anything else.

"I think he could tell himself before that what he allowed, he allowed because it would have been wrong to kill his brother. And now that he sees me like this—maybe he's realizing that it was only ever because he was scared of me, after all. And it's easier to take it out on the pathetic new me than to be angry with himself."

"It's still wrong," Marit said.

"Not as wrong as eating people."

"Wrong," Marit repeated. "Wrong to defend a monster, then turn around and attack a weak, sickly boy, no matter what the boy's done. I wouldn't care how he treated you now if he hadn't treated you so much better before."

She retreated to her chair by the window to eat her roll, unwilling to listen to Davey further defend Harald, and equally unwilling to continue defending Davey after the reminder of the lindworm.

She forgot, sometimes. Other times, what she remembered was that the lindworm had not been unkind to her. But he had still eaten two others.

♛

They were on time for breakfast the next morning.

"The wedding is soon," the king said. "Marit, would you like your family to attend this time?"

"Yes, please," she said. She was still angry, at being forced into two weddings now, at sharing breakfast with the man who had condemned her to death, but she missed Greta and her father horribly, and would take any chance to see them.

"Very well," he said, and then he turned his attention to Ida. "We'll need David standing for quite some time. He can manage it?"

Davey looked up from his plate. "I'll try."

"Trying isn't good enough, David," said the queen. "We can hardly have you collapsing in the middle of the ceremony. Can you do it, or not?"

"We'll make it work," Marit said.

"David?"

"We'll make it work," he repeated dully.

Harald was silent throughout the meal. Marit watched him, and thought about how much he seemed to hate Davey, and wondered how many other people, unbound by family ties, hated him just as much. She wasn't sure their official story was convincing. She knew, because Smilla had told her, that most of the servants, at least, knew the truth. Smilla didn't seem to care, but Marit doubted that was the prevailing sentiment.

♛

They went to church on Sunday. There was a chapel built into the palace, and there were two priests assigned to it. The royal family sat in the front row, all in a line, with Ida there to separate Harald and Davey, and Marit on Davey's other side. Marit, marveling at stained glass scenes different from the ones at the church in the city, wasn't looking for trouble, and didn't see it coming until it was too late.

The communion bread and wine were passed around the room. Marit had always gone to the front of the church to take communion before, and wasn't sure if it was always different here, or if the king had ordered the change so that the whole room wouldn't see Davey make his slow, unsteady way to the priest and back. It didn't matter; all eyes were on Davey soon enough, still.

The bread went well enough. Then he took the cup from Ida, or tried to, but fumbled. It slipped through his fingers, and he sat shaking, red wine dripping from his fingers, soaking into the front of his white shirt, while Ida collected the cup and passed it on to Marit.

"Take, drink, this is my blood," he murmured, and then he fell apart. Marit was frozen, wine goblet still in her hands, watching him as he shook, mumbling almost silently, and then with increasing volume, about blood—blood on hands, Christ's blood, his blood, his blood on the sheets, on the floor, blood of a princess, blood on the floor, blood in his mouth, no, blood on his hands, no hands to bleed, the blood, the blood, there was always blood.

Finally the priest stopped speaking, as no one was listening to him. Ida tried to take Davey's hands, but he pulled violently away, and then laughed, hysterical.

"I'm fine. I'm fine. It's only blood. I've seen blood enough now, haven't I?"

"Everyone is here," Marit whispered.

Davey looked up at the priest. "I'm sorry. Please do continue."

He did, and Marit passed the goblet on, though there was not enough wine left in it for the whole congregation. When everyone had gone, Davey stumbled up to the priest, who refused to speak to him. It was not the priest who had performed their marriage, but the other, who had absolved Marit before the wedding. She had confessed to hating the king, to hating the lindworm, and he had told her God understood. There was no penance necessary.

Watching Davey stumble away again, she liked the priest less than she had. They did not return to church the next week, or for many weeks after, and the queen did not try to press the issue as she had the breakfasts.

Chapter Five

The second wedding was more elaborate. Davey was taken to another room to get ready, Ida trailing anxiously behind. Marit stayed in their room, but was joined by several tall, elegant women, possibly the same ones as before. She was made to take a proper, thorough bath, and they fought her more this time on her mother's wedding dress, which was very plain by their standards.

Marit was insistent, and finally they left her alone in the room.

She didn't know if she was meant to take herself downstairs or wait to be collected, and so chose to wait, not eager for another wedding. She went to the mirror to see what the women had done to her—she had grown accustomed, by then, to her own reflection, and it was no longer so exciting.

They had covered up her freckles with something, and pulled her hair back so tightly that her curls were gone. Her scalp ached with it, but she was afraid to let it down, knowing that would send the jewels they'd braided in scattering across the floor, not confident she could find them all again, and not sure how much money they might be worth.

Smilla came to the room not long after the women left, bringing with her Marit's father and sister, both in their best clothes, and letting Marit know how much time there was before they needed to be in the great hall.

She thought of asking her father to sneak her home and away, but that would never work, would only get them all in trouble. She hugged him instead, and told him the king's instructions for the night.

"What about me?" Greta asked.

"You. You do not talk to Davey. At all. He's already on edge. You'd think he'd be used to this by his fourth wedding, but all those people, looking at him—Ida stopped by to tell me he's nearly confessed everything twice."

"He didn't seem upset last time."

"I know. But he's less composed today, and we can't afford any problems."

"Fine," Greta said. "Do I get to meet Prince Harald? Now that we're related?"

"No."

"Why not?"

"Because Prince Harald is evil."

"All my friends say he's brave and merciful and open hearted. And handsome. Of course."

"Of course," Marit repeated. "Well, none of your friends have ever eaten breakfast with him. He's dreadful. They all are."

Greta folded her arms over her chest. "I hate this. There were supposed to be charming princes and fancy balls and pretty dresses."

"Well, we can probably manage a dress. They keep sending up beautiful, silken things that I can't get into without help. You're not so much smaller than me—I think one would fit."

"I don't want to be a princess anymore," Greta said, but she let Marit help her change, and spent some time before they were required downstairs staring into the little wardrobe mirror and running her fingers down the soft, fine material of the dress.

When they reached the great hall, Davey was already there before the priest. She didn't know how he'd gotten down all the stairs—maybe someone had carried him again. He stood with his back to the crowd, swaying like a sapling in strong wind, and she was struck by the familiarity of the situation, with him thin and pale and out of place, wearing a crown, and was almost afraid.

But it was only Davey, and that Davey was also the lindworm seemed unimportant. Ida had been right, that they could be friends. He and Smilla were the only friends she had here. And it was a different crown, though likely just another spare—too large, slipping down farther on his forehead than the king's did, or Harald's.

They stood closer together than was traditional, which the wedding guests could choose to interpret as romantic. But really it was so that she could support most of his weight when his legs gave out, as they inevitably would if he was swaying already.

The ceremony was as much a blur as last time, though she at least managed to answer the priest before he had to repeat himself. She was focused mostly on keeping Davey upright without looking like she was, and a little on the pain in her head from the too-tight braid.

This time they walked to the banquet tables together, and a man came and showed them where to sit, near her father and Greta, but also too near the king and queen and prince, who had been far away before. Ida had disappeared again.

The prince, at least, seemed uninterested in tormenting Davey tonight. He left their table quickly, and Marit saw him later in a crowd of well-dressed people near his age.

Davey picked at his food, while Greta rambled excitedly to anyone within hearing distance how good the food was, and how beautiful the clothes. Marit stared at their wedding cake, identical to the first, and thought a little longingly of their last wedding, even knowing it was foolish.

She had been on her way to death. But at least she had had her anger to sustain her, at least she had—it was foolish. She knew it was. But the two weddings were equally meaningless, equally false, and at least last time it had been common knowledge, and she had not had to pretend.

Would she spend the rest of her life staring out windows while Ida coddled her husband?

It wasn't that she wanted this marriage to be real. It was just—she had wanted a real marriage, someday. She had wanted to share a bed and raise children. To have a small farm not too far from her father's, where they would keep a few chickens and perhaps a goat. To sit in a rocking chair near the fire with her mending on long winter nights, to bake bread with the unneeded help of small, filthy hands, to braid a little girl's hair and kiss a little boy's bruises. All the things she hadn't thought of before, she found herself thinking now, and she tried, and failed, to let go of them.

She would never have children with Davey, who was bright and kind but too consumed by his own guilt, who hardly knew how to be a person, much less a man, a husband, a father. And she thought, even if there were children, they would not be allowed to raise them. There would be nurses and tutors, people the king would pay to steal her family from her, as he had stolen her from her family.

Greta was sitting beside her, but it would never be the same. Marit was a princess now, would always be a princess, and the fact she hadn't the faintest idea how to be one did not lessen the divide that she knew would grow with time, as Greta worked hard and grew up into a normal life, while Marit sat in a tower doing nothing that mattered, except pretending to be the wife of a prince.

She didn't want to be there, wished Davey could just say they were done and take her away like he had before. But Davey didn't have the confidence of the lindworm. Which made sense—he didn't have the size or the teeth anymore to back up that confidence. And it was stupid to miss anything about the monster who would have eaten her.

People began coming to congratulate them, a few of the same people from the week before, but mostly new ones, people who must not have been invited to the last event, and could only meet the new prince now. A few people she recognized from church, which was...unfortunate. That had not been Davey's best moment.

They were sitting on long wooden benches, so it was easy enough to slide closer to Davey, to slip her hand into his and smile shyly up at the people coming to meet them. She wanted them to think they were in love—that was Ida's plan, wasn't it?

Davey was awkward with her closeness and affection, clearly didn't understand what she was doing or why. Marit pulled back a little, worried that people would see his confusion and think that she was an ambitious peasant taking advantage of a prince who didn't understand. That would be no help.

"Davey," she said, after a moment, and he looked over at her and smiled. She saw that people around them were smiling too, and thinking it the best opportunity she would have to display convincing wifely affection, she leaned in and kissed him very quickly on the cheek.

"Ew," Greta said, with great feeling. Someone in the crowd laughed.

Marit leaned in again to whisper to Davey, "They have to believe we're in love," and after that he tried to be more cooperative, although she could tell he was still uncomfortable.

She was uncomfortable, too, but someone had to carry this lie, without Ida there to help, and it certainly wasn't going to be Davey, who, she thought, still didn't much care about the possibility of being found out and summarily executed.

It was a long night, already too long when they were finally allowed to leave, and she realized that a large crowd of people intended to follow them, in a congratulatory sort of way, up to their wedding bed.

It didn't matter that they would certainly leave them in private to consummate, or rather not consummate, their relationship—they couldn't be allowed to see Davey try and badly fail to make it up all the stairs. And she was worried that, leaving them at their door, it would occur to people to wonder why the rescued prince was using the same bedchamber the lindworm had.

It was Prince Harald who saved them from that mess, Harald, stumbling and laughing, apparently happy to be celebrating his brother's wedding, who led them and their crowd down an unfamiliar hall to an unfamiliar room, following them inside and closing the door firmly on everyone else.

The cheerfulness faded out of him when they were alone. "You'll stay here for the night," he said. "I've drunk far too much to even think of getting you up the stairs." He slipped out the door without waiting for a response.

Marit realized when he was gone that she hadn't said goodbye to Greta and her father. She didn't know when she might see them again.

She looked around the room, half expecting Ida to be there waiting for them, but they were alone, and she was a little afraid they'd be alone until morning—it was their wedding night.

There was a large fireplace, which Davey was already sitting in front of, on the wooden floor, legs tucked under him. Davey liked the fire. She left him there and went to examine the rest of the room. There was, unsurprisingly, only one bed, as large as the one in their room, with a canopy and an intricately carved headboard. There were two doors besides the one they'd come through, one leading to an empty closet several times larger than theirs, and one leading to a small room with a mirror, a chamber pot, and a basin of water.

She went back to Davey, a little surprised to find him still sitting up instead of collapsed on the floor. She sat beside him and began taking down her braid, collecting the gems in her lap. "There's only one bed."

"We could have a second one brought in," Davey said.

"No," Marit said, "we couldn't. It's our wedding night." There was a small table with a decorative bowl near the fireplace. She stood, gems caught up in her skirt, and spilled them into the bowl.

"We've been married for weeks, and we've never shared a bed before."

"Davey, it's our wedding night," she said again, more slowly. He stared blankly at her. She remembered his insistence on having her shifts off, and then remembered that he had been following instructions from Ida, and sighed. He really didn't know how to be a husband.

"We can't ask for a second bed," she told him. The specifics were for Ida to explain.

Davey shrugged. "You should sleep in the bed, then; you always have the small one."

"Because the cot can't fit you and Ida both, and I don't want to share with either of you."

She did take the bed, though, and left Davey there on the floor, hoping Ida wouldn't scold her for it later.

They were woken in the morning by Ida bringing them breakfast. Apparently newlyweds weren't required at family meals. Marit had half expected her to join them in the night and, waking to find she hadn't, decided to be cross with her.

"You said it would be a marriage in name only. That I would assume no wifely duties."

"It was one night in a room alone. I'm sure you had no trouble."

"No, no trouble, if only because my husband doesn't even know what my wifely duties are."

They both looked over at Davey, sitting again by the fire. He was staring into the flames, his breakfast untouched, apparently uninterested in their conversation. Ida changed the subject abruptly.

"We'll need to find help for the stairs."

"I can do it," Davey said quietly.

"You couldn't a week ago," Marit said.

"We've nowhere else to be today; I can take my time. I don't want to be carried by Harald again."

It took them most of the day to get up the steps at Davey's pace. Marit was bored, a once-unfamiliar sensation she'd experienced with increasing frequency since coming to the palace. At home, if there was no immediate work to be done, there was usually at least work that would be better done now than later. And if there was somehow no work at all, there would still be people to talk to, or the forest to explore. There was never nothing to do.

She wasn't sure of the way back to their room yet; it was a long, winding journey, and they'd only made it a few times. She could ask Ida to take her to the room and then come back for Davey, perhaps, but thought Ida wouldn't agree. She wouldn't want to leave Davey unattended anywhere, but especially on a staircase, where a momentary loss of balance could mean serious injury or even death.

So she spent the day after her wedding waiting for her husband to climb the stairs. He was, at least, not sick this time when they reached their destination, though he did fall down immediately into his place before the fire, and slept for some time before their supper was delivered.

♛

The days that followed were quiet. They went to breakfast, where the queen was distant, and the king kind, if reserved. Harald often said cruel things, though Marit thought he didn't always mean to; sometimes there was a moment, after he spoke, when he looked surprised by what had come out of his mouth. Marit knitted, and wove, and grew thoroughly, thoroughly sick of thread and yarn.

She could see through their window that it was a beautiful spring, though she had not been outside since the day the king came for her. She longed to do—oh, so many things. To feel the grass on her bare feet, to pick berries with Greta, to milk the goat and chase chickens through the mud. She wanted to make her own food and wash her own clothing.

Instead, she took bits of charcoal from their fireplace and doodled on the stone floors of their room, ignoring Ida when she scolded her for making a mess.

Davey spent his time wandering about the room, becoming slowly more accustomed to his legs. As the days lengthened and the light began to shine more often through their window, he sometimes sat at the chair Marit had set there, but more often lay on the ground below it, soaking up sun like he was a reptile still. It was warm enough, by then, that there was often not a fire in the fireplace all day.

One day, when Ida was gone, probably talking to the king, planning their lives for them, and Marit and Davey were sitting on the floor eating their lunch, Davey dropped an apple, which rolled away under the bed.

Marit went to fetch it, not confident in Davey's ability to crawl around grasping for it in the dark. Behind her, he said, "I could have gotten it myse—" stopping abruptly as she lifted the bed skirt.

She retrieved the apple and, turning back to face him, found him pale and looking a little ill, arms wrapped around his knees.

"Davey?" She held out the apple, and he didn't take it. "Are you all right?"

She looked down at the apple, a little dirty. "It's only dust."

He shook his head, eyes squeezed shut.

"Davey, what's wrong?"

There was long, silent moment before he said quietly, "I forgot about the skins."

"Oh." He must have seen them over her shoulder when she lifted the bed skirt. They'd been there since the day Ida came; Marit hadn't thought much about it. Probably they should get rid of them. Burn them, or take them into the forest and bury them, perhaps.

"I'm sleeping every night on top of my own remains."

Marit frowned. "That's not—I mean, they aren't—you're not dead yet."

"No," he agreed. "Not yet."

"Davey—"

He stood, and went to the other end of the room to throw himself onto the ground below the window, where there was a small patch of sun. Neither of them mentioned the incident when Ida returned.

The next morning on the way to breakfast, Davey stopped at the top of the stairs, swaying slightly—odd, as he didn't usually have trouble on this route anymore. He said quietly, almost dreamily, "I wonder how it would feel to fall."

Ida took his arm in hers, and didn't release him until they reached the bottom step.

Marit thought they would talk about it after breakfast. But after breakfast Prince Harald jogged to catch up with them in the hallway, grabbing Davey's shoulder and whispering something in his ear.

Davey flinched. Harald was jogging away again before Marit or Ida could react. Davey wouldn't tell them what Harald had said, but he was trembling, and when they got back to their room he went to lay face-down on the floor in front of the unlit fire, where he stayed for several hours, unmoving except for the occasional shaking of his shoulders. Marit thought he was crying. Ida tried once to talk to him, but he only shrugged her off, and she left him to himself.

It was only one bad day, Marit thought. And perhaps it would have been only one bad day, if the letter hadn't come that evening.

A maid brought it up, a little before sunset, and Ida glanced over it quickly before saying, with much too measured calm, "Davey, sweetheart..."

Still lying on the floor, he reached out an arm, and she handed him the letter. It hadn't occurred to Marit that a lindworm would be able to read—Marit wasn't. But then Ida had always known that Davey was also a prince, and of course a prince, even a sickly, unwanted, spare prince, couldn't be illiterate.

"Oh," he said quietly, a minute later. "Well, of course you have to go."

"Davey," Ida said.

"You'll leave in the morning—if you hire a wagon you can be at the harbor by evening, and there's a ship headed southwest at least a few times a week, at this time of year."

"Davey," she said again.

"You have to go, we both know that. Marit and I will manage."

"What's going on?" Marit asked, and Davey held out the letter in her direction. "I can't read that. Just tell me."

"We have friends who need help badly," Ida said. "The sort of help that only someone like me can provide."

"You're leaving us?"

"I'll be back as soon as I can."

Marit looked back and forth between Davey and Ida. She didn't want to have to mother Davey, but he was mostly beyond needing it now, and it would be good, she thought, for her if not for Davey, to have some time away from Ida. "Davey's right, then. We'll manage."

♛

Ida woke them the next morning. She spent a long time fussing over Davey, and told Marit to take good care of him, and then she was gone. Davey seemed to be handling it well, calmly tolerating Ida's fussing and assuring her several times that he would be fine.

Marit turned to him after she had locked the door behind Ida. "I suppose we'd best prepare for breakfast."

"I'm not going to breakfast."

"The queen won't like that."

"Damn the queen," he said, with feeling. "You can go without me."

He went back to bed.

Marit didn't know what to do.

After a few minutes of consideration, she decided that she probably should go. Better to try to explain to the queen before she came looking for them, and maybe Davey would like to be alone in the room for a while, to be sad without an audience.

But then there was the problem of clothing. She'd been wearing her borrowed finery instead of her own things since the queen had commented for the second time on her unsuitable attire, but all the borrowed dresses had to be done up in the back, which Ida always did for her. Even if she was comfortable asking Davey, and even if he wasn't in a bad mood, unlikely to cooperate, she didn't think his fingers were dexterous enough yet for buttons.

Finally, she put on her own best dress, and bundled her hair into the most elaborate braid she could manage, hoping that would balance out the dress a bit.

"You'll have to lock the door behind me," she told Davey, knowing he wouldn't. She went to the sunroom and sat down quietly in her usual seat.

"Where is my son?" the queen asked.

"Ida left this morning. Davey's...upset."

"Left?" the king repeated. "Where did she go?"

"All they told me was southwest."

"Without telling anyone? Well, when will she be back?"

"Oh, what does it matter, Olaf?" the queen said tiredly. "Better to have her meddling with someone else. Marit, you may tell David that being upset is not an excuse to miss breakfast. I expect him here tomorrow."

"I'll try," Marit said. She didn't know what state Davey would be in by tomorrow. She'd seen him, before, work himself up so badly that he was sick as well as upset.

The queen sighed. "You'd best not leave him alone. Not everyone believes our story. I doubt anyone will assassinate him in his bedroom, but best not take chances. We'll have food sent up for you."

Marit hadn't thought—she was only a farmer's daughter, she couldn't be expected to think of assassinations. She hurried back to their room. Not that she would be much of a deterrent, if there was an assassination.

As she'd expected, Davey hadn't gotten out of bed to lock the door behind her, but he hadn't been assassinated, either. He was crying, quietly, head turned toward the wall, and Marit left him there. Ida was the one who handled things when he cried; Marit didn't know how to, and didn't much want to, either. That fell too much in the category of mothering.

It was a long, quiet day. Marit took their food from the maid at the door, and left Davey's share on the bed beside him, where it sat untouched until the next meal came, and Marit set it aside to be eaten later.

In the night he woke screaming, as he often did, and Marit pulled her blanket over her head and ignored it.

They didn't make it to breakfast the next morning, and the queen didn't come to scold them for it. She must have understood that Marit wasn't Ida, and couldn't force what was technically a grown man to go anywhere.

She and Davey ignored each other, again, and he continued ignoring his food. It was a cool, rainy evening, and he finally stumbled out of bed when she made a fire.

"Better?" she asked as he spread out in front of it.

For several minutes he didn't answer, eyes closed, laying probably too near the heat. "You know," he said, "last time I spent more than a few hours away from Ida, I ended up eating two people."

"Fortunate, then, that you've barely the strength to manage two flights of stairs now."

"I suppose so."

"I'm sure she'll be back soon."

He shook his head. "She'll be months. The travel time alone—and it won't be a quick problem to fix. And when it is fixed, she'll find a dozen more. It's been many years now since I was small enough to travel with her, and almost as many since it's been safe to leave me unattended. She's neglected her other duties."

♕

They made it out of their room the next morning, but not as far as breakfast. Harald was waiting for them at the bottom of the stairs.

"I heard the old lady left," he said. "What happened?"

Davey didn't answer.

"She finally get sick of you?"

"Leave it," Marit told him. "It's nothing to do with you."

"Nothing to do with me?" he repeated, still addressing Davey. "You were her mess to clean up, and she's gone off with her broom and left us alone."

"Her broom?" Davey asked. There was something almost dangerous in his voice, something that reminded her, for a reason she couldn't name, of the lindworm, and she saw the path of the conversation unfolding before her.

"Her broom to clean up the mess," she said quickly, laying a hand on Davey's arm.

"No," Harald said, "her broom because she's a witch."

Marit remembered calling Ida a witch, to her face, and meaning it, so long ago now, remembered Davey's sharp look.

He shook her arm off, and shoved Harald into the wall. He was much weaker than Harald, but he was angry, and had taken him by surprise, and Harald looked pained at the impact. Marit thought he was going to kill Davey, maybe kill them both. He laughed, not even slightly amused, and she was so afraid.

Marit missed whatever Harald said next, too focused on trying and failing to find a way out of this mess. Whatever it was made Davey shout, "Shut up, you bastard," and shove him again, less effectively now that he was expecting it. He strode away, going the wrong direction down the hall, away from their breakfast, disappearing around a corner.

"Well," Harald said, "he's your problem now. I suggest you learn to control him."

He went in the opposite direction, and Marit hurried after Davey. She found him not too far away, sitting on the floor, back against the wall.

"What do you do when you're angry?" he asked.

Marit considered this for a moment. "Well. Pick fights with people more powerful than me, lately," she said, feeling a little sheepish after seeing him do the same thing. "At home I was only ever angry with Greta, usually, and we just shouted at each other until we were both over it."

"I don't think I'd better do that again."

"Probably not," Marit agreed, sliding down the wall to sit on the floor beside him.

"I used to eat mice," he said after a moment. "Rats, when I was bigger, or any large rodent I could find."

Marit stared at him blankly—why were they suddenly discussing his dietary habits?

"When I was angry, Marit. I'd catch them and swallow them and feel the bones crush as they went down."

"That's awful."

"I am a snake," he said.

"You were a snake," she corrected him, and he shrugged.

"I suppose we'd better go back to our room."

♛

They made it to breakfast, finally, the next morning. Harald didn't speak to them at the table, but followed them down the hall when they left.

"They're your parents too," he said, instead of anything particularly cruel, and Marit realized he was offended on his mother's behalf at being called a bastard.

"You think I care? All they ever did for me was make me a cannibal."

"Davey," Marit said, warningly. Harald had been too shocked to retaliate yesterday; anything could happen now.

"Keep your worm on a leash, Princess, or I'll have him on the end of a fishing pole." Harald spun on his heel and strode away.

When they got back to their room, Marit's cot was gone. They'd expected people to be in the room while they were gone; it was the morning when the maids came in to clean, one more simple thing Marit wasn't allowed to do for herself. And if they were tidying up, taking away the spare bed of Davey's now-gone nursemaid was to be expected, she supposed. But it hadn't been expected. That was her bed.

"It doesn't matter," Davey said. "The bed's so big, we could lie on either end, spread our arms, and not meet in the middle."

He understood her need for space from him, at least, if not what they were actually supposed to be doing in their bed. She probably should have suggested that Ida have a conversation with him before she left—Marit certainly wasn't going to be the one to explain.

And so that night she shared a bed with her husband. It was two nights before she came to the unfortunate discovery that his screaming nightmares were also thrashing nightmares. At least he had been right that the bed was large enough. Wrapped in her own blanket on the opposite end, it was no worse than Greta's occasional light kicks her sleep.

Chapter Six

"I want you back in church on Sunday," said the queen the next morning, thinking, rightly, that Marit would be easier to command than Ida. Perhaps she had forgotten exactly why they had not been to church more than once.

"Yes, Mother," Davey said, before Marit could remind her why it was a bad idea, and she looked over at him in surprise.

They sat in the back, this time, at the king's suggestion. Davey was anxious and fidgety, and Marit took his hands in hers to still them, and set her head on his shoulder to stop him shifting on the bench. It was scandalous, being practically on top of each other in public at all, never mind at church, but it was the best she could do.

She was still worried; Ida had wanted the court to believe they were in love. But Davey was too young, for all that he was three years older than her, in a body he didn't quite fit into, not quite sure how to be a person. She had watched people talk to Davey—servants bringing their food, people at the wedding, and had heard their voices go a little higher, a little softer, like they were talking to a child. Marit didn't want to be thought more predatory than loving.

There was no one to talk to about it. Ida was gone, Davey's inability to understand was the root of the problem, and Smilla was too new a friend for that sort of conversation. She hadn't seen her family since the wedding, and thought she might not for some time; it was a busy season.

Everyone walked to the front of the church to take communion from the priest this time, and Marit and Davey, by silent agreement, stayed in their seats.

It was the priest who had married them, today, married them twice. Davey had, she remembered, wanted to speak to the priest, last time, the other priest, and he had turned him away.

Marit and Davey stayed seated as the service ended and the room emptied, and when everyone else was gone, Marit left Davey at the bench and went to the priest.

"You read me my vows and condemned me to death," she said to him.

He opened his mouth to answer, and she didn't let him, not sure she wanted to know whether he would apologize or defend himself.

"So, I think that means you owe me."

"Owe you what, exactly?"

"My husband. He wanted to speak to a priest weeks ago, but the other one sent him away."

"I would be glad to speak with Prince David."

"Good." Marit paused, remembering, suddenly, stories of lashes and hair shirts and men punishing themselves, and thinking it might be a good way to get back at someone otherwise untouchable. "Don't give him any physical penance."

"I am not in the habit of encouraging disturbed and deeply unhappy young men to hurt themselves."

"Good," she said again. "I'll return to our room so that you can have privacy. Please see that he makes it safely back when you're done."

She left them both in the chapel, making her way back to the room eventually, although she did take a few wrong turns along the way; it was only her second time at the palace chapel. Davey had gotten them there easily enough in the morning, and she thought he must have spent more time exploring the palace when he was still a lindworm.

It had been long enough that she was beginning to be worried when there was a knock on the door, and she opened it to reveal Davey, holding a book, and the priest, with a firm grip on Davey's elbow. They must have had trouble on the stairs; Davey had done well enough earlier, but they lived near the top of the palace, and going downstairs was much easier than coming up.

"All right?" Marit asked.

Davey nodded, and the priest smiled, a little strained.

"I'll see you next week, David," he said, and left.

Davey went to his usual spot on the floor, opening the book very carefully. He didn't seem to be reading it, just slowly flipping the pages.

After a few minutes Marit went to sit beside him. "Was he nice to you? I told him to be nice to you."

"He was fine. He was confused, then he was sad, then he was confused again, but he gave me a Bible." He flipped another page. "I could never read by myself before. Ida had to turn the pages for me."

He spent a long time turning pages without reading them—practicing, Marit thought, so he wouldn't tear anything. It was a beautiful book, with intricate illustrations in the margins and golden lettering on some pages.

Maybe, she thought, Davey could teach her to read. It would be something to pass the time.

♛

Davey didn't fight with Harald again. He was quiet and increasingly distant, and ate little. Twice he suggested that Marit go home, now that Ida was gone, and Marit dismissed this. She told him the king would only drag her back, especially now that they were married a second time. And that was true, but it was also true that she was fond of Davey, and didn't want to think of him struggling to manage alone.

She had thought, though, that she might enjoy their time

together more with Ida gone. After all, most of their best conversations had happened when she was out of the room. And now he would barely talk to her—not, she thought, because he was upset with her, but just because he would barely do anything.

Marit hadn't accounted for how dependent Davey was on Ida, for how much time Ida had spent, while Marit busied herself with anything else she could find, comforting him when he was distraught and convincing him to eat. Those were things Marit didn't know how to do, and things she half-resented being expected to try.

His nightmares were getting quieter, at least, and he spent some time reading his Bible when he was between periods of staring blankly at the walls, and the walk to and from breakfast seemed less difficult each day. He talked to the priest after church again, and seemed a little happier after, for a few hours at least.

Marit convinced Smilla to bring her a spindle and some wool, thinking that making yarn might be less tedious than making things out of it had become. She left Davey to do, or not do, what he pleased, thinking it would probably get better when he was more used to life without Ida.

Breakfasts had become more difficult. Every morning the queen said, "Good morning, David," and waited until he had said good morning back before allowing anyone to eat. Some mornings she insisted on a "Good morning, Mother," but all mornings, for many days, the rest of the meal was spent in silence.

Marit had almost forgotten the sound of the king's voice by the day he said, "The court is very concerned about your health. Should we be concerned about your health, David?"

Davey was always nervous about speaking to the king and queen (and the prince, outside of those two strange days when Ida had left), and so Marit expected him to mumble something no one could hear, leaving her to assure them that he was fine.

But instead he looked up at the king and said, "I'm sure I would feel better if I could eat a few more princesses. They tasted wonderful, you know."

"Davi—"

"I wonder how much better a king would ta—"

Marit recovered enough from her surprise to kick him under the table, hard, knowing it was too late. She looked across the table at the royal family, saw shock turning to rage, and she didn't—she didn't—Davey had just made himself a threat, and she had to—she had to make him stop being a threat, so they wouldn't think they needed to—if he cried. They'd never seen him cry, the way she had, over the dead girls and his lost body, how young he could be and how vulnerable and—she needed to make him cry. And she'd spent weeks listening to everything he'd ever cried over.

She leaned forward and whispered in his ear, not quite quietly enough, the cruelest things she could. "You didn't even know their names. Think of the blood in your mouth, the crunch of their bones in your throat. The way their flesh stuck between your fangs. Imagine how their fathers mourned."

It worked. It worked, and she hated herself the way she had the first night when she lifted the whips, watching the stricken look on his face, and then the crying she'd known would come. She wrapped her arms around him as he broke down, not satisfied with the move she'd made, not sure what choice she had, and stared steadily at his parents, waiting to see what they would do next.

Finally the queen said, with surprising gentleness, "David, perhaps you should return to your room until you can...compose yourself."

Marit stood, pulling him to his feet in the process.

"Just David," the queen clarified. "Marit, we'd like to talk to you. In private."

It had not been so long since the queen had scolded her for leaving him in their room alone, since she had suggested assassins; Marit certainly wasn't going to let him wander the halls weeping after what she suspected had been a bizarre attempt at suicide.

"He's not going anywhere alone. Not like this."

"Fine. Harald, would you escort your brother back up to his room, please?"

"Absolutely not," Marit said. Harald was little better than an assassin.

The king and queen exchanged a glance. The king sighed and said, "Harald, I have that meeting with the count soon. I'd like you to go and fill in for me."

Marit thought it was a rather obvious attempt to get rid of him, but Harald left without a word. She turned her attention back to Davey, trying to calm him, trying to be with him the way Ida had been. "Davey. Davey, sweetheart, I'm sorry. It's all right."

But Marit was not Ida, and was not surprised that she was unsuccessful. Her own way, then. They were in a sunroom, and Davey was fond of the sun. She herded him to the largest, brightest patch of it on the floor, and left him there, returning to her seat at the table. He was probably too distraught to pay much attention to their conversation.

"He was baiting you," she said. "He's been...off, since Ida left. He's—he's talked before, about—about not being dead yet, or about—"

She stopped, not sure what she was saying, not sure of anything except that Davey couldn't have meant what he'd just said, that he could only have said it to make them angry, and he—she knew that he hadn't been well lately, she knew, but—

Small moments were coming together in her head. Not dead yet. The little shrug when she'd said he used to be a snake, as if it didn't matter whether he was a lindworm or a man. Trying to send her home. Things she'd seen and Ida hadn't, because he hid them from Ida, because Ida knew him well enough to understand what they meant, and Marit hadn't yet, then. And there was that moment at the top of the stairs when he wondered about falling, that moment that had so upset Ida—and the priest, having just come up the same stairs with Davey, that tight grip on his elbow when usually Davey was fine there—had he seen the same thing Ida had, the thing Marit had missed?

"You don't think he wonders about my taste?" the king asked, expression unreadable.

She took a moment, this time, to compose herself, to pick out the best words. She looked over at Davey, who was sitting in the patch of sun, still crying but clearly trying to pull himself together.

"I think that you should be concerned about his health," she said. "I think that you should be very concerned about his health, because I think he has just tried to make you angry enough to have him killed."

"David?" the queen said. "Is that true?"

"Why do you always do that? Can't you just leave him alone?" He wasn't in a condition to speak to Marit, then, much less the queen, who he was afraid of.

"David is twenty years old. He is fully capable of speaking for himself, and I fail to see how we will ever get past this if we persist in treating him like a small child. David, do you want to be treated like a small child?"

He looked up then, very slowly, and took a few deep breaths before he could answer. "I just want to have my head chopped off."

There was a long silence as they all processed the confirmation of Marit's suspicions. Davey was done crying for the moment, and stared at the king, waiting. But it was the queen who recovered first.

"Well, I'm afraid that's not an option. If you want to atone for your sins, David, you can start by coming to dinner, and by coming to the ball next month, and by being the prince we've told the kingdom you are."

"I am very sorry."

Marit wasn't sure what he was apologizing for; perhaps the queen understood. She sighed. "It's not entirely your fault. Olaf, why don't you take David off for some bonding time? I'm sure that would be beneficial, and I would like to speak with my daughter-in-law alone."

The king hauled Davey to his feet, and Marit didn't have the energy left to object. She was almost more concerned about herself alone with the queen than she was about him with the king. He had an arm around Davey's waist, helping him as he stumbled reluctantly forward. They'd be all right.

The queen said, "Ida was afraid in the beginning that he would kill himself."

Marit hadn't known that. It seemed she hadn't known a lot of things.

"It was why we waited so long to introduce him to the court—in case he didn't survive." The queen glanced away for a moment, then met Marit's eyes again. "You understand," she said softly, "it would have been better if he died."

"Better for who?"

"Better for the kingdom. For all of us. We could announce that the lindworm was dead, apologize that we had not been able to kill it before lives were lost. We could claim the brides were meant for Harald and the lindworm took them. If only we didn't have this boy rising up from the lindworm's demise. It's suspicious, you must see that. Ida should have taken him and disappeared. He should never have been left here. He should never have been our responsibility."

"He's your son."

"I gave birth to him, yes. I don't know how much he was ever mine, with the magic. How much either of them—I would like to believe that I would have loved him the way I love Harald, if I had been given a chance. I would like to believe I could have seen past his monstrousness, if I had known him as a child. But he slithered out of me and out of the room, and I did not see him again. I confess I screamed. I was in labor; I would have screamed no matter what he looked like. He was hardly bigger than a salamander, and I convinced myself it was only my imagination. I knew I'd disobeyed the wise woman's instructions, and I'd been dreaming of something like it for months." She took a breath, composing herself. "He has a mother; he doesn't need me."

"Ida—"

"Ida loves him beyond reason. As a mother should love her children. But queens do not have that luxury."

"Love is not a luxury," Marit said, though, remembering the princesses, she thought she understood.

"Marit. A bad mother will hurt one or two children. A bad queen will hurt thousands. I have already let two mothers' children die for David. I cannot allow more. Do you understand?"

"I understand."

"It doesn't matter. It would have been better if David had died before we introduced him to the court. Just a body and a story to tell, and no one guilty and alive to cast suspicion on himself, and on all of us through him. But we have introduced him to the court. We have made him a part of this family, and we need him to be a part of it. We need him to be a prince."

"He can't—he's not like Harald. He can't be—"

"He has to. Marit, Ida chose you to do this, and I admit you are not who I would have chosen, but I believe Ida could see—"

Marit interrupted her, a low, swooping feeling in her stomach. "But Ida didn't choose me. The king did."

"Oh," said the queen. "Of course, she wouldn't have said—Marit, I am sorry."

"Sorry for what?"

"Ida chose you. When the lindworm demanded a third bride, and Olaf went into the forest, to think what to do, Ida met him there. She pointed out your father's farm and recommended his oldest daughter. She told him your name, Marit."

She wasn't—it wasn't as if—Ida loved Davey. Loved him beyond reason, the queen had said. And Marit had known that she was just another option that happened to work out, that if she had disobeyed the instructions Ida wouldn't have spared a sad thought for her. But they had—for weeks they had shared a room, a life, and if Ida—it was personal, then. Ida had condemned her to death as surely as the king had.

The queen handed her a handkerchief, so fine and white she was afraid to use it, and wiped her nose on her sleeve instead. The queen did not comment on this.

Both of them in tears at the breakfast table today. What a disastrous marriage this was.

"I will let you go in a moment," the queen said, "and collect yourself, but I need you to understand. We are on the brink of two wars. Half the court suspects the truth, and the only way to convince them is to convince ourselves. We need to be a family, the five of us, and David needs to live. If he died of an illness, perhaps—but if he falls down the stairs or slits his own throat with a bread knife, it will be one thing too many for our rule to take. I need you to protect him; Ida chose you because she saw you could. But protect him from himself, Marit. Don't protect him from us. I know Ida will have told you to protect him from us, to hide him from us. But if I am hard on him it is because I see no other way to make him become the man I need him to be. And if you keep secrets from me, I cannot do my part in keeping all of us safe. Do you understand?"

"I understand."

"Good. Go upstairs, wash your face, and change into a clean dress. You may keep the handkerchief. Olaf will bring David to you when he's finished."

Marit returned to her room and did as the queen said. It was no use, she thought, being angry with Ida, who wasn't here to face it. If she let herself nurse the anger, she would only say something that would hurt Davey. She would save up her anger, and tuck it away, and someday, when Ida came back, there would be a lot of shouting.

The king brought Davey back the same way the priest had, with a book and a tight grip on his elbow.

"I'll see you in the morning," he said. "Tell me what you think of the book."

"Thank you, Your Majesty." There was a pause. "Thank you, Father," he corrected himself, finally, and the king left, closing the door behind him. Davey threw himself onto the floor still clutching the book.

"So?" Marit asked. "What was it like?" She was trying to be normal—she didn't know how things were between them, if Davey would be mad at her. He had a right to be, but she thought she had a right to be a little mad, too, after what he'd tried.

"He patted my back a lot and talked about the sanctity of life."

"And what did you say?"

"I told him that sanctity of life is why we have the death penalty."

"Of course you did." He probably hadn't meant it to sound like he was talking back. Not in the state he'd been when they walked out. "And then what?"

"He got really quiet and patted my back some more. What did the queen want?"

Marit sat down beside him, tucking her legs under her skirt. "She was worried about you, I think."

Davey looked unconvinced.

"Well, she said that the whole kingdom being all right depends on you being all right. I think. There was a lot—I cried."

Davey sat up. "She made you cry?" he demanded, sounding awfully upset for someone who Marit had made cry not much longer than an hour ago.

"It wasn't her, just something she said."

"How is that different?"

"It is. She didn't mean to hurt me. Not like I meant to hurt you."

Davey waved this away, unconcerned. "I meant to hurt myself worse than that."

"Yes, that." Marit sighed. "We need to talk about that."

"What about it? I took a chance, and it didn't work out."

"The problem is that you took the chance at all. Davey, what if they'd taken you outside and hung you?"

"Then I'd be dead and you could go home to your family."

"Damn my family," she said, meaning it then, if she wouldn't a moment later. "I don't want to go home if it costs your life."

"I don't care much about my life," he said, as if this had not become obvious over the course of the morning.

"Because Ida is gone?"

"I suppose so. Not—not that life without Ida isn't worth living, but that—that she isn't here to stop me fixing things in the only way

I know how."

"No. The queen—the queen said dinner. If you want to atone for your sins you should go to dinner."

Davey, staring at the wall beyond her, didn't answer, and she had a sudden, horrible thought.

"Davey, atoning for your—did the priest—"

"No," he said quickly, turning back to her. "No, the priest is kinder than I deserve. He talks about repentance, and all the good that has been done by the worst of sinners."

"Good."

They sat together in silence for a few minutes, Davey running his fingers absently down the spine of his new book while Marit thought.

"You can't die, Davey. Can you imagine what Ida would do to me if she came back and found I'd let you die?"

He shrugged. "I won't kill myself, or try to get myself killed. I think I'll die regardless; the beheading would have been faster."

"Faster than what?" She didn't know how much more she could take in one day.

"I'm dying, Marit," he said, and pulled off his shirt.

She hadn't seen him undressed since—well, she tried not to see him undressed. She hadn't properly looked at him without his shirt on since the first night, and he was far thinner now than he had been then, nearly skeletal, each rib standing out clearly. She'd known—she'd known he wasn't eating much, but he was eating, he wasn't refusing to touch food the way he had sometimes for Ida, but—

How had she failed in so many ways to see how he was struggling?

"Davey—"

"I've not been starving myself on purpose. I can't—I feel sick thinking about food, never mind seeing it, I can't stop thinking about the princesses, and it's not—it's not just that."

"What else is it?"

"The nights I haven't woken you with my nightmares. How

many nights is that?"

"Three of the last five, maybe?"

He nodded. "Those are nights I haven't slept."

"Davey."

"Ida used dark magic to save me."

"I didn't think you heard that conversation."

"I didn't hear any conversation. I don't need Ida to tell me what black magic looks like. She raised me; I know my magics. And I know magic has a price."

"And you think the price of saving your life is—is your life?"

"That spell wasn't to save me, it was to change me. And you're the one who carried it out, so I think we should both be grateful the cost is falling to me."

"So because I tortured you, you have to die?"

"You didn't torture me, Marit."

"I did. You know I did."

"You did what Ida told you to do. As did I. The difference is that what you did changed one person, and what I did killed two."

"Why should you be hurt by a spell Ida started and I finished?"

"Because I am an impure being put into a pure body, and it doesn't want me here."

"How are you impure?"

"I'm a monster, Marit."

"You were a monster."

"I am a monster. The spell changed my shape, not my soul."

"You were—when you were the lindworm. You told me to run."

"And if you hadn't run and you hadn't obeyed Ida, I would still have eaten you, no matter what I said."

"You're not a monster."

"It doesn't matter what you think I am, the fact—"

"No." Marit stood and took a breath. She walked across the room, giving herself as much space from the situation as she could, and then walked back. She looked down at Davey, still sitting on the floor.

"No," she said again. "Here is what I think. I think you were raised on the magical, and I was raised on the practical. And I am done listening to your magic and nonsense, and I'm going to be practical again. Your body is failing you because you haven't taken care of it. Your body is sick because your mind is sick. And I don't know what to do about your guilt and your fear and your pain, but tomorrow I'll tell the king and the queen that you need a doctor."

"Marit—"

"You just need a doctor. Now put your shirt back on and tell me about the book the king gave you."

"We were in his—I think he said it was his study. And I didn't want to hear any more about the sanctity of life, so I started pulling down books. History and records, things like that. The older ones were printed and bound, like this, but some were handwritten—I think they were more recent. He wouldn't let me look at those. I wanted to see if I was there. I think he thought it was morbid."

"Well, it is, a little."

"I was just curious. I know what I did. It doesn't—he wanted to know how much I knew about the history of the kingdom, and I said not much. And he said that I was a prince; I should know where I came from. And besides, I must get bored. This would take my mind off things. So he gave me this one to read. Said it was the most interesting. Wars, I think."

"He gave you a book on wars to take your mind off of the way you killed people?"

Davey shrugged, apparently not seeing why that was strange. She left him to his book.

♕

"Good morning, David, Marit."

"Good morning, Mother," Davey said.

"We need a doctor," Marit said.

"A doctor?" the king asked.

She didn't want to have this conversation in front of Harald, but she didn't want to waste the time to have him sent away, either. "We never finished discussing Davey's health. He's not eating or sleeping, and I think he'll die if we don't do something."

"Olaf," the queen said, and the king gave a tight nod.

"We'll arrange for the royal physician to see you after breakfast."

"Thank you," Marit said, and the king nodded again.

"Would you rather wait to join us for dinner until your health has improved?" the queen asked.

"Yes, please," Davey said quietly.

"Very well. I had intended to send for the tailor this week, but perhaps we will wait. Marit, I do expect you to be dressed properly for dinners."

She sat up a little straighter, surprised; the queen always addressed Davey and ignored her. They'd spoken yesterday, but yesterday had been...odd.

"The dresses that have been sent to me," she said, a little hesitantly, "I can't put them on myself. They all have to be done up in the back. I can't reach, and Davey's fingers can't manage it." She also did not care to have Davey see her in shift ever again, but was reluctant to explain that to his parents.

"We will assign you some ladies' maids," the queen said after a moment. "It should have been done before now. A few men for David, as well."

"Won't work," Harald said. It was the first time he'd spoken that morning.

"Harald?"

"They haven't got a suite. It's not as if they can store the servants in the closet when they're not being used."

"A new set of rooms, perhaps," the king said.

Davey and Marit exchanged glances. Their room had become home, and she didn't want to be taken away from another home. She doubted he did, either.

"Couldn't Marit have different dresses?" asked Davey. "If we—if we're to have our own clothes made. Couldn't they be made like her own clothes? So she could dress herself?"

"You would rather not change rooms?" the queen asked.

"I would rather not," he said. "I would—I would rather not be surrounded by strangers every day, also. And I don't think Marit would like it either."

"You do have many secrets that would need to be hidden from the staff. Very well, then. You may keep your room and your privacy, and Marit, your dresses will be made in a different style. You will need a few for large events that will require some assistance; a few women will be sent to help you on those nights."

Chapter Seven

The doctor came in the afternoon, with two assistants. He had Davey stripped down to his underthings, and began poking and prodding at him and asking questions.

Davey shot panicked looks at Marit as the questions kept coming; they'd forgotten to agree on a story to tell the doctor, and probably they weren't supposed to mention Davey was the lindworm.

Marit hadn't thought they'd need a story, really, but the doctor kept asking questions about Davey's health in childhood, which of course he couldn't say he'd spent as a perfectly healthy lindworm.

"He was kept in a dark, dank cave with other dragon treasures," Marit said at last. "I doubt his health was ever good, though there was no doctor then to treat him. You understand these are painful memories to draw on merely to satisfy your curiosity."

The doctor glared at her. "It isn't curiosity. It is standard, princess, to establish a medical history."

"He's always been weak and sickly," Marit lied. "He's plagued now by nightmares and insomnia, and finds it difficult to eat and to keep food down."

The doctor finished his prodding, and went to the other end of the room to consult with his assistants.

"We will stay tonight for observation," he said. "I am going to fetch more supplies; we will return before you retire for the night."

Marit felt awkward and ill-at-ease that night, preparing for bed. The cots brought in for the doctor and his assistants took space, and his various supplies took more. She couldn't speak freely to Davey, and when she climbed into bed, saw one of the assistants looking at the gap she left between herself and her husband.

"He's a restless sleeper," she said, perhaps more defensively than needed.

It was the sort of night when Davey woke screaming, arms flailing as they did when he was still half-asleep and couldn't quite remember what they were or why they were attached to his body. The doctor had him up and out of bed for more poking and prodding, which Marit thought was only preventing him from getting any more sleep.

Preventing her, as well.

In the morning the doctor sent an order to the kitchen for soft, bland foods, and he mixed up a sleeping medicine. And then he told Marit, firmly, "Fresh air. You take him out into the sun, for an hour or more each day. I'll tell the king and queen. We'll return in the afternoon to look him over, and every afternoon until he's well."

"There," Marit said when the doctor and his assistants were gone. "Did he say you were going to die?"

"No," Davey said.

"You aren't going to die."

"Wishful thinking, I suppose."

"Oh, don't start that. Get dressed; we'll be late for breakfast."

The doctor had woken them early, giving enough time, Marit saw, for his orders to be carried out. There was a special plate for Davey at the breakfast table.

She explained to the king and queen that they were to go outside each day, and the queen said that Harald would show them to the royal gardens after breakfast.

Marit ate quickly, eager to be out of doors for the first time in months. Harald led them out of the sunroom, not speaking until they were away from his parents, when he said, "The garden is on the ground, of course. Am I going to have to carry you again?"

"I can manage down the stairs," Davey said, not mentioning that he almost certainly wouldn't be able to manage going back up.

"I don't think the doctor would want you to overexert yourself," Marit said, earning her glares from Harald and Davey both.

"Perhaps you should build your strength before the garden," Harald said. "There's a balcony near here."

Davey agreed to this, and Marit gave up, for the moment, on her dreams of being properly outside. She wouldn't want to be carried up and down several flights of stairs by Prince Harald, either, especially if he was as cruel to her as he often was to Davey.

The balcony was nice. It was good to feel the sun directly, without a pane of glass in the way. They hadn't brought anything along to do; Davey sat soaking up the sun, as he did, though there wasn't quite room to lie in it. Marit ran her fingers over the ivy growing on the railing and along the wall, relieved to finally be touching something alive again. The palace was all stone and dead wood, and this was better, but she wanted so badly to be in the garden, if she couldn't be in the woods.

They needed someone who wouldn't be angry to help Davey, someone whose help he wouldn't be embarrassed to accept. Someone the king and queen wouldn't object to, as she was sure they wouldn't appreciate the rumors likely to be spread by nearly anyone who could do it.

The idea came to her that night, as she lay awake next to Davey, sleeping the sleep of the heavily drugged. She had grown accustomed to his occasional kicks and soft sounds, and found it hard to sleep without them.

It didn't matter—it was good that he was sleeping so soundly.

"Your Majesty," she said at breakfast, not sure if she was addressing the king or queen or both. "I was—I thought my family might visit, if they could spare a day of work."

"Whenever you like," the king said easily. "We'll let the gate know to let them in."

"Thank you."

"Would you like to write a letter to be sent to them?" the queen asked.

"I can't write."

She frowned. "Another thing to remedy. I'll arrange a tutor for you when I have the time. And for now we'll send a messenger. David, do stop fidgeting and eat your breakfast. The doctor said you were to finish your plate."

"Sorry," he mumbled.

Neither the king nor the queen asked about the gardens, sparing them from admitting they hadn't made it that far, or explaining why.

The next day, in the early afternoon, Marit's father and Greta were brought to their room. She forgot all about Davey for a moment, hugging them and asking about the neighbors and the chickens and the patch of flowers Greta had begun tending in her spare time last summer. She was a little embarrassed when she'd heard all the news and looked over to see Davey still sitting on the floor with the book the king had lent him.

"I thought we might go down to the garden—they've hardly let me outside—but Davey's not strong enough to manage all the stairs by himself."

"I can help with that," her father said, as Marit had known he would, and Davey sighed, but let himself be half-carried.

Marit realized too late that she didn't know how to get to the garden, but it was another thing Davey must have learned while he was the lindworm; he directed them without trouble. He led the way, supported by Marit's father, while she and Greta hung back on the stairs and caught up more.

"He's so thin," Greta said, not quietly enough. "You could carry him yourself, I think—he can't weigh anything at all."

"If I threw him over my shoulder, maybe. He's too big for me to manage with any dignity, though. It's the height, not the weight."

"He's shorter than you, too."

"Not by much. He's too near my size; it would be awkward."

The garden was...pretty, which Marit supposed was the point of a royal garden. Probably their carrots and cabbage were brought in from elsewhere. The oranges would have to be brought in by ship from other countries, at least when Marit had just arrived and it was still practically winter. They'd had apples, too, out of season.

The garden was flowers and trees, well-trimmed grass and winding stone paths. Marit found a stone bench near a large rosebush, wide enough that she could sit there between Greta and her father, and Davey spread out on the ground just below them. Marit had been worried about how to include him in conversation, but it had been a long, difficult walk for him, and he fell asleep.

Greta spent several minutes examining the rose—she was fond of flowers, and it was a city rose, bigger and fancier than the forest roses, as was often the case with things from the city. It had more petals than a wild rose, so many that a flower in full bloom was nearly round, and Greta wanted to pick one to take home; if she hung it upside down in the sun it would dry and she could keep it forever.

"That one is the nicest, I think," Marit said, pointing to one of the fuller blossoms.

"But won't the king be mad if I pick his roses?"

"I think a rose is the least thing the king owes us for all this."

"It's not going too badly?" her father asked, as Greta carefully broke off her chosen flower.

"Not too badly."

"The prince doesn't seem well."

"He's a little ill," Marit said. "The doctor said fresh air would help. But he's having trouble adjusting to all—" She paused. They were in public; there was no one nearby, but she could see several people milling about not too far away, and one of them might hear. "There have been a lot of changes lately."

"It's just as well," her father said, very quietly. "If he looked a little less sick and sad, I imagine more people would want to hit him."

"He is rather hard to stay mad at. Except for the prince. The prince is almost always mad at him."

"Well, Prince Harald has been stopped from getting married twice now, and Prince David has you."

"I suppose. You can just call him Davey; he is your son-in-law."

"Me too?" Greta asked.

"He's your brother-in-law."

"All right. Davey." Greta poked him very gently with her foot. "Davey, are you awake?"

"Leave him alone," Marit said. "The doctor's giving him a sleeping drought at night, but I think it lasts into the day sometimes. And the stairs are hard for him."

"Fine. Why are you never dressed like a princess when we see you?"

"I don't like the dresses. They're hard to put on."

Greta sighed. "It's such a waste. If I had princess dresses I'd never wear anything else."

"If you never wore anything but princess dresses, they would be covered in mud half the time, and your friends would tease you."

"My friends tease me anyway. It would be nice if it was because I looked good, for once."

"Are you having troubles with your friends?" their father asked. Greta wouldn't have talked to him about something like that, especially if it was because of her clothes; those conversations were for sisters.

"Astrid and Kaia are both the oldest in their families. They don't have to wear their sisters' old clothes."

"Bring me one of two of your dresses next time you can come," Marit told her. "I'll embroider them a bit, make them fancier without taking away from their practicality. I've nothing else to do with myself all day."

"When can I come again?"

"Whenever Father can spare you. The king said they'd let you in at the gate now."

"We can both come next week," Greta said. "Can't we? Money's not so tight now; we can spare a half day's work every week."

"All right," their father said. "Next week. You should wake your prince, Marit—the back of his neck is burning."

"Oh." She nudged Davey with her foot, a little harder than Greta had. Snakes didn't sunburn, so probably lindworms didn't, either; she doubted it was a sensation he'd appreciate. "Davey, wake up."

He sat up in one fluid, serpentine movement, which might have reminded her of the lindworm if he hadn't then smiled brightly.

"This is better than the balcony."

"Because there's enough space that you can sleep in the sun like a snake?"

"It is a small balcony."

"We'll come back next week, when my family visits again."

"All right," he said. "Do we have to go back already?"

"No. I just didn't want you to burn."

"Burn?" He looked around, obviously confused. "There's no fire here."

"Sunburn, darling," she said, a little loudly, seeing a man walking not too far away. "Not something you would have experienced when the lindworm kept you in his lair."

"No," Davey said, "I suppose not."

The man walked past them, bowing briefly as he went.

"Can you walk a little?" Marit asked. "I'd like to see more of the garden."

"I can walk." Davey stood. "There's an orchard, um, that way, I think?" He gestured vaguely leftward. "It's supposed to be a quite nice orchard."

It was a quite nice orchard, and they spent an hour in it before Greta and her father had to go home. They helped Davey up the stairs before leaving; he didn't need carrying, but did need a lot of support and several short breaks.

One week. In one week Marit would see both her family and the outside again.

♛

Greta brought two dresses the next week, and Davey made it up and down the stairs with a little more ease. The doctor came every evening to check on him, and said that it was good they weren't making the walk every day, that the balcony was fresh air enough. Marit was disappointed, though not surprised. Davey, medicated, spent more time sleeping, and Marit spent most of hers embroidering Greta's dresses. The queen had not mentioned a tutor again. She and the king both, Marit thought, were making more effort to engage Davey in conversation at breakfast, though it often didn't go well.

"You need a haircut, David," the queen said one day, and he flinched, whether at the criticism or the idea itself, Marit didn't know. She remembered, with sharp clarity, the first time Greta had needed a haircut; she was two years old, and had got sap in her hair. Marit, seven then, had held her head still while their father did the cutting, and Greta had screamed and screamed, though their father had been careful, and it should not have hurt her.

Marit didn't think Davey would scream, but he did wince again when the queen said, "I'll send a barber to your room in the afternoon."

"I can do it," Marit said quickly. "I do for my father, at home."

The queen frowned, but after a moment she nodded. "I'll have scissors sent up for you, unless you have them already."

"I do, for my sewing."

"Very well. The doctor says you're progressing nicely, David, and I see you've put on some weight. Harald's clothing is fitting you better. You'll need to see the tailor soon, if he's to have time to finish your clothing for the ball."

Marit had forgotten the ball; no one had mentioned it in many days. They had not heard more about dinner, either, since Marit had asked for the doctor. He was still managing Davey's diet, and Marit suspected the king and queen didn't want their court to see his special meals.

"I trust you're well enough for the ball?" the queen asked. "You managed well enough for your wedding."

Davey didn't answer right away, and Marit almost answered for him—she knew Davey could make it through a party, though he wouldn't likely enjoy it. But the queen wanted Davey to speak for himself, and she would only ask him again if Marit answered for him.

"I'm sure it will be fine," Davey said finally, though Marit could hear in his voice that he was not sure at all.

"Good. I'll let you know when the tailor can see you."

Davey went with the king to his study after breakfast that morning, as he did once a week or so, now. He had an hour or two with the king most weeks, and the same with the priest, and Marit was jealous a little, though she didn't know what for. She had time with her family each week, and perhaps she would rather not share all that time with Davey, but there wasn't anyone else she would like to spend time with. She couldn't imagine an hour or two alone with the queen would be enjoyable. She did enjoy talking with Smilla, but Smilla was at work in the time they spent together, and Marit knew they were not close enough that Smilla would want to spend her time off with her.

She went to her room alone, and remade the bed as she had nothing better to do; they'd been running late for breakfast, and had left the sheets in a tangled heap at the foot of the bed. When Davey came back they would go to sit on the balcony for a while. He would read whatever book the king had given him this week, and she would work a little more on the elaborate flowers she was embroidering around the collar of Greta's best dress. They would return to their room for lunch, Marit would cut Davey's hair, and he might fall asleep in front of the window while she searched for something else to occupy her time. The doctor would come, they would eat supper, and then they would go back to bed, another, slow, lazy day.

She was so sick of slow, lazy days.

♛

The tailor came to their room later that week, and with him came two seamstresses and Prince Harald.

"Neither of you knows a thing about clothing," he said. "I'm to see to it that everything runs smoothly."

Everything would run much more smoothly, of course, if Harald wasn't there. He frightened and embarrassed Davey.

The seamstresses wanted to take Marit to the little private area where their chamber pot was kept, which was usually where she dressed, to take her measurements without the men seeing her in a state of undress, but she didn't want to let Davey out of her sight with Harald there.

She wasn't sure how to explain to the seamstresses that she couldn't trust her husband to his brother's care, and was relieved when Davey distracted them by removing his shirt at the tailor's instruction.

He was still far, far too thin.

"Don't you eat anything anymore?" Prince Harald asked.

Davey flushed and looked away.

"Make the clothing too big," Harald told the tailor. "He's supposed to be gaining weight; we don't want to do this all over again in a month or two."

The tailor nodded and began his measurements. One of the seamstresses remembered herself and tried again to take Marit away.

"I'll be fine," Davey said when he saw her hesitate. "You aren't even leaving the room."

He did seem fine, when Marit and the seamstresses came back. They left with the tailor; Harald stayed.

"We're ordering proper crowns for you both, as well. The tailor will give the goldsmith the measurements. David, I suggested Father have yours set with rubies."

"I don't want rubies," he said, which surprised Marit; he hadn't argued with Harald since Ida left, and she wouldn't have thought he cared much about a crown.

"They would suit you well," Harald said, Marit thought a little reluctantly. "You have our father's coloring."

"Not rubies," Davey repeated. "I had rubies before."

Marit had nearly forgotten the lindworm's crown, though it wouldn't have mattered; she knew little of gemstones.

Harald shrugged. "Emeralds, then. I'll tell Father."

♛

Their crowns arrived in time for the ball, Davey's gold with green stones, Marit's small and silver, made of several thin bands woven together in an intricate pattern. Prince Harald had said she'd have a crown, but somehow its arrival had still surprised her.

Their room was crowded with people to help them get ready. They dressed Davey in gold and white, which Marit thought made him look even paler than he was, and the doctor came by to fuss a little, and remind him not to overdo it. Marit watched Davey as best she could while she was having her hair tugged at, and being laced into the most beautiful and the most complicated dress she'd ever seen, a shimmering blue cloth embroidered all over in silver and gold, which seemed, from the tugging at her back and at her sides, to need to be laced up in three different places. They braided pearls into her hair this time, but didn't pull it so tight as at the wedding, at least.

She felt very much like a princess, but she didn't think it mattered much how she looked; everyone would be paying attention only to Davey, who most had not seen since the wedding, and who was clearly a bit unwell, though not as bad as he was a few weeks ago.

The ballroom was not quite as far away as the great hall, but the doctor was a little worried about the stress of the ball. He had his assistants help Davey down the stairs, and said that they should be called back when Davey went back to their room.

They weren't expected to actually dance at the ball—Marit had checked that with the queen in advance, knowing that Davey couldn't manage it, and that neither of them would know the steps, either. There were chairs lining one long wall of the room, and

Davey and Marit chose two to sit down in. The music was bright and beautiful, and Marit listened, and watched the flying skirts of the ladies as they danced and spun.

A few people tried to come and have conversations with the new prince and his wife, but Marit and Davey were neither of them good conversationalists, at least not here; at home Marit could talk for hours to anyone, but no one in the palace cared about the kinds of things she knew about.

They had been there for maybe an hour when Prince Harald approached their chairs with a large group of young people who must have been his friends.

"David," Harald said, "may I borrow your wife for a dance?"

Davey hesitated, but there were too many people watching to refuse. "Of course," he said.

Marit grabbed his hand and squeezed it before Harald pulled her away, trying to be reassuring; she didn't like the idea of him alone with so many strangers.

"It's an easy dance," Harald assured her as they stepped out onto the floor. He had been there when Marit reminded the queen that neither she nor Davey had learned to dance. "Only two steps."

"I shouldn't have left Davey alone," she said, annoyed with Harald for making her.

"He's with my friends. They're very nice."

"I'm sure they're very nice to you."

"They're very nice," he repeated, "and after you dance with me, you're going to dance with a few of them."

"I can't be away that long," she said, though he was right that the dance was easy, and she was enjoying it.

"You can't spend your life babysitting your husband, Marit. You could be queen someday, and my friends are the people you need to know you and like you before that happens."

Marit stumbled. "I won't—I won't be queen. Why would I be queen?"

"David is ten minutes older than me," Harald said bitterly.

"I can't be queen," Marit said. "I won't." She pulled away from him in the middle of the dance and went back to Davey—it had only been a few minutes, and he was fine.

When she sat down he leaned close to whisper, "Are you all right?"

She nodded, though she wasn't. Shaken, she went over the idea again and again. She had told Ida she wouldn't bear Davey's children; she had never told her that she wouldn't rule his kingdom, because it had never occurred to her that anyone might put a lindworm and a peasant girl on the throne.

Harald's friends spent several minutes trying to make conversation—with her as much as Davey, maybe more than Davey, probably because Harald had told them to, probably because he thought she would be a little better, at least, as queen than Davey would be as king.

She was too distracted to maintain the thread of conversation, even when they tried to keep it to the weather, which should have been simple enough. When Harald didn't return they wandered slowly away; Marit did not see Harald again that night.

They stayed in their seats for long hours, until the king came to send them away. He was fatherly and gentle, as he sometimes was in his best moments; he wrapped an arm around Davey's shoulders and walked him out the door, Marit trailing behind. The doctor's assistants were waiting just outside the ballroom. Davey was shaky and too-hot by then, and they frowned at her and the king both, as if they had allowed Davey to do something he shouldn't—he had only sat there all night.

The king said goodnight, and the assistants helped Davey upstairs. It wasn't until they were alone that Marit realized getting undressed would be just as difficult as getting dressed had been. She looked into the hallway, but at this hour there was no one milling about in case they might need help. She thought there might have been, in the first few weeks, but they so seldom needed help that it was a waste of staff, leaving someone each night to watch their otherwise empty hall.

She kicked off her shoes, and took her crown and Davey's to

sit on a little shelf in the wardrobe. She took down her hair and collected all the pearls, then unclasped the matching pearl necklace, and finally, with no other options, explained to Davey that she was trapped in her ballgown.

He managed the first set of laces, tired as he clearly was, a little clumsy, but well enough. Marit knew there was more lacing, and the dress was not yet loose enough that she could slip out of it, but neither she nor Davey could find it in the mess of ruffles and flounces and embroidery.

"We could cut you out," Davey suggested a little hesitantly.

Marit shook her head. "I'm sure this dress is worth more than my father's farm. I'll just have to sleep in it—we'll find someone to help before going down for breakfast tomorrow."

In the morning it took Smilla an hour to find and undo the two remaining sets of lacing.

Chapter Eight

"Father," Harald said at breakfast, "we need to discuss the succession."

The king hesitated. "David is older, but that's hardly common knowledge." He cast a nervous glance at Davey, as if he would suddenly change back into the lindworm and eat him for trying to deny him the throne.

"David is utterly unsuited to rule," the queen said dismissively. "Harald has the training for it, and the...better equilibrium, of mind and body both, as well. David will be second in line."

"No," Davey said quietly. The entire family turned to stare at him, and Marit suppressed a sigh. Why did he have to be difficult? She couldn't imagine he wanted to be king.

"You think you'd make a better king than Harald?" the queen asked, something a little dangerous in her voice.

"No. I think I'd make a terrible king. I won't be second in line—I won't be in line at all. If something happens to Harald, the crown can go to whoever would have gotten it next if I'd never come."

The king and queen exchanged a glance. After a moment the king nodded.

"Very well," said the queen. "Harald will rule. No one will find it odd that the line skips our poor invalid prince. The court knows he is...ill."

Marit knew the queen's short pauses before words like ill were her way of saying "not right in the head." She didn't know if the queen thought Davey was of unsound mind, or only knew her court did. Surely she wouldn't have assigned the daunting task of making Davey more like a man and more like a prince if she believed him too...ill for that to be possible.

Marit wondered, a little, what the court thought of her, but didn't dare ask the queen. She was only glad Davey's difficulties would protect her from any unwanted responsibility.

"Did you bring my book back, David?" the king asked when they were nearly finished with breakfast.

"I forgot."

"I'll get it," Marit said quickly, wanting to spare him the extra trip up and down the stairs after the ordeal that had been yesterday.

When she came back to the sunroom, Davey was gone. They were all gone. It was not the day Davey usually went to the king's study. The king and queen would not have left Davey alone, but they would have left him alone with Harald.

Where would Harald have taken him?

She found Harald down the next hall, without Davey.

"He had a meeting," Harald said. "I'll take the book back for you."

"Where is my husband?"

"He said he was going to sit on the balcony."

"And you let him go alone?"

"He's not a child, Marit."

"He's not a man either."

"And he's not my responsibility. If he wants to sit on the balcony I'm not going to stop him. I told him I'd tell you he was there; now how was I going to do that if I followed him?"

Harald stomped away, clearly angry with her. She didn't care. She needed to find Davey.

He was sitting on the balcony, leaning against the railing, and he smiled when she came to join him. She frowned back.

"You should have waited for me."

"I knew it would only be a few minutes. I wasn't going to throw myself off the edge without you to watch me."

"The queen has mentioned assassins."

Davey shrugged. That he was not going to kill himself did not mean he would care much if someone else killed him.

"You worry too much," he said.

"You're a very worrying person." She sat down beside him, and admitted quietly, "I half expected to find you had gone over the edge, and Harald had thrown you."

Davey shook his head. "He may mock me and insult me now that I'm not the lindworm, but he won't kill me now any more than he would then. Besides, he's pleased today. I won't be stealing his crown; I suppose he's worried about that for months now."

"I don't like him much, but he'll be a better king than you would."

"Definitely. Though you could have been a good queen."

"No, being a princess is bad enough. I don't think the queen ever wears anything that doesn't take multiple people to get her in and out of it."

♛

It was a few days later that Davey, in a patch of sunlight on the floor below Marit's chair, slammed his book shut and sat up.

"I am so sick of wars and grain taxes."

"I'm sure the king will give you something new to read tomorrow."

"Yes, and I'm sure it will be more of the same; this kingdom's history seems to be nothing but war and taxes."

Marit looked down at the knitting in her lap; she doubted Davey's fingers could manage any of the things she did to pass the time. "I'm sure there must be other books somewhere, in a place like this? More interesting books?"

"A library," Davey said. "I think I've seen—I didn't bother going in. There was no one here to turn the pages for me. But I think I know where it might be."

Marit set her knitting aside. She had seen only a handful of rooms in the palace, and would much rather see more than make a mitten. "Is it near enough that you can manage?"

"There are a few flights of stairs, but I think—I might need to take a few breaks."

It took them not quite an hour to get there. Marit didn't mind the time spent waiting for Davey; it was all halls she had not been down yet, and she was enjoying it all—the paintings on the walls, the rugs on some floors and the tiles on others, the windows of different shapes and sizes.

The library itself wasn't of much use to her, a room full of prettily bound scribbles, but Davey was as happy as she'd seen him, and it was good to see him happy. He ended up with a small stack of books that she carried back to their room for him, not trusting him to maintain his balance on the stairs with anything in his arms.

After that they were often in the library. Marit wandered down aisles and looked at pictures in margins. Davey lay sprawled on the floor with a book open in front of him, or two or three.

Mostly no one else came when they were there. Once they had arrived to find someone already there, and Davey had turned immediately to go back to their room. Another time they'd heard someone coming, and fled through a different door.

They'd gotten a little lost, that time.

They had an argument, one day, when Davey decided he needed a book off the highest shelf. Marit didn't think he was steady enough for the ladder.

"I'll get it for you," she said.

"You don't know what it looks like."

"You'll fall and break your neck."

"It's not so high. I used to be taller than that."

Marit threw up her hands. "Fine! Risk your life for a bundle of paper."

He did, climbing carefully up the ladder while she watched from below, ready to try and catch him if he fell. He took a long time searching for the right book, and Marit was distracted from her watching by her sister appearing in the door.

"Greta." She ran to hug her. "What are you doing here? It's the wrong day."

"Father said I could; I didn't think you'd mind."

"Of course I don't."

"A man from the gate showed me how to get here."

"Marit?" Davey called, a little wobbly. "I think I might fall."

"Don't be a baby, Davey. You used to be taller than that."

He glared down at her, and she laughed. Everything seemed easier with Greta there.

"Come down, then," she said after a moment. "I'll find it for you."

"You don't know what it looks like," he said again. He took a deep breath and stayed very still for a minute, regaining his balance, then resumed his search. A few minutes later a book came flying to the ground, landing a few feet from Marit and Greta, and Davey made his way slowly and carefully down the ladder.

"Go talk with your sister."

"I can't leave you alone."

"Just go down a few rows—you should have some privacy. I'll shout if anything happens."

"What if Harald—"

"I'll throw a book at his head. Go."

"He seems cheerful today," Greta said when they were alone, sitting on the floor with their backs against a bookshelf.

"He's getting better. The doctor seems pleased."

"Good. All my friends are jealous of my dresses now." She changed the subject abruptly, and Marit was glad; sometimes, for a few minutes, everything did not need to be about Davey.

♛

Harald met them in the hall on the way to the sunroom. "Breakfast is cancelled. There was an urgent meeting."

"All right," Marit said, and started turning to go back up the stairs.

"You could–" Harald paused, looking uncomfortable. "You could come and eat in my rooms. If you liked."

"Davey?" Marit asked. She didn't think it was a good idea, but she thought Harald was asking Davey more than her, so she would let him answer.

"I suppose," he said slowly, "I suppose we could do that."

"Good. Come on, then."

They followed him; he took only a few steps before stopping and turning around. "There are three flights of stairs, if you can manage? Only one of them is very long."

"I can manage," Davey said. Harald looked over his shoulder at Marit, who nodded; he probably could.

In his rooms, they sat down carefully on overstuffed arm chairs and waited for the food to arrive. The space was huge and ornate, with corridors and hallways and high vaulted windows, and half a dozen men and women drifting about, lighting fires and dusting and bringing in clean clothes. There were velvet curtains above the windows, and soft cushioned seats below them, and Marit counted three fireplaces.

It was somehow both empty and crowded, and she was glad for their own simple room.

Davey was clearly nervous, picking at his food–the doctor had let him go back to usual meals for breakfast, and he had been better lately about eating at least most of the food he was supposed to.

Harald tried a few times to start a conversation, but Marit and Davey were both too nervous to cooperate, and they mostly sat in silence. Davey fumbled a bit and dropped his fork; a maid picked it up before either he or Marit could.

"Are you all right?" Marit asked, and he nodded.

"I am trying to be nice," Harald said, clearly irritated; Davey flinched.

"You're being nice," Davey agreed quietly.

"Good. Have you ever ridden a horse?"

Davey shook his head. "I ate one once. It didn't taste very good—I think it was sick."

Marit was surprised a bit that he'd mention anything to Harald from when he was the lindworm, but looking at his face, she understood; he was testing how far Harald's niceness would go, trying to decide if he was safe.

Harald didn't seem bothered by what Davey might have eaten. "I'll take you riding after breakfast—give your poor wife some time to herself."

"I'm fine," Marit said, not liking the idea of Harald and Davey unattended.

"You haven't been alone since you got here," Davey said quietly.

"I'm fine," she repeated.

"It will be fun," Harald said. "Just, do finish eating first, David. I don't want you taking a bite out of one of my horses."

They went down to the stables. Marit, unable to stop Davey, had to ask one of the people in Harald's room how to get back to her own, and then waited there for Davey to come back, only mostly sure that he eventually would.

♛

"Horses are evil."

Marit looked up at Davey, standing precariously in the doorway. "Did you have a good time?" she asked, as lightly as she could manage.

"Horses are evil," he repeated slowly.

"Well, what about Harald? How was he?"

Davey stumbled over to the bed and sat down. "Strange. Different. Nice. We could probably be good friends if I could stop wincing when he looks at me."

"You should work on that, then. It would be good to have friends."

It would be better to have friends who hadn't bullied him for months until learning he wasn't a threat to their future kingship, but they were not in a position to be particular; Marit would take whatever friends they could manage.

♛

The next day at breakfast was no different than any other, Harald eating in silence while the king and queen made idle small talk, occasionally trying and failing to involve Davey in the conversation. But the morning after that, Harald came to their room before breakfast.

Marit opened the door when he knocked; Davey was still getting dressed.

"What do you want?" Marit asked without letting him in, aware she was being rude, far past caring about rudeness to royalty, not sure she trusted the other day not to be leading up to something awful. She'd had more time to think, and was no longer as willing to settle for whatever small decency he might offer.

Davey walked into view of the door, still struggling with the buttons on his vest. "Marit I—oh." He stopped, staring at Harald, clearly nervous.

"May I come in?" Harald asked, and Marit stepped reluctantly out of the doorway.

"Am I in trouble?" Davey asked.

"What would you be in trouble for?"

Davey shrugged. Marit went to help him with the vest buttons, unable to reassure him when she was also uneasy.

"I just came to say you shouldn't go to breakfast," Harald said. "Mother and Father are having a nasty fight, and if you show up in the middle of it, they'll start blaming each other for your existence, and I don't—I'm sorry, about—the horses were a bad idea."

"It was all right," Davey said.

The three of them stood in silence for a moment, awkward, before Harald turned to go. Marit followed him into the hallway, carefully closing the door behind her.

"I know we should be thankful for whatever kindness we're given. But you have been very cruel, before."

"And you don't trust me."

"I don't."

"You're worried that I'm only being kind because he's been removed from the line for the throne, and the next time I feel my position is threatened in some way, I'll go back to being cruel."

Marit nodded. "And it will be worse, if he's begun to trust you a little."

"I'm sick of being angry. I'm sick of—" He paused, shaking his head. "I don't like the person I've become since the lindworm came into my life. But that's not really his fault. Is it?"

"You've made your own choices," Marit agreed.

"You asked me for help. The princesses didn't; I suppose they knew better."

"I don't need help anymore."

"You don't need rescuing. I think you still need help. I think that your marriage to a former lindworm has left you both isolated and alone, and I think you both need a friend. One who can help you make a place for yourselves in the court." He took a step back. "I'll give you both some space, and visit again when my brother is a little less frightened of me."

He was polite, after that, and more friendly at breakfast, but did not approach them again at other times. The doctor declared Davey "As well as he was likely to become," which Marit took to mean he thought Davey would always be a little weak and a little prone to illness, though he could just as easily have meant the same thing the queen did with her little pauses.

Davey could, by this time, manage more stairs with more ease, and the queen began to require their presence at dinner multiple times each week, though not every day.

It was not so bad, though it was not so good, either. They sat usually near Harald, who held the attention of everyone near him; Marit thought this was his way of helping, and was grateful. She and Davey were both anxious in the crowd, both unsure of court manners. Davey's clumsiness got worse when he was nervous, which made him embarrassed, which made him more nervous. Marit focused most of her attention on him at dinner, a little because she worried about him, but mostly because concern for her husband was a good excuse to ignore the rest of it.

It was nice to have one more thing breaking up the monotony of their days. This was beginning to feel a little like a proper life, with the breakfasts and the dinners, the balcony and the garden and the church and the library. But it still felt mostly like a life for Davey, one where she was only tagging along. She wasn't a real princess; she didn't belong at breakfasts with the king and queen, which was made clear by the way they seldom addressed her. She didn't belong at court dinners or in libraries full of books she couldn't read, and after church she went to their room alone while Davey stayed with the priest. She was glad that Davey was beginning to have a life beyond sitting in the light being guilty and sad, but she was afraid of being left behind.

Marit woke later than Davey one morning, and found him sitting on the floor with a few of the lindworm's skins pulled out from under the bed. She slid down beside him.

"What are you doing?"

"Just thinking."

"Morbid thoughts?"

He shrugged. "Some people under curses like mine can take their skins off and put them on again, switch back and forth between forms."

"What would happen if you put one of the skins back on?"

"Nothing," he said, in a tone that made her wonder if he'd tried it while she was still asleep.

"Davey..."

"I still feel more like a lindworm than a man."

"It will take time, that's all."

Davey shook his head, she thought more dismissing it than disagreeing. "Ida wasn't sure—she knew something like me would happen if the queen didn't follow her instructions, but she didn't know the specifics. We spent a lot of time researching together, when I was still small enough to travel. We met a few selkies, and a man named Hans who used to be an oversized hedgehog. They all—

they all missed it. Forever."

"A hedgehog?"

He nodded. "His wife burned the skin so he would stop going back and forth. She didn't like being married to a hedgehog."

"Was he angry?"

"Not by then—it had been many years. He was an old man when we met him."

"Would anything happen if we burned your skins?"

"You mean, would I feel more like a man?"

"I suppose."

"Probably not," he said. "And it would be a waste."

"You think the skins would be useful for something else?"

"Lindworm skin has healing properties. When I was a child I brought a women back to life by molting in the wrong place."

"You resurrected someone?" She hadn't spared much thought for Davey's childhood as a lindworm, but she hadn't imagined it would be so exciting.

"It was a disaster. She came back wrong. She tried to kill her husband, and nearly destroyed her kingdom before she died again. I've been careful of where I molt, since then. Ida collects my skins, and sometimes donates them to churches or infirmaries."

"Should we—"

"No," he said quickly. "No, not yet. They're all I have left to show for twenty years of—it wasn't so bad, until the last year or two. I know how to be a lindworm, even if I can't do it anymore. I've still no idea how to be a man."

"It takes time," Marit said again, though she wasn't sure there was time enough in the world. He was not so bad at being a man, and getting better all the time. But if Marit was turned into a bird tomorrow, she thought she would keep feeling like a girl no matter how long she spent as a bird. Ida had said Davey was always meant to be a man, but Marit understood that what he was meant to be wouldn't matter to him as much as what he was.

"You're doing well," she added.

He sighed, and began pushing the skins back under the bed;

Marit helped. They were nearly late for breakfast.

♛

They weren't having dinner with the court that day, nor seeing Marit's family, which left several long hours stretched out before them. And Davey could manage many flights of stairs now, though going from their room to the great hall still left him winded.

"We should explore," Marit said.

"Explore?"

"I've lived in a palace for months now, and hardly seen it."

Davey sat up, closing his book. "Where do you want to go?"

She took a moment to think it over. "Did you see everything, when you were the lindworm?"

"Not everything."

"Then I want to go somewhere you haven't been."

Half an hour later they were thoroughly lost. Marit didn't much care; eventually they would find someone who could point them back toward their room, or they would turn down a hallway Davey knew. She was trying not to take too many stairs, not knowing how long they would be out, and not wanting to strain Davey early on.

"I know this hallway," he said suddenly, sounding more excited than Marit felt the situation warranted. She was a little disappointed; she has thought being lost for a bit would be fun.

Davey must have seen the disappointment in her face. He added, "I've never been down it. It was in one of the books the king lent me. A famous artist came from another country to design it, a few hundred years ago—it used to be in a more central part of the palace."

He had gotten used to calling the king and queen Father and Mother to their faces, but only ever used their titles when alone with Marit. He was telling Marit more about the artist, and she was listening, a little interested but mostly humoring him, when they heard voices.

Davey went a bit pale. "Oh," he said. "Oh no. What—we need to—"

They hadn't encountered anyone yet, but it was inevitable that they would; Marit didn't understand his panic until the owners of the voices came around the corner, and she saw that it was Harald and his friends.

Harald split off from the group when he saw them, coming forward and grabbing Davey's shoulder; Davey stumbled a bit. Harald was smiling.

"Davey," he said. "I've been meaning to talk to you all day. You weren't in your room this morning."

He had been in his room this morning; they'd only just left. But Marit didn't mention it. Harald was turning back to the friends.

"I'll see you later, all right? I need some time with my brother."

The small crowd dispersed, and Harald let go of Davey.

"They're nice, really. But you didn't look as if you wanted to talk to them."

Davey nodded slowly. "What did you—what did you want to talk to me about?"

"What?"

"You said you were meaning to talk to me."

"Oh, that. Nothing. I just wanted them to go away."

"Oh."

"Are you all right?" Harald asked.

Davey nodded.

Harald frowned. "You're not," he said. "You're nearly as white as the lindworm. Am I so terrifying?"

"No," Davey lied, and Harald sighed.

"What are you doing here? You're nowhere near your room, or anywhere you'd have reason to be."

"I wanted to explore," Marit said.

"Come with me, then. I can show you much more interesting places than this."

Marit hesitated. "Davey?"

He nodded. "Let's see something interesting."

Harald took them everywhere. All of the rooms Marit had expected to find in a palace but had never seen. There were hidden corners of thin patterned wood, and elegant dark rooms with high ceilings and cold stone floors. He showed them portraits of his ancestors, a long line of square smiling people with blonde hair, and then the queen, willowy and dark haired, more severe, and himself, like his father with his mother's hair. There was no portrait of Davey, and Marit was more interested in the rosemåling throughout, and especially the designs on the ceilings, the thick dark beams of wood with carvings barely visible. And Harald slowed down when he noticed Davey was having trouble, and told them interesting things about the palace, but also boring historical things that fascinated Davey.

She wasn't quite sure when he'd learned that Davey was fascinated by nearly any new information, however dull—he must have been paying attention to the books the king gave him. (It had taken Davey a long time to grow tired of grain taxes.)

Davey was tense beside Harald for several minutes, but had relaxed fully by the time they returned to their own room, hours later.

"I've got to get ready for dinner," Harald said, dropping them off. "You're not coming tonight?"

"Not tonight," Marit said.

"All right. Goodbye, Davey. Marit."

Chapter Nine

"Of course," said the queen, "there will have to be a ball."

Marit looked up from her plate. "The kind of ball Davey and I have to go to?"

The queen sighed. "Haven't you been paying any attention? A ball to celebrate Harald and David's birthdays. You'll need new clothing, of course. David, will the tailor need to retake your measurements?"

"He should be fine," Harald said. "I had them make the clothes too large, before. They're still fitting, Davey?"

Davey nodded.

He had got better at controlling his emotions, and Marit didn't realize until they'd gone to the balcony after breakfast how upset he was about the ball. She knew he didn't like things like that—she didn't either—but they'd been attending dinners for some time now, and she thought he would be resigned to it.

"It won't be so different from the last one," she said, and he shook his head.

"We don't even know what that was a ball for. This is—it's about me. Like the first time, when I could barely stand, with all the people in the endless line to meet us. But it'll be worse, because we've been at dinner, and they'll expect us to be able to talk with them by now, and probably to dance. A ball is a punishment for being born." He paused, frowning. "I suppose they do have reason—my birth was not a wonderful occasion."

"You and Harald are twins. It's a party for him, and I'm sure no one spared a thought for you in the planning of it."

"I suppose not. Is it too late to throw myself off the balcony?"

"Far too late."

When they returned to their room, Harald was waiting at the door.

"Oh, good," he said when he saw them coming down the hall. "I thought maybe you were in there and ignoring me."

Marit unlocked the door—she'd demanded the key weeks ago, though she doubted it was the only copy; most likely someone could still lock them in. Harald followed them inside.

"We're to coordinate our clothes, Mother says. For the birthday. I thought—I know neither of you cared what the tailor made, last time, but I wanted to be sure, before I told him what I wanted—you didn't want red stones in your crown. Is it red in general you don't like, or was it only the rubies?"

Davey, clearly surprised to be asked, didn't answer right away. "I don't—I don't think it matters," he said finally.

"Blues and greens, perhaps," Harald says. He turned to her. "Unless Marit minds?"

"I don't mind."

"It's settled, then. I thought—" He paused, then started again. "I thought you and I might spend the day together tomorrow, Davey. I know I make you nervous, but you and your wife have hardly been apart since the first wedding, and I know she hasn't been home to see her family, because I know you can't walk that far."

Marit was annoyed when the king and queen spoke past her at breakfast, addressing themselves only to Davey; she was annoyed that Harald was talking about her and not to her, as well, but not for the same reason. Having decided that Marit should go to see her family, he had also decided that it would be easier to make Davey feel guilty so he would insist she go than it would be to convince her.

It worked, of course.

"I'm not sure—" Marit started.

"It will be fine," Davey said.

"You'll leave after breakfast," Harald told her, "and I know you're not expected at dinner tomorrow, so you may stay as late as you like."

"Fine," Marit said. She did want to see her family alone, and to see her home for the first time in months, the forest and the animals and their little cottage.

♛

She wore her own clothing to breakfast for the first time since her new things had come from the tailor; the queen raised an eyebrow but didn't comment.

The king and queen always left the table first, and as soon as they were gone Marit tucked a few things in her skirt—interesting and expensive foods to take home to Greta and her father—said goodbye to Davey, and hurried down the stairs, trusting Harald to manage for the day.

She knew the way from the sunroom to the garden, and thought she could work out the rest once she was outside. It would be good to surprise Father and Greta, and to take back her share of the work for what was left of the day.

She got a bit turned around, not sure where all the gates were to lead off the palace grounds, or which one would take her back toward the forest, but a man she thought was a gardener helped her, and once she was through the gates everything was easy. She was a little worried there would be trouble getting back through the gates in the evening; she didn't think she was a very recognizable person, and surely there would be different guards stationed by then.

It was a worry for later.

As soon as she was safely among the trees, beyond where she expected the guards to watch her, Marit slipped off her shoes. She left them sitting beside a stump, half-hidden by the thick, twisting roots of the tree it had once been, and went on barefoot. They were old, worn shoes, and if they were stolen it would only be by someone who needed them much more than her; if she came back to find them gone, she would assume they had been taken by someone in need, and not by a squirrel. There were plenty more shoes at the palace.

Summer was well underway, and it was good to have her toes in the grass and dirt and moss. All the flowers were in bloom, and the forest smelled right and alive. She let herself run a little, though there was no hurry, just to feel a little more alive herself—she was thoroughly sick of stillness.

When she had run enough to feel a bit more like herself, she took the rest of the walk slowly, savoring it. She listened to birdsong and collected some wildflowers she knew were Greta's particular favorites, careful to keep her skirt bunched up with one hand whatever she did, so as not to spill the food she'd brought.

By the time her home was in sight she felt more herself than she had in months, probably since the day the king had first come, and she ran again the rest of the way.

Neither Greta nor their father was in the house, so she put her food on the table and her flowers in a cup. She watched out the window until she saw them coming through the trees, and ran to meet them.

It was a wonderful day. She took care of all the household chores that Greta, young and careless and used to her help, had allowed to pile up, glad instead of annoyed for the extra work. She petted and made much of all the animals, the ones she knew as well as the new goat and her kid. The chickens did not appreciate her displays of affection, but she didn't much care. The small cat that wandered between their house and the woods came close enough that she could pick it up; the cat tolerated this with the air of a creature doing Marit a great favor.

She milked the goats and made supper, and talked to her family about all the things she couldn't in front of Davey, or in the palace at all; how sometimes she loved Davey and sometimes he drove her half mad, how out-of-place she still felt, how betrayed she had felt by Ida since her conversation with the queen, how she wanted to trust the prince but wasn't sure she should. She had not had a moment truly alone with them since first being taken to the palace, and it was such a relief to finally describe the first wedding night, the tangled jumble of terror and resentment and sympathy and guilt, the blood, everywhere blood, and how she'd made a monster weep.

The days were long this time of year, so she could stay for many hours before she had to go or risk walking the forest alone in the dark. She petted the pets one more time, and let the little goat butt its small head against her hand, then hugged her father and her sister and went back; it would only be three days before she saw them again at the palace.

Her shoes were where she'd left them, and she slipped them onto her filthy feet. The guards at the gate let her in when she said her name, though she was fairly certain there was dirt on her cheek and a twig in her hair. She was in an excellent mood until she returned to the palace and ran into Harald down several hallways and three flights of stairs from their room. He was alone.

"You said you would spend the day with him," she said, furious with herself for trusting him.

But he looked confused, not malicious. "I did. Until just a few minutes ago—he was tired. He said he could go back to your room himself."

"And you let him?"

"He's nearly twenty-one, Marit. You coddle him as badly as that witch some days."

"He's not been alone for more than a few minutes since he changed, and never outside our room."

"Then it's about time, isn't it?"

"The queen mentioned assassins."

"That was weeks ago. He's been seen by all the court over a dozen times since then; they know he's too small and meek and—

and ill to have been the lindworm."

"Yesterday he joked about throwing himself off the balcony."

"A—a joke," Harald said, sounding, finally, a little unsure.

"I thought he was joking, but I've thought so before and been wrong."

"Then we should stop arguing and find him."

Finally in agreement, they both went quickly toward Davey and Marit's room, and found him sitting on the next staircase, three steps up. He smiled when he saw them.

"I'm sorry I went alone, Marit," he said. "I should have known you'd worry."

"I wasn't worried," she lied.

"And that's why you've both just come running down the hall?"

She shrugged.

"What are you sitting here for?" Harald asked.

"I realized I've never been on the stairs without someone right there in case I slipped, and I got nervous. I was working my way up to it."

They took the stairs together, and Harald walked with them to their room, still feeling bad, Marit thought, about leaving him alone, though it had turned out fine.

Of course Davey was in a state of utter panic by the night of the ball. A small troop of women had shown up to deal with things like Marit's hair, as they had for the last ball, calmer than the ones from the weddings. Harald had appeared, about half ready himself, to help with Davey, who was not panicking any less under the ministrations of half a dozen maids.

Although Marit suspected it was also propaganda. Stories about Davey so far had mostly focused on his relationship with her, though Harald had been mentioned in some versions of how he'd been rescued and brought home. Now everyone would be talking about how the brothers had helped each other button their shirts, and how Harald had fixed Prince David's hair, and held his shoulder and talked him through the details of the night when he looked nervous.

They would be good stories, and more true than the ones about Marit.

Davey was getting better at buttons, too.

She convinced them to let her hair hang loose, although they would insist on a heavy string of pearls around her neck. Her dress was blue and white and green, and swished about her legs when she walked. She did not mind these maids so much, and was still in a good mood from her day at home. She was nearly looking forward to this.

When it was time to go down to the ball, Harald arranged them carefully, himself on one side of Davey, Marit on the other, and kept his eyes on them as he walked into the ballroom. He told a joke just as they entered, and got a laugh out of Davey, and they must have looked like a real little family.

Maybe they could be one.

Harald looked up, as if he had forgotten about everyone else until that moment, and waved. "Thank you for coming, everyone." Then he turned back to Marit and Davey. "There'll be chairs in the back corner, and food just to the left of that. The cake won't be out until later, and you'll need to be here then, but you can probably slip away for a bit in between."

Davey nodded.

"I really should be talking to people. Now I could go and do that, and leave you here, and probably some other people will come to talk to you. Or I could stay with you, and let them all come to us. More people, but me and Marit between you and them. What do you think?"

Davey looked over at Marit, who shrugged. "Stay. Please," he said.

"Of course."

Most of the people who came to speak to them were older, or clearly foreign—people, Marit thought, that were not a part of Harald's daily life. She was surprised not to see many people she thought were his friends, but perhaps they saw enough of him at other times, or perhaps he'd asked them to give her and Davey space.

For all he had accused her of coddling Davey not long ago, Marit thought Harald was doing little better. He let Davey mumble and stare at his feet, and answered for him when people asked questions. She didn't really mind, though the queen would surely disapprove; Harald answered questions for Marit, too.

The three of them had spent much time together in the last few weeks, and Harald had taught them both to dance. Marit trusted him, mostly, and could almost forget how angry she'd been with him so many times.

Many people said they were glad to see Davey looking so much better, as if now that the danger was past they were finally allowed to mention how ill he'd seemed. Many also said how glad they were to see the two princes together, and Marit wondered if everyone in the court had been able to see the months of tension between them, Davey's fear and Harald's anger.

It didn't matter; it was done with, now.

Davey refused to dance, though he'd been taught. He was certainly not a good dancer, and Marit couldn't blame him. Harald left them occasionally to dance, and after a while came back to sit with Davey, and sent Marit to dance with a few friends he'd picked out. They were all kind, graceful where she was clumsy, and she felt rather like the princess she was supposed to be.

The cake was eaten and toasts were given, and the queen came to speak to them, looking in a better mood than Marit had seen her before.

"And how are my boys on their birthday?"

Harald stood to kiss her on the cheek, and assured her that they were both well. "And how are you, Mother?"

She laughed. "Better than I was twenty-one years ago, certainly."

"I'm sorry," Davey said immediately, and the queen raised an eyebrow.

"Whatever for? Being born?"

He nodded, slowly, a little unsure, and she laughed again.

"David, that was certainly more my fault than yours. In a...variety of ways."

Davey looked upset. Marit wasn't quite sure why; she supposed there were any number of reasons to be upset. He'd been born a monster, he'd grown up a monster, he hadn't met his family until he had become too much a monster to love.

The queen reached out a hand; for a moment Marit thought she would touch Davey, and then she pulled back.

"You've nothing to be sorry for."

"I've many things to be sorry for," Davey countered.

"As do I," the queen said, which was almost an apology. Marit still didn't know exactly what the queen had done to lead to Davey's birth as a lindworm.

"Have a good night, David," the queen said, and left.

♛

Two days later Harald walked into the library, trailing extravagantly ornamented young people, and sat down at the table across from Davey.

"So, I thought it was time you got to know my friends."

Marit tried to glare at him without the friends noticing. Davey just stared up, frozen, one hand still lifted to turn a page.

Harald plowed ahead, unconcerned. "Everyone, this is Prince David. Davey. My twin. And this is his lovely wife, Princess Marit. Davey, Marit, this is Gertrude, Helga, Kirsten, Erik, Felix, Jon, and Katrina. Don't feel like you have to remember all that right away. Half the time I still get Felix and Jon confused, and it's been eight years."

Davey lowered his hand slowly, and looked intently down at the book. No one said anything. Davey wasn't trying to be rude, Marit knew; he was only panicked by the ambush in a place he felt safe.

Harald tried again. "Gertrude's father is an ambassador. Trudy, tell them about where you come from. Davey loves learning about new places."

Trudy was a little blonde in a yellow dress, and Marit had seen her before. It took her a moment to remember—she'd called the first wedding dreadful, and called Harald Harry.

"Well, it's not so beastly cold as here, but it rains more, and I—oh, do tell us about the lindworm, Davey. Was it very horrible? Did you ever see him, you know..."

Davey looked up. "Eat people?"

She nodded.

"Just twice."

They stared at each other for a long moment, then he looked down again, and Marit grabbed his hand under the table.

"I told you specifically not to talk about that," Harald said, irritated.

"I'm sorry," Trudy said, addressing herself to Davey still. "I'm sorry. Only no one really knows what happened to you, and we all worry so much—you're always so pale, and skinny, and sad and quiet, and I just—"

She was too close, as well as saying all the wrong things, and Davey was clearly uncomfortable.

Harald grabbed her arm and pulled her back. "Trudy. Back off, or I will have you deported."

"I'm sorry," she said again.

Harald released her, and perched on the table in front of Davey. "Are you going to be all right?"

"I'm fine," Davey said. "I'm fine."

"This was a bad idea," Harald said. He sounded both apologetic and angry. Marit was angry too, and not ready to accept apologies.

"We don't talk about the lindworm," she said.

"I'm sorry," said Trudy again.

Things were quiet and uncomfortable again, until Harald said to Davey, "Tell me what you're reading about."

"*Skáldskaparmál.*"

Someone—Erik?—leaned over and pulled the book towards him. "How far are you?"

One of the girls turned to Marit, and she let herself be distracted. Davey could handle talking about books.

"Have you ever milked a cow? Or a goat?"

"Every day for nine years."

"Really? Is it as fun as it looks? Do you churn your own butter?"

They spent nearly an hour cooing over her romantic peasant life, while Davey held his own in conversations about traditional literature. Harald's friends were nice. A little overwhelming, but nice.

♛

Harald appeared on the grass beside Marit later that afternoon, when she and Davey were in the garden. Alone this time, thank God. Davey was a few feet away, sprawled out on the ground, still soaking sun like a snake.

"I really thought it would be good for him, meeting more people our age," Harald said.

"You could have warned us."

"He would have panicked. More than he did. And it was all right, wasn't it? After Trudy shut up? He seemed like he was having a good time." She didn't answer. "And I talked to them later. I told them the truth."

"The truth? Are you mad?"

"I told them that he was the lindworm, and that he ate the princesses. I told them that he was under a spell, and that he had no control over what happened, and that he's traumatized by it. I told them not to tell anyone. And they won't."

"You can trust them?"

"They wouldn't be my friends if I couldn't."

"You could have asked us about that, too."

"I suppose I should have. But I trust them. And they won't be asking any more insensitive questions."

"They'd better not."

"Trudy's a really sweet girl, you know."

"Mm hm. Now go apologize to Davey."

Chapter Ten

"I'm going to learn how to write."

Marit nodded absently; she was focused on the drama in the garden below their window. Some young couple was having a fight. "Have fun with that."

A few minutes later she heard a crash, and looked up. There was a black splotch on the wall, and broken glass on the floor beneath it. "Um...everything all right over there, Davey?"

He shrugged, looking sheepish. "I got upset."

"Looks like it."

"Hands are stupid."

She left the window and plopped down on the floor beside him. "Let me see." She slid the paper away from him. "Looks all right to me."

"You don't know how to read, Marit."

"So?"

"So they may be very nice looking squiggles, but they aren't actually recognizable as any specific letters."

"Well, you'll get it, I'm sure. It's only your first time." She paused, then asked, "You got upset?"

"I got upset."

"You got upset."

"All right, I got very upset."

"And you broke an ink pot by hurling it at the wall."

"I think that's already been established, Marit."

She shook her head. "I just never know what you're going to do when you're upset."

He was quiet for a moment, then said, "I suppose it depends who I'm upset at?"

"Who are you usually upset at?"

"Myself."

"And who are you upset at now?"

"My hands."

"And that's different how?"

He shrugged. "I can't—it's been months. When will they start feeling like my hands, and not something that got stuck on me by a spell?"

"I've had hands for almost eighteen years, and I don't think my first time writing would go any better. Even if I could read." She stood up. "You're cleaning the ink yourself."

♛

They had been going to dinners often enough, by then, that Marit didn't worry much about Davey. They weren't always seated together, and someone was about, if she wasn't, to see that he managed, that he ate his food and didn't say anything he shouldn't. Harald was there, or the king and queen, or Harald's friends, who were beginning to be their friends too.

Marit was talking to Katrina in the time before everyone sat down; she lost sight of Davey, and found him again across the room, standing unhappily beside the king.

He should not be so obviously unhappy in public.

He smiled when she appeared beside him, at least.

"Your Majesty," she said to the king.

"Marit. Meet Sir Tomas. He's just returned from the south."

She attempted a curtsey, badly. "It's lovely to meet you. Could I have my husband back, sir? It's nearly time to sit down."

"What's wrong?" she asked when they were safely away, out of the room so they could speak in private.

"Sir Tomas."

"Yes?"

"He's a very famous monster hunter."

"Oh."

"He's been working in other countries for the last few years. Otherwise they probably would have brought him in to kill me."

"They wouldn't have. They could have killed you. Without him. They didn't because you're their son."

"Harald couldn't, the way the prince is supposed to when dragons lay waste, because I'm their son. If there had been someone else to bring in—if they could have gotten rid of me, and kept the family connections out of it, they would have. They would."

She shook her head. "Harald loves you."

"Harald loves me now."

She left it, for now; she didn't think they would ever have had him killed, any more than they would have killed him themselves, but it wasn't a conversation to have just outside a court dinner.

"Why is a monster hunter here? Why now? There are no monsters."

"Only me," he said quietly, and then, a little louder, "He's hunted monsters across the world, but this is his home. He's come back to help with the war."

"War?" No one had mentioned the threat of war in so long, and they had been with other people, people who should have known about such things, often enough.

"They don't speak of it in front of us. Even the ones who believe I was never the lindworm know it's my fault; if the king didn't feed the monster because it was his son, he did it to save his son. But we will be at war, someday soon."

"It's been so long. Shouldn't a war have already come, if it was going to?"

"Kingdoms move more slowly than men. Even when war is finally declared, it will likely be months before there are battles."

Marit dismissed thoughts of war, for now; there were more

immediate concerns. "Why would the king introduce you to a famed monster hunter?" She could see a still-angry Harald doing such a thing, or perhaps the queen, to make some point, but she wouldn't have expected it of the king, who was always gentle with Davey when he acknowledged him at all.

"Sir Tomas asked to meet me."

"He doesn't–"

"I don't think he knows anything. But I am afraid, Marit."

"We'll go back upstairs, and have dinner sent to our room. The king will understand what happened."

♛

"I wouldn't worry," the king said at breakfast, though no one had mentioned worrying. "Sir Tomas was quite concerned to see you leave last night. He thought it was his fault, you see."

"It was his fault," Marit pointed out.

"Marit, he has no idea. He's one of our best soldiers, and soldiers–I could hardly tell him not to come back." He turned from her. "David, you must know we would not put you in danger. He thinks that you are angry with him, and have every right to be, because in twenty years he never managed to kill the lindworm and save you. He didn't even know about the lindworm, and has taken a blow to his professional pride."

Davey laughed, more relieved than amused.

♛

The queen had never gotten Marit the promised tutor. She was busy, Marit supposed, with their secret war. Wanting a distraction, Marit asked Davey, finally, to teach her to read, and they spent long hours lying on the floor surrounded by scraps of paper and charcoal, and occasionally pots of ink, though Davey had learned that writing was easier when one wasn't using a liquid.

They could ask for a desk, or they could work in the library, perhaps, but Marit rather liked the casual mess of it all. The room was becoming more and more their home, less stifling now that they also spent time outside it. They'd had a shelf brought in, which held Marit's tangled bundles of yard and tools, whichever books

Davey was reading at the time, and a few little trinkets Marit had brought from home, her favorite a little bear her father had carved when she was ten.

"I told you," Marit said, shoving away her scrap of much-smudged paper, "that it would be just as hard for me."

"It would be easier for you to learn your letters if I could write them more neatly for you to study."

"I don't mind; it's better to learn along with you than from some stuffy tutor used to teaching noble children."

Davey scribbled idly on Marit's discarded paper. "I still find myself, some days, trying absently to flick a tail I don't have. The muscles for it are gone, and my whole spine seizes up in confusion when I try."

"But it is good to have hands, isn't it?"

"I do like turning my own pages." He pulled out a fresh sheet of paper and tore it in two, sliding one piece toward her. "Here, let's both try the alphabet again."

Harald burst in while they were working, Marit focused carefully on her M; the last time she had got over-excited, and given it an extra hump.

"I'm getting married," Harald said, waving about a thin sheaf of papers.

"I thought no one would have you?" Marit asked, regretting it immediately as his face fell a little.

"No one near enough to hear the rumors would. But we sent off—I shouldn't have kept it a secret, but I was in the habit of keeping it a secret already before we were friends; I suppose I didn't want the lindworm to steal another bride."

"I'm sorry," Davey started, and Harald waved him off.

"She's from the other end of the world, and it will be months yet before we meet her, but she's written me a letter along with the formal acceptance of my proposal, and a small painting."

"May I see?" Davey asked, and Harald selected a few sheets from his bundle.

"That's the translation. She has a different language, of course, but a different alphabet, too. I've the original letter, but it's only pretty symbols to me."

While Davey was reading the letter, Harald sat on the ground between them and offered Marit the painting. It showed a girl with dark hair and dark eyes, narrowed as if in the middle of a laugh, though her mouth was only upturned a little.

"What is her name?"

"Suhki," Harald said, then repeated it twice, pronouncing it a little differently each time. "I've only seen it written, and the writing of it was only our translator's best attempt to fit the sounds into our letters. I'll have to wait and see how she says it."

Davey handed back the letter. "She seems nice, but is it safe to bring her here?" It was the closest either of them had come to mentioning the coming war that apparently they were not supposed to know of.

"She won't come until midwinter, at least. It could be this is all over by then."

"It hasn't even started yet," Davey said.

"The second princess you ate was the fourth child of a small, weak king whose second daughter was married to Sir Tomas ten years ago, after he saved the kingdom from a band of ogres who had kidnapped her. She died of a fever six months after the wedding, but Sir Tomas loved her very much, and has remained on good terms with her father. He will remind his father-in-law of how many people he allowed to be hurt trying to save his own daughter, and he will advise him not to make him choose which of our two countries holds more of his loyalty."

"That is only one of the princesses," Davey said. He met Marit's eyes, briefly, and she knew they were both uncomfortable to think of his meal as not just a girl with an angry father, but a girl with older siblings she must have loved, one dead now, and a brother-in-law who would be at dinner tonight.

Harald, excited still, shrugged off their concern for the war and the dead girl both. "It was Suhki's father who chose a date for her to come; I thought it would drag on longer, a year or more."

Marit had given the painting to Davey, who handed it now back to Harald; Harald reorganized his papers and stood. "I've work to do, but I wanted to tell you as soon as I read it. You mustn't tell anyone; only Mother and Father know yet, and the people who've helped us with the arrangements."

♛

They went to dinner that night, or tried to. Davey saw Sir Tomas as soon as they entered the room, and took a shaky step backward, running into Marit. His face, when he turned so she could see it, was as white as the lindworm had been. Marit, looking around for someone who would understand, caught the eye of one of Harald's friends. She couldn't remember his name, but the important thing was that he knew the truth. She gave a sharp nod to the door, he looked at Davey beside her and nodded back. Marit wrapped an arm around Davey and led him out of the room, trusting whoever-he-was to tell Harald that Davey was ill and returning to his room.

"He's going to be at dinner," Marit said when they were safely in front of their fireplace.

"Then I'm not," Davey said. He was still pale and trembling, and Marit didn't argue. She would save her arguing for tomorrow, when they explained to the queen that they would no longer be attending dinner.

Smilla brought them food, and they slept for a little, until Davey woke up them both with a screaming nightmare like he had not had in weeks and, refusing to go back to sleep, lay in front of the fire for the rest of the night.

In the morning he was clumsier than usual with exhaustion, and battled with his fork while Marit told the king and queen he wasn't well, and would not be at dinner for a few weeks.

"He doesn't look well," the king agreed, and that was settled.

Davey was very frightened of Sir Tomas. Of course, Marit supposed that for lindworms, even lindworms who were meant to be men, fear of dragon slayers was best instilled at a young age. And it was reasonable that such a fear would be difficult to overcome. If Marit were told she was inflammable, she would not immediately throw her whole self in a fire to test it. Ida had probably warned Davey to beware of monster hunters in the same way her father had warned her to respect old women in the woods. And even after several long weeks of companionship, it was only in moments of sudden anger that Marit had been able to shake off such respect, with Ida standing before her.

She thought the king was right that Sir Tomas was harmless, as long as Davey was a man. She did not think learning Davey had not always been a man would make Sir Tomas attack him, either; she thought that if Sir Tomas did demand Davey's death, it would be by hanging, rather than a sword through his throat. He was a slayer of dragons, not quiet, clumsy boys with charcoal stains on their fingers.

♛

If their relationship with the royal family had been damaged by their retreat from dinners, there was no evidence. One day the king had stood to leave nearly a quarter hour earlier than usual, and said, as was fairly normal, "Harald, I need your help with those forms from the governor." But after that he had said, "Would you like to come, David?"

Davey glanced over at Marit, just for a moment, then stood and followed them down the hall.

Marit sat staring at the queen for all of twelve seconds before she stood too.

"Surely you haven't finished breakfast yet," the queen said.

"I'm sorry." She sat back down.

"How have you and David been lately? Is everything going well?"

"Yes, Your Majesty."

There was a pause. "He said good morning first yesterday; did you notice that?"

"Yes, Your Majesty."

She sighed. "Oh, go on upstairs, then. I won't keep you."

Davey had friends now—Harald, Harald's friends. And he got on well enough with the king. And Father Gregor—that was the priest they liked. Marit liked Harald, too, and his friends were very nice, if sometimes overbearing in their romantic enthusiasm for her old life. But she was not yet ready to befriend the queen.

She fled the room.

♛

Their library was invaded the next afternoon. It was invaded by Sir Tomas, bowing, so sorry to intrude, so sorry to hear the prince had taken ill the other night, searching for a book on dragons.

Davey looked as if he might take ill again, but knew where the dragon books were—knew because he'd read them all himself, two weeks ago, despite Marit's warning to leave lindworms alone—and showed Sir Tomas the way, though with, Marit thought, an obvious reluctance.

She remembered what the king had said about his professional pride, and hoped he would think that Davey resented him instead of fearing him. He seemed a nice enough man, and one who might end half their war before it started, and had done nothing to earn resentment. But she did not want him to know Davey was afraid. She did not want him to wonder why.

♛

After the library, Davey did not want to venture anywhere for fear of meeting Sir Tomas. They went to breakfast, and after breakfast he could not be convinced to go onto the balcony or down to the garden. They went to church, and he did not want to stay after to talk to Father Gregor. By the day her family was to come, Marit had had quite enough of being hidden away, and left him alone in the room, locking the door behind her.

Autumn was near, and soon Greta and her father would not be able to spare her a half day each week. And after autumn was winter, when the snow was heavy on the ground and such a long walk in the woods so frequently was ill-advised.

She tugged gently on Greta's pigtails as she teased her about the cobbler's son, and did not think for a few hours of her husband or the war that would soon be fought over him.

When her family was gone and it was time to go back into the palace, she was restless still, unready to be cooped up with a brooding, anxious Davey, and thought she might take a different, longer route back to her room.

It was a large palace, and she had seen much of it, by now, but there were halls she had not walked down, and many more that she had taken only once, guided by people who knew better where they were going. She was quickly lost, and not quickly found again.

This corner of the palace was empty, and she resolved to ask directions of the next person she met.

At last she saw a figure inside an open door, and did not realize until too late, when she was standing already in the doorway, that the figure was the queen.

She was sitting at a desk making notes in a little book with a feather pen, and looked up when Marit crossed the threshold. "Marit," she said. "I did not expect to see you here."

"I'm lost," Marit admitted reluctantly, not sure if the queen's comment had been a rebuke or merely an observation.

"I'm working now, but in a moment I'll send for someone to escort you to your room."

"Thank you," Marit said, and stood awkwardly in the doorway for a minute or two while the queen turned back to her book.

"What sort of work does a queen do?" she asked when it seemed the silence had gone on forever.

The queen looked up again. "I'm settling our accounts, today. You may help, if you like."

Marit shook her head. "I know my numbers well enough, but Davey's only just begun teaching me letters; I would be of no use to you yet."

"I see."

"You'll have a real princess here, soon."

The queen frowned. "No more real than you," she said, and Marit was not sure whether it was a compliment, or an insult to her soon-to-be sister-in-law.

After a moment, the queen closed her book and set aside her pen and ink. "You must know I was a foreign princess once, too. I know it is an adjustment for you, who have never been a princess. It was not so hard for me; my language and my culture were near enough to Olaf's that I learned quickly, and we had a language in common already when we met. But it will be much harder for Harald's wife than it has been for you, who at least knows our language and our customs, who can even see her own family once or twice each week."

"I didn't mean—I only meant—"

"You meant that I should be pleased to have a new daughter who was born a princess, because I do not much like you." The queen sighed; she looked suddenly sad, and rather old. "This is not my homeland, Marit, though it has been home for nearly thirty years. I am still unaccustomed—affection and friendliness, the way they are expressed here, perhaps especially as they are expressed in the less formal settings that have been home to you and David, do not come naturally to me. And David's presence has, from the start, caused many difficulties, which do not leave time for...bonding. I do not dislike you."

Marit didn't know quite what to say in response, but felt oddly warmed, and did not yet want to leave the queen's doorway. "Do you think it will be very difficult for the new princess?"

The queen peered around Marit into the hallway, and then motioned for her to step into the room. Marit did, and at another gesture, closed the door behind her. There was a second chair in the room, and after a moment of hesitation Marit sat in it. The queen appeared, briefly, lost in thought.

"It's an odd business," she said. "Harald is ignoring the oddness because he has wanted this so badly for so long, and Olaf because he has wanted it for him. And it is true that it will be good to have an heir on the way as soon as possible. Olaf was an only child, and already king when he married me, and it took us too many years to produce an heir. I would not give our people such a time of uncertainty again so soon. But we made the offer to feel we were doing something; I did not expect it to be accepted. There has never been a match made between our corner of the world and theirs. If Olaf and I had not had a language in common when we wed, we would have had a priest or scholar to translate. Harald and his wife will have a sea merchant we are paying to stay on land until they can manage for themselves. She is bringing no one here from her own household, and will likely never see anyone she knows again. Her country is not a poor one, and the bride price we offered was not overly large."

"You think there is something wrong with her."

The queen shrugged delicately. "She is a year older than Harald, but we do not know at what age her people are traditionally wed. She is beautiful enough to my eye, but we do not know what features they value. She has written a letter to Harald, but her alphabet is not our own, and we have only the merchant's word for what it says. I do not believe she is a first child, or even a first daughter; perhaps he has several dozen, that he can send one off with such ease."

Marit thought for a moment of the queen saying Ida should have taken Davey away from the palace, and then felt unkind; surely this foreign king had known his daughter since her infancy, and surely his entire kingdom was not hanging by one small thread that she could snap without effort, or even by accident. Surely his daughter had never eaten a person. Besides, the queen had said she did not dislike Marit. Marit did not need to be told the queen preferred Davey to her; that meant she must like him, at least, if she still did not love him.

"The arrangement has been made very quickly," the queen continued, "considering the distance that must be travelled for each small bit of communication. We have sent a proposal, and her father has sent an acceptance. To reach our port by the date the acceptance named, she must leave home on the same ship that brings our acknowledgement of the acceptance, if not sooner, and there are usually many more exchanges. There are negotiations for what each parent will offer, what—and often who—the princess will bring from home. We do not know if her father will send men to witness the marriage and then return home, but he has indicated that none of her own people will stay with her."

"Harald is very excited," Marit said slowly.

"As he should be. He is to be wed; you needn't fill his head with worries over it. We will accept whoever we are sent; we have already accepted a lindworm." She stood abruptly. "I have earned a break, I think; I will take you to your room myself."

Marit followed the queen slowly down the winding halls; they did not speak again. She wondered if silently escorting Marit herself was the friendliness she knew how to show, or if she had just wanted to be done talking to her.

She had to unlock her door when they reached it, and felt rather silly for locking it behind her, for locking her husband in; surely she could have left the key, and Davey could have locked the door behind her, then opened it when she knocked. There were two locks on the door, the outside one and the inside one, and the only key was for the outside lock. If something had happened, Davey would have been unable to get out. Locking it as she had was foolish.

Davey looked up when Marit and the queen stepped in; he was sprawled on the floor, hair tangled and shirt rumpled, with a large smudge of charcoal on his forehead, and another on his cheek. He tried to sit up quickly in a more respectable position, but could do nothing about the rest of it. He looked very unprincely.

"Hello, Mother," he said, nervously.

"I got lost," Marit told him, "and your mother showed me the way back."

The queen, to her surprise, crouched on the ground in front of Davey. She reached out for a moment and then pulled back, just as she had at his birthday. "You are filthy," she told him.

"Yes, Mother," Davey said, sheepish.

"And your wife has mud on the elbows of her gown. I'll have a bath sent up for you both."

The queen stood and swept out while Marit was still twisting for a view of her elbows. The ground had been a bit muddy, she supposed.

♛

They saw less of Harald, these days. Marit didn't know if he was busy preparing for war, or busy preparing for marriage, or if it was only that they so seldom left their room, and Harald could not be expected to always be the one to come looking for them.

There was still breakfast, but Marit was surprised to find she missed their dinners, and the library full of books she couldn't read, and Harald's friends, with whom she had nothing in common.

She worried, too, for Davey's health; he was having many nightmares again, and was reluctant to eat. He had no fresh air and little exercise. Marit thought they should be living their lives again, but she knew he was very afraid, and did not want to force him into a situation that might be more dangerous than she expected. She did not know what signs there might be, to a trained eye, that he was really a lindworm, and she did not care to find out.

She had hoped that by autumn he would be strong enough that they could go a little ways, at least, into the woods, to see the changing colors and jump a little in the crunchy leaves. But she knew that even if he could be coaxed out of the room, a Davey who had barely even been on the stairs in weeks could not manage such a walk.

Greta and her father had no time to visit, busy doing all the things that must be done before the snow fell, and she was lonely. She had gone for another visit, on a day when Harald could spend several hours with Davey, but had felt awkward and out of place in her childhood home. She found that she no longer quite fit into her old life, and she knew that this was not because of the king or the lindworm, or anything that anyone could be blamed for. It would have been the same, eventually, if she had married a farmer or a shepherd or a blacksmith; her father and her sister were no longer the people she shared her daily life with, no longer the people who knew her the best. It was a part of growing up, but, she thought, a cruel part.

Davey could not manage the forest, and Greta had not the time, so Marit settled instead for long, lonely walks in the orchard. The gardeners raked frequently and with enthusiasm, and she could seldom find sufficient crunchy leaves to stomp on. But the colors were bright and beautiful, and it was in her autumn wanderings that she stumbled upon the royal greenhouse, and finally learned how there had been fresh fruit so early in the season. It was a large space to her peasant eye, but much smaller than the orchard, or any other part of the garden, and it was about half filled with orange trees. A gardener she asked one day told her that the queen was particularly fond of oranges, which had been more easily grown in her homeland; the king had built the greenhouse for her when she carried his first child, who had been stillborn.

It was on the first truly cold day of the year that she next encountered Sir Tomas.

She had stuck her head out the window before going down to breakfast, and so had known it was cold; she had dressed as she was expected to dress for breakfast, and had, after a half-hearted attempt to convince Davey to come along, changed her clothes before going to the garden.

Her own old clothing was warmer, and easier to layer for additional warmth. She wore a hat that she had knitted in her endless first days at the palace, and two hastily-grabbed mittens that were not from the same pair.

She had not been outside for long, but when she reentered the palace her breath came out in little bursts of fog. She felt oddly giddy, and was not paying much attention to her surroundings; when someone called her "Princess," she was badly startled, and even more startled when she realized that someone was Sir Tomas.

She was still not accustomed to being called Princess. The king and queen and Harald called her Marit, and Harald's friends did because he did. Servants would call her princess, sometimes, and the elegant people she met at dinner. But it was more surprising than usual, too, because she had not expected to be recognized by anyone who did not know her well, bundled heavily in old clothing, with her orange curls tucked away beneath her hat.

"Sir Tomas," she said, trying to sound a little dignified.

"I am sorry; I did not mean to startle you."

She wasn't sure how to respond to that with dignity, and so didn't respond at all.

"Is your husband well? You have not returned to dinner in some weeks."

"David has a poor constitution," Marit said, which was true; he was much better than he had been, but still prone to exhaustion and mild fevers. "I am sure he will be all right."

"I am glad."

Marit hesitated a moment, but, well, it wasn't as if she would likely have many opportunities to talk with the man who so terrified her husband. "Harald told me that your wife was held, once, like—like David was?"

"A bit like," he said gravely, "though the ogres did not hold her for nearly so long, and many more people died for it. The ogres killed a man each day as long as their demands were not met, and it was nearly a month before I came and was able to slay them."

"What were their demands?"

"Their leader wanted to be married to Viktoria, and inherit the kingdom; he thought his argument would be strengthened by having Viktoria already in his possession, but it only made the king wild with worry, and unwilling to listen to anything the ogres said, even as the corpses piled up. Marriage to a monster is a bitter thing, and our women's bodies are not made to bear their children safely." He did not say this like a man who knew his queen had born a monster, nor one who thought Marit was married to one.

"Viktoria was your wife?"

Sir Tomas smiled, briefly. "She was, for a time. Her constitution was poor as well, and made no better by a month in an ogre's den."

"I'm sorry."

"It was long ago, now. But you may tell your husband that there will be no war from that quarter. I have only just heard back; I go now to tell my king. But I saw you on my way, and I remembered—it is said your husband has been sick with guilt over the girls his captor ate, and the war it will cause. I thought it might bring him some peace to hear the news now, instead of whenever he may next see his father."

"Thank you," Marit said. "I will tell him."

"That's all very good," Davey said when Marit told him, "but it doesn't make Viktoria's poor sister any less dead."

"It gives you perhaps several thousand fewer deaths to feel responsible for. And you brooding over it won't make the girl less dead, either."

"Oh, don't be like Ida."

"Ida would say eating her wasn't even your fault. I'm only saying that, having already eaten her, it's not productive to continue obsessing over her."

"I am not meaning to obsess."

"But you have been, ever since Sir Tomas came. I do hear the nightmares."

"I'm sorry."

"You always are." She kissed him absently on the cheek as she went past him to the wardrobe, calling back as she put away her hat and mittens, "We're going to dinner tomorrow night." It was too late to go that night; there wouldn't be plates set for them.

"Will Sir Tomas be there?"

"Yes, he will, and so will we."

She closed the wardrobe and came to sit in the chair across from him, this being one of the rare occasions when he was seated instead of sprawled on the floor.

"I know you're afraid of him, Davey, but we've seen no evidence that he isn't a perfectly nice man, he's just averted a war for us, and if you really think he might suspect something, I think going into hiding as soon as he came to court was a rather suspicious course of action."

"What if he knows something? What if he's just waiting—"

"Waiting for you to attend dinner in a very public place so he can chop your head off in front of several dozen witnesses including you parents the king and queen? If he wanted to kill you, surely the best way would be to sneak into our room in the night?"

"Maybe," he conceded.

"Besides, I talked to him today, and he didn't seem like he knew anything at all. He was worried that you might be ill, and he told me about the war before he told the king, because he thought you would be happy to hear it. And, Davey, I am so sick of being locked up in this room living half a life."

"You can go out without me. You do; you could do it more."

"It's lonely, going to the garden or wandering the halls alone, and it would be lonelier, going to dinner without you, no matter how many other people were there. You're my friend; they're only people I know a bit."

"Harald is your friend."

"Harald is my friend. He is also the crown prince, and cannot spend every evening neglecting his guests to keep his sister-in-law company. And he isn't you."

"Fine. Dinner tomorrow. If Sir Tomas kills me I shall haunt you."

♛

He had not walked all the steps to dinner in some time, and was therefore more clumsy and slow than he had been. He complained all the way down, whining about the stairs, Marit thought, to distract himself from anxiety over Sir Tomas and the dinner.

"Legs," he said decisively, when they took a moment for him to recover between stairways, "are the most ridiculous, unnecessary thing. What kind of deal was it, I wonder, that Ida made? I could have the bloodlust taken away, but must accept legs instead? You know, I would have been quite satisfied if I could rid myself of the bloodlust and still be otherwise a lindworm. I was quite a good lindworm, I think, as lindworms go, and I am rather a poor example of a man."

"You're only grumpy because you've let your legs go weak again. In a week or two you won't mind so much."

"I suppose," he agreed, and took the next staircase.

♛

Sir Tomas greeted them politely, and otherwise left them alone. They took their seats near a few of Harald's friends, who Marit thought had missed them; they were eager to share all the gossip of these last few weeks, and especially of Harald's coming bride, who was by then common knowledge.

(Harald had memorized the translation of her letter, and often recited bits of it when they saw him. Marit, who loved her husband as a friend, was a little jealous that he could stir up so much romantic feeling in an arranged marriage with a complete stranger. But mostly she was content with what she had. If she had not married Davey, she would have married some boy she had known all her life, and she thought she knew them well enough to say she would never have been in love with any of them.)

Chapter Eleven

It had been a long summer. The weather was warming, already, when Marit went to the lindworm so many months ago, and by now it was something of a relief to see the snow fall again. The eternal summer had ended. The world was changing.

She went to the bed and shook Davey; he sat up groggily. "Come see."

He stared out the window with that sort of joyful, puzzled fascination that was her favorite thing about him. "Snow."

She grinned. "Snow."

When he spoke again, there was a hint of sadness in his voice that she couldn't understand. "I forgot about snow."

"Well, it's been long enough. Let's go outside."

"It's cold. It's snowing."

"Yes," she said.

"I can't go out in the snow. I'm cold—" He stopped abruptly. "I'm not. Marit, I'm not cold-blooded."

"You aren't," she agreed.

"I can go out in the snow!" He ran to the door, stumbling a bit in his enthusiasm, and she had to grab him by the tail of his shirt and tug him gently back.

"You will need a coat."

"Oh."

"You've never been in the snow?"

"I'm never been outside in the winter at all. It isn't safe; it would freeze my cold blood and kill me. I spent last winter slithering around the palace wondering when Ida was going to come back for me, and whether it would be before or after the king finally did the sensible thing and chopped my head off. It was...lonely."

"Well. The queen said we would have clothing for warmer weather delivered this week, but for now perhaps Harald has a coat you can borrow? I'll be fine; I brought all my warmest clothing back the last time I was home."

It was early yet, and they were not expected at breakfast for over an hour. Harald did not answer his own door; he seldom did. There were always people in his rooms for things like that. The man who answered today said Harald was still in bed, but fetched an old coat from his closet for Davey.

He descended several flights of stairs with far more enthusiasm than she had ever seen from him before. Marit had to pull him back again at the door, shoving mittens onto his hands and pulling a hat down over his head. There had been many times, over the course of their marriage, that she had felt he was acting childish; today it was adorable instead of irritating.

Davey's foot sank deep into the snow when he first stepped outside, and he turned back to look at Marit, face full of surprise and delight.

"Well?"

"I've never been this cold in my life." He took a few more steps. "It's amazing."

She could hardly get him inside after that. There were snowball fights, and snowmen, and snow angels, and eternities spent just sitting in it, until she had to drag him inside to prevent frostbite.

Winters were long here—the last year had been abnormal in every way. Usually summers were brief and glorious, a flash of lightning in an endless black sky. They had all grown tired of this warmth, but she had not expected Davey to thrive in their usual cold darkness.

It was best when he went out with Harald or his friends—she hadn't thought she could ever be sick of snow again, but Davey could hardly be dragged from it. He seemed never to be cold.

It was wonderful, the way he'd turn around, knee deep, to smile at her. He was very nearly handsome when he was happy.

It snowed often and hard, the first two weeks of winter, and it was with great difficulty that Marit kept him inside during blizzards.

♛

On Sunday Marit left Davey with Father Gregor after the service, and didn't think anything of it when she was alone in the room for several hours. If he wasn't with Father Gregor anymore, he would be with Harald, or perhaps Felix or Jon, outside or in the library. He would be fine. They were long past the time when leaving him unattended was unsafe.

She was playing with his pen and ink, attempting letters and making the most horrific blots, when Harald burst in without knocking, half dragging and half carrying Davey, who looked damp and dazed. He dumped him into the nearest chair, and Marit stood, spilling the ink.

It didn't matter.

"What happened?"

"I found him lying in the snow. Just like that. No idea how long he was out there. Too long, anyway." He crossed the room to the fireplace as he spoke.

Davey was still wearing the green sweater and breeches he'd had on this morning—not at all appropriate for church in a palace, but if he'd grown up in some hole in the ground, the lindworm's prisoner, no one could expect him to know better.

They were even less appropriate for sitting in the snow for extended periods of time.

"How long?"

He stared blankly up at her.

“Davey. How long were you outside?”

He shrugged. “I don’t know. A while. It wasn’t cold.”

He was soaked, and ice cold, shivering. Harald was crouched down, feeding the fire; Marit hadn’t been paying it any attention while Davey was gone, and it was nearly dead.

“It is not possible,” Marit said, “that you are not cold.”

“I don’t feel anything, really.”

She needed to get him out of the wet clothes. Davey was unfocused, his limbs floppy and uncooperative. Marit managed to strip off his soaked sweater, and the shirt beneath, then balked at the inevitable next step; she hadn’t seen him naked since the night of their awful, awful first wedding.

“Harald,” she called, “come get him dried off and changed. I’ll take care of the fire.”

They switched places, and after a few minutes Harald brought Davey back, changed into his blue sweater. His hair was still wet, and he still seemed dreamy and far away. Harald pushed him gently onto the floor in front of the fire, where Marit wrapped their warmest blanket around him and took his icy hands in hers.

“Idiot,” she said, softly, rubbing his palms with her thumbs. “We warm blooded people can die of cold, too.”

Harald stepped out of the room; she could hear his voice, faintly, talking to someone in the hall.

“It was very nice,” Davey said.

“You’re numb with cold, now. In a few minutes it will hurt. Why were you outside alone?”

“I only meant to be a few minutes. I’d just left Father Gregor, and it had snowed again last night, and the sun was shining on the snow, and it was—it was sort of warm and cold at the same time, sitting in the sun.”

“You’re lucky you don’t have frostbite.” She turned around; Harald had come back. “He doesn’t have frostbite, does he? You got a better look at him.”

“No frostbite. Someone is going to bring up some hot chocolate.”

"Good."

The shivering worsened; by the time the hot chocolate came he was shaking too hard to be trusted with his own mug—he had broken several over the months—and Marit held it to his lips.

"Are you cold now?"

"Very," he admitted.

He came down with a cold, of course. The first time he sneezed he thought he was dying, and he continued to panic about things leaking, no matter how many times Marit told him runny noses were normal.

He hadn't panicked when he leaked tears.

He whined a lot, mostly about the unanticipated downsides to humanity. He was annoyed that she wouldn't let him go outside again until he was better.

He could have gone out sooner if he hadn't spent so much time sticking his head out open windows.

He was crabby and miserable for a while. But it was better than other forms of misery, and Marit was entertained, at least, by the crabbiness.

She distracted him from his cold by asking for stories, of which he had plenty, collected over a lifetime with Ida. He told her of a boy who did not know fear, and of a girl who wept pearls and blood.

"Did he learn to fear in the end?" she asked.

"No. I suppose his wife did. Those who have not seen fear can seldom learn kindness."

"I am not afraid," she said. There were many things to fear—the war loomed ever closer—but today she felt light and happy, bundled up with Davey beneath heavy furs, in front of their cheerful bright fire.

"I am."

"Don't be. I will tell you a proper love story, with no blood or tears."

"Do you know one?"

"I do. You know the Hulder?"

"Everyone knows the Hulder, Marit." They were troll maids, beautiful, but with animal tails or backs that were hollow like rotted trees. They had no souls, and were said to seduce men in the woods.

"Once there was a Huldra maid," she told him, "who met a young fisherman. She would have had him, and killed him, but he was very polite to her. He saw her fox tail hanging below her skirts, and knew what she was, and he did not run. Instead he told her that her petticoat showed, and continued to make conversation when she had hidden her tail again. She told him where to cast his nets, and he came home that night with many fish."

"That is hardly a love story," Davey said.

"Hush. I'm not finished yet. For many days she met him and told him where to cast his net, until one morning he asked her to sit in the boat with him. She was surprised, and reminded him what she was, but she had done nothing untoward in all these days they had spoken, and had been kind to him, and he wished to spend more time with her."

"And I suppose they were married in the spring, and with her human wedding the Huldra maid received her soul, as happens in these tales. But would you have told me the second half, when the Huldra grows old and loses her beauty like anyone else, and her husband is unfaithful? She still has the strength of a troll, you know, and will rip his head off when she knows, and then she will be an outcast among humans and trolls, for she is a man-killer without her old beauty."

Marit sighed. He had often been in a foul mood these last few days; it was the illness, but she thought it was something else, as well. She did not know what. "Must you ruin everything?"

For a long time he only stared at her.

"Once there was a human maid," he said, "who saved her husband and tried to make him human. It did not quite work, and he was rather dreadful. She was not in love with him, but she cared for him very much, even when he did not deserve it, and he was very grateful. That is a proper love story, I suppose."

She put her head on his shoulder, and watched dancing embers in the fireplace, and they both fell silent for a while.

"Christmas is coming," the queen said at breakfast.

It took them a moment to realize a response was required. "Yes, Mother," said Davey.

"There will be a ball, of course. Olaf, did you—"

"It's all ready. Of course, dear."

"Of course," she repeated. "Marit, your family is welcome. It hadn't occurred to me before, but we must have—do you think we should give them titles?"

"I don't think they'd like that, Your Majesty. The titles, I mean. I can tell them about the ball."

"Well, I suppose you know best. You might want to bring them in for fittings. The crown will provide wardrobe, of course." She turned to the king. "Olaf? I suppose you need the boys today?"

"If they have nothing better to do, yes."

"I'll see you all at dinner, then." She swept out, the king quickly following with Harald and Davey.

Marit was left at the table alone. It was good, she thought, that the king had time for Davey again. He had been busy lately. But she wished—she thought for a moment, then went to find the queen. She needed help. She thought the queen would be glad to give it, even if it meant being interrupted in her office. Davey remained rather terrified of her, and Marit could change his mind if anyone could.

"Would you help us with the dresses, Your Majesty? My sister and I? For the ball? Usually the tailor—I thought it would be nice, for Greta, if she could have some say in her first ball gown. Only we don't know anything about clothes, really."

The queen smiled, just slightly. "I would love to. Whenever it's convenient for your sister."

The queen arranged for them to meet the tailor in his shop, in the city. Marit was a bit worried that it would be too much for

Davey—a long walk, and his first time in the city, and an afternoon spent with the queen. But she wanted to be in the city, and Davey didn't object, just wandered around the room looking miserable for a while, so she decided to let herself have this.

Davey had probably never been into the city. Certainly, Marit would have heard if there were a lindworm slithering in and out of shops along the main way. It would be good for him.

The three of them walked together to the palace gate, where they met Marit's family.

It was not too cold a day, and the queen looked very elegant in her fur hat and gloves. Marit and Davey were both in wool hats that she had knitted, and looked decidedly less elegant, and Greta and her father less elegant still, but the queen didn't seem to mind.

Davey had never walked farther than the palace grounds, and it was a few blocks yet to the tailor. They walked slowly, and the queen did not speak for some time, so the rest of them did not, either. Marit did not think she meant to be rude. It could not be often that she talked to farmers and their young daughters; perhaps she didn't know what to say.

Davey hesitated, a little, as they prepared to turn onto the first proper street, and the queen turned to him.

"Is everything all right, David?"

"Yes, Mother."

"Good. You needn't talk to anyone. It's unlikely they'll approach, although they should all recognize you, even crownless and dressed like that."

"How?"

She smiled. "Because you're with me, dear. Greta, do you know what colors you'd like?"

"Colors?" she repeated.

"For your ball gown. I think you'd look quite nice in pink."

"I love pink."

Greta had no strong feelings about the color pink. But she was young, and romantic, and pleased at the idea that her queen might think she looked nice in anything.

Her queen, who had just called Davey "dear." Marit looked over at Davey. He shrugged; he had noticed it too.

Being in the city was almost as good as being in the forest—she'd not been here since last summer, when the lindworm was only a strange rumor. Even then, she'd been on the edges of the city, where the people like her—poorer people, whose shops would never be visited by a queen—lived. Marit only found herself on the main way for events like parades. It was beautiful here, sparking and clean. There was not much snow just now; the roofs were clear, and she always loved to see the terra cotta waves of them, so different from the thatching and sod of the roofs she had grown up beneath.

"What are we walking on?" Davey asked.

Marit looked down. "Cobblestones, Davey."

"Oh."

"We need to get you out more."

The shop had been cleared for them, and Greta wandered, stroking fabrics, while their father was taken to the back to be measured.

"Marit, look at this," Greta called. "Have you ever seen anything so beautiful?"

The queen walked over. "That's satin. This tailor does all of the crown's business. David, do you need a new overshirt? The red silk could make a lovely vest."

He tilted his head. "Marit? Do I—"

"That would be wonderful, Your Majesty. Thank you."

She nodded. "Of course. And Marit, green for you this time, I think. A lighter green. Greta, go to the back now. They'll be ready to measure you soon."

"Marit?" Greta asked. "Will you come with me?"

She glanced over at Davey, who nodded, and then followed her to the back. When they came out again, Davey was sitting on a countertop, looking over the queen's shoulder at a collection of drawings. Her father was talking to the tailor; it was anyone's guess what they might have in common to talk about. Marit perched on the counter too, and Davey's arm snaked around her waist.

"Having fun?" she asked.

"Yes. Watching my mother choose clothing for my wife. Lovely. Are we almost done here?"

"A prince ought to have a say in his own wardrobe," the queen said. "You ought to have a say in something. Anything."

"Because there have been so many opportunities for that in my life."

"I'm sorry. I know. But it's been months, David. I need you to be a prince."

"Does Harald pick out his own clothes?"

"Yes. He does. Greta, come here and tell me what you think about these patterns. Marit, there's a pile over there. I had help, so you'll have to let me know what you think of your husband's taste in clothes."

Christmas was coming quickly, and Marit was more homesick than she had been in months. All of her Christmas traditions were things she would never have again. She would not be allowed into the palace kitchens to bake. She would not make her own candles. She would not have porridge to set out for the nisser. They had æbleskivers to eat, but the flavor was just a little off, and surrounded by cheerful people, Marit was still so lonely.

"What did you and Ida do for Christmas?" she asked Davey. He'd just come in from snowshoeing with Harald—a short walk through the gardens to get a feel for it before a few of them went farther the next day—and was struggling to get his feet out of the shoes.

"It depended where we were." He collapsed into a chair, still struggling with the snowshoes, and Marit bent to help him. "We didn't often spend winters here, when I was small enough to travel; most of Ida's friends are abroad, and these are long winters, hard on a restless dragon child."

"I've never seen a baby lindworm. I wonder—you were terrifying, full grown. What did you look like when you were small?"

"When I was very small, the wings could lift me a little. Ida hated that. But my body grew much faster than my wings, so it didn't last long. I don't think people were afraid of me, but most people we met knew Ida well, and were used to me. I suppose strangers we met might have thought I was her familiar. I—I grew like a human child, though. Not my body, but—I think lindworms are mature much sooner, and don't need parents. When I was a small lindworm I thought and acted like a small child, and I'm sure that made me less frightening. Unless I was having a tantrum, but I think I did not often have tantrums."

"Do you miss Ida?" Marit asked.

"Sometimes. She had left me for many months before you came. I am much happier without her now than I was without her then. I think—I think she knew that she needed to be gone a while, now, that I would better learn how to be a man without her. She has always babied me; she would think it easier to leave than to stop."

"When do you think she'll come back?" Marit did not want her to come back. She was still angry, when she let herself think about it, which she tried not to do; now was not the time to tell her husband that she hated his mother for choosing her specifically, of all the girls in the world, to feed to him. She did not think there was a time to tell one's husband such a thing.

"If we look to be losing the war she'll come and try to whisk me away somewhere."

"Try?"

"I shan't go into hiding while my kingdom fights a war I caused."

They'd gotten far off the topic of Christmas, and Marit did not want to think of war today. "Tell me about your Christmases," she asked again, and he did.

♛

The ball was on Christmas Eve. Marit was glad she would spend the night with her family, but she felt awkward, too, at the thought of her old life and her new one coming together so. She was worried that her father would think the ball shallow and silly. She was worried that Greta would spend the night answering questions about her chores. She was worried that no one would dance with Greta, and equally worried that people would, since Greta didn't really know how.

She was, overall, far more nervous than Davey, who was quiet and calm. She did not think he was hiding any special dread, but she had never seen him so willing before to endure a large social event. It helped, she supposed, that he fully trusted Harald by now, and shared many of his friends.

It wasn't right, spending Christmas like this. They should be tucked safely away at home, having their own quiet celebrations in front of their own small fire.

But she did have an awfully pretty dress to wear, and she did like her husband's taste in clothes; he hadn't let the queen pick anything too difficult to get in and out of, remembering how she'd spent her night in her gown before.

They had people to help them. Greta and her father, she thought, must have people to help them too, though Marit had not seen them yet. Smilla had told her they were in the palace, being attended to in another room. There were no other rooms near Marit and Davey's, and she wasn't at all sure where they could have been taken. Hopefully she would see them soon.

The room was crowded with their helpers. Davey let a man button his shirt and lace his boots, although he was perfectly capable by now of doing it himself. Marit let them braid her hair, which she could have done herself, too, though not so elaborately, and a woman moved to lace up the back of her dress.

"Let me," Davey said.

The maid stepped aside, and Marit turned. "Can you do it?"

"I think so. My fingers are much better now." He tugged on the laces, and the woman stood back, giving them space. "They've restrained themselves, tonight," he said quietly. "The braid isn't so complicated."

"It's not even making my head hurt yet. Though I wish they would stop filling my hair with jewels. I'm sure I've cost the kingdom a fortune by now, losing them in the carpets when I take down the braids."

His fingers stilled, and he took a step back. "How did I do?"

Marit shifted her shoulders, then turned to face him. "Well, I think. I've no idea how it looks, but it feels right."

"It looks right, as far as I can tell. You look very nice."

"Thank you." She kissed him on the cheek. "You and your mother have made me a lovely dress."

There were new people to meet at the ball, of course. There were always new people, just when Marit thought they were finally done. Davey's outward calm remained, but this was not like court dinners, and she thought that he was quietly terrified.

He was holding her hand.

And there was Greta, of course, who was not calm at all. Marit had made Harald promise to dance with her; hopefully he would show up soon. Marit didn't have the energy for this. Her father was no help, even more out of place than her and Davey. They could all have been at home now, setting out porridge for the nisser.

Palaces, she supposed, had no need to appease the household trolls. There were humans enough here to take care of things themselves.

Harald came soon enough, and swept Greta off for a dance immediately—the first time he had stopped to talk to Marit and Davey while her family was there, Greta had stomped on his foot, still angry on Marit's behalf, but they'd made up, and she was delighted to be the prince's little sister-in-law.

Harald came back without Greta; he had handed her off to Erik. He said he'd arranged for a long list of young men to dance with her, all of whom would be polite and gentle. They did not see much of her for many hours.

Marit had one dance with Harald, and then coaxed Davey into one, as well, but mostly they sat in the chairs at the edge of the room. Neither Marit's father nor Davey were dancing, and she was reluctant to leave them there.

The ballroom was beautiful tonight, glittering with a thousand candles, the light bouncing off the snow outside the high, arched windows. Marit liked dancing well enough, but did not miss it much. It still took her effort to remember each step, and it felt more Christmassy, she thought, sitting between her father and her husband among the sparkling lights. She liked to hear the music, too; it was harder to appreciate when she was struggling to dance to it.

Trudy convinced Davey to dance with her, with somewhat more difficulty than Marit had. Harald took breaks from the dancing to sit and talk with them, and was there when the queen came.

She wished them a merry Christmas, kissing first Harald, then Davey, on the cheek. She smiled at Marit, tight but sincere, before leaving.

The night was, Marit hoped, nearly over by the time they saw the king. She had never attended a ball until its end, but surely it must be nearly over? Greta was back from the dancing, nearly asleep on their father's shoulder. Harald had come and gone again—he seemed tireless, but Marit supposed he had been raised for this. She could walk for hours and work all day and lift heavy things, but loud music and large crowds of strangers were exhausting. She'd had a second dance with Harald and a second with Davey, and was quite done.

The king squeezed Davey's arm in what Marit thought was a fatherly way, and suggested that they all go upstairs to bed. Two cots had been sent up for Marit's family, and a fire was being made ready; Marit and Davey had no true valuables, and she did not leave their room locked when it was empty.

The cots weren't needed. As soon as they reached their room, Davey collapsed on the rug in front of the roaring fire, without even taking off his boots or unbuttoning his vest. By the time the rest of them had changed into nightclothes, he was fast asleep. Marit left him there, and brought Greta and her father to the bed so they could huddle together as they would have a year ago, Greta whispering about the ball until she fell asleep mid-sentence.

Marit woke when it was still night, and saw Davey was awake, sitting by the fire. She crawled carefully over her sleeping sister and went to sit on the floor beside him. He had a blanket, and readjusted so it would cover her as well.

"I'm sorry we crowded you out of the bed."

"You didn't crowd me out; I fell asleep here. And I don't mind—I never slept in a bed when I was a lindworm."

Marit leaned forward to put another log on the fire. "It was a nice party. Everyone seemed happy."

"I wonder how many of them will die in the war."

"Don't be morbid. Not on Christmas."

"War doesn't stop for Christmas."

"War hasn't even started yet. Maybe it won't."

"It will," Davey said.

"I know." They sat in silence for a few minutes. "It's not your fault," she said quietly.

"I ate the princesses."

"And the queen made you a lindworm, somehow, and Ida put you in a situation that she knew would lead to princess-eating, and the king gave you the princesses to eat. Many people have made many mistakes to bring us here."

"I suppose."

Another long silence, and Davey said, "The queen kissed me."

"I saw."

"There wasn't even anyone important paying attention then."

"She is your mother."

"I suppose," he said again.

Marit woke late in the morning in front of the dying fire, tangled in Davey and their blanket. When she sat up she saw that Greta and her father were already up and dressed, eating a breakfast that must have been brought by Smilla. (The king had told them not to come down for breakfast; everyone would be too tired.)

Davey was still asleep. Marit left him there, building the fire back up before she crossed the room to join her family and eat her own breakfast.

"You'll have to go home soon?" she asked.

Her father nodded. "The animals have been alone too long already."

"It was good to have Christmas with you."

They left soon after breakfast. Davey had not woken up yet, and Marit, still tired and with no other plans for the day, lay back down beside him.

Chapter Twelve

"We had a message this morning from the ship sent to collect your wife, Harald," the king said at breakfast.

"Is she nearly here?"

"The messenger estimated ten days."

"How did a messenger get here before the ship?" Marit asked; she knew nothing of seafaring.

"They would have sent a small boat ahead through a narrow channel at the last port," the queen explained. "It's a shorter trip, but the ship is too big, and has to take the longer way around."

"It seems Suhki has spent most of the journey working on language," the king said. "Our messenger says she has quite a solid grasp by now."

Harald frowned. "I don't want her to be making all the changes and sacrifices here."

"You'll learn her language when she arrives with the translator; we would have started you sooner if it were easier to find people who spoke both languages."

"I know."

There was silence for a while before the queen said, "We've finally learned why her father was so eager to send her so far away."

"I told you I don't care about that," Harald said, irritated.

"It's nothing so terrible, dear."

"And you're going to tell me, whether I want to hear it or not. Well, go on then."

"She is not officially a princess. The king is her father, but the queen is not her mother. When the king received our offer for one of his daughters, this one had only recently joined the royal household, after the death of her own mother, and the queen resented her presence. Accepting the proposal was a way to appease his wife, and give his illegitimate daughter a marriage above her station. It's doubtless why she's being sent alone; no one here need know the truth if she does not want it known."

"All right," Harald said. "Ten days?"

"Approximately. We'll have the wedding in two weeks, I think."

He smiled.

"It will be nice to have a wedding that the bride and groom are both looking forward to," the queen said.

"Is she looking forward to it?" Davey asked. "Or was it only about her family drama?"

"I think she's happy with it," Harald said, "from the letter. I hope she is."

"I'm sure she'll love it here," the king said.

♛

The next several days were filled with wedding preparations. Everyone in the palace—possibly everyone in the city, though Marit seldom knew anymore what was happening outside the palace—had known for weeks that the wedding was coming, but now that a day had been chosen, there were menus to make and wardrobes to tailor and rooms to decorate. A suite was prepared for Harald's bride to live in for the few days she would be there before the wedding. The queen came to Marit and Davey's room to discuss what they would wear and to remind them that weddings were the sort of events where crowns were required; they both had a habit of forgetting them. Harald talked of nothing but Suhki, until everyone they knew was thoroughly sick of it.

Father Gregor was performing the ceremony. It occurred to Marit that she had not seen the other priest in a long time. She wondered, idly, if he had been sent away for not cooperating with their story, for turning Davey away; she thought he had probably known the truth. Father Gregor had known it already, when Davey had tried to tell him.

(Davey had told her about this weeks later, and she had shouted. He had asked what the point of a confessional was if you weren't allowed to confess your worst sins, and said this was why he'd waited so long to tell her about it, and that it didn't matter anyway, since Father Gregor had already known. She had given up the shouting, though she was still unhappy.)

Davey was the only one to seem at all unhappy now, aside from some annoyance over Harald's boundless enthusiasm. He told Marit, quietly, one night when they were alone in front of their fireplace, "I'm not sure it's fair, bringing a new girl into a country that's about to go to war. I'm not sure her father would have agreed to send her, if he hadn't been too far away to hear the rumors."

Marit frowned. She'd been thinking more, she knew, of Harald's happiness that of his bride-to-be's. She didn't like the thought of a fourth girl being endangered by marriage into this family.

"Harald's too excited to have thought of it. I don't know if the king and queen haven't considered it, or if they just don't care. Maybe they think if we're tied to this other royal family, they'll have to help us in the coming war. But I—I won't mention it to Harald. I've stood in the way of his marriage enough times."

"I'm sure it will be fine," Marit said, though she suddenly wasn't sure at all.

♛

Suhki arrived twelve days after their breakfast conversation, two days before her wedding. There had been talk of a grand procession from the dock to the palace, but ultimately everyone had agreed that it might be a bit overwhelming for a possibly-seasick girl just arriving in a foreign land to spend the rest of her life with strangers, and they decided to save all celebrating until after the wedding.

Marit thought the king and queen had probably greeted her when she first arrived at the palace, but she seldom knew or cared exactly what the king and queen were doing when she was not at breakfast or dinner with them.

As Suhki arrived in the midafternoon, on a day when Marit and Davey were not scheduled to have dinner with the court, they didn't hear about it until breakfast the following morning. Harald, apparently, had not yet met her. The three of them had been out in the garden yesterday, along with several of Harald's friends, having a snowball fight; probably it was during that time that she'd come.

The entire meal was spent listening to Harald go over the wedding plans they had all long since memorized, and when they were done he followed Marit and Davey back to their room. Marit was a little surprised; she'd have expected him to run off to meet his bride as soon as possible.

"Will you talk to her, Marit?" Harald asked. "Please?"

"Why me? You're her husband."

"What if she doesn't like me? What if I knock on the door and she lets me in but it's only because she thinks she has to? Someone who isn't me should meet her first. And it should be another girl, I think, and—you'll probably understand her better than anyone else, Marit. All my other friends have grown up here, or in places like here. Trudy's come from the farthest away, but she's spent half her life in our court, and I know you're from only a few miles away, really, but it's still—it's different, isn't it? The palace was a strange place for you; probably it's a strange place for her too."

"All right, I'll talk to her, if she doesn't mind. You'll have to show me where she's staying."

The three of them went down to her room together, and Marit shooed the boys away before knocking on the door.

A young woman opened it a moment later, familiar from Harald's small painting, with smiling eyes and messily braided black hair.

"Hello," Marit said, feeling a little awkward. She hadn't expected Suhki to open her own door, somehow, though she knew Suhki had come here alone, and the translator was a man and therefore wouldn't be sharing a room with her the day before her wedding; she wasn't expecting a visitor, so of course he wasn't there. "My name is Marit. I'm—I'll be your sister, I suppose."

Suhki took a step back, making room for Marit to come through the door.

"I thought there were two princes?" She spoke slowly and carefully, with an accent Marit has never heard before.

"Yes, there are—I'm married to the other one."

"Oh," she said, and then, even more slowly and carefully, "the—the dragon?"

Marit was frozen for a moment, before she shook herself out of it enough to look back and see that Suhki had, at least, shut the door, that she hadn't spoken into the hall. She hadn't thought the rumors would travel so far.

"Yes," she said, "he was a dragon, but—a secret dragon." How much of their language had she learned? "You understand?"

Suhki nodded. "I am a secret daughter. Why I was sent."

Marit looked around the room—rooms. It was a suite, with a few doors Marit could see branching off, one of which must lead to the bedroom itself; dignified people, the queen had told her once, didn't leave their beds on display for any guests to see. A suite, but smaller and plainer, she thought, than Harald's. She would only be in it for two nights, one already past.

"Harald is very excited to meet you. He's waited—having a dragon for a brother makes marriage hard."

Suhki nodded again, as if she understood; Marit didn't know how much she knew about the lindworm, and was not ready to ask.

"He is—" She paused, frowning, before she chose her next word. "Nice?"

"Yes," Marit said immediately, discounting her awful first months here as something Suhki didn't need to hear about when she was new and nervous. "He is nervous too."

"Nervous?" Suhki asked, frowning. Marit wasn't sure if it was the first word she didn't recognize, or only the first she found important enough to ask about.

"Scared. But excited."

"Oh. I will meet him at the wedding?"

"You could probably meet him sooner if you want? He wouldn't mind."

Suhki frowned again, and there was a long silence; Marit thought she was working through the words in her head. "I will meet him at the wedding," she said, finally.

Marit didn't press her, not sure if it was nerves or a cultural thing or something else. "All right. He—he wants to learn your language. But the only translator we know was with you, so he hasn't had a chance to start."

Suhki nodded.

"Did you want to come here?" Marit asked. She was afraid no one else had, no one else would.

"Yes," said Suhki. "I asked to."

"Good. I'll see you at the wedding tomorrow."

She found Harald and Davey in the library.

"Well?" Harald asked as soon as he saw her.

"She seems nice. She knows about Davey. She wanted to come here, but she doesn't want to meet you before the wedding."

"Do you—do you think she'll like me?"

"I'm sure she will."

The queen was standing in the hall, apparently waiting for them; she frowned. "I forgot to send anyone up to help you get ready."

"I thought we did all right ourselves," Marit said. They could have—probably should have—asked for help, but it was nice, not having their room crowded with bustling strangers. "I put on one of the nicest dresses—see? Davey can lace them up now."

"It is a lovely gown," the queen conceded. "David, your crown is crooked."

She straightened it, and tidied his hair a little; it was getting longish again, and Marit probably should have cut it, but it was almost the same gold as his crown, and she thought the way it curled around it was rather adorable.

Marit was glad to be free, for once, of tiny, priceless, easily misplaced gems in her hair. She'd braided it around her head, making a nest of sorts for her crown.

"All right," the queen said when she was satisfied with Davey's hair. "We should go in; Olaf will be waiting."

♛

It was a good wedding, Marit thought. Better than either of hers, at least. Suhki was beautiful in a golden dress cut like nothing Marit had seen before, and Harald was so excited he was nearly bouncing in place. Marit sat with the royal family at the front of the room, all of them in a row—king, queen, Davey, Marit.

When the ceremony was over she followed them to the banquet hall, where they were joined by the translator. By unspoken agreement, everyone gave Harald and Suhki space to get to know each other. (It would be nice if Marit and Davey had been given such space at their wedding. She supposed it was common knowledge they'd shared a room for weeks before the wedding, and therefore didn't need to get to know each other. It must have been a scandal, but probably there were newer, more exciting scandals by the time they left their rooms often enough to hear any gossip.)

Marit spent the evening talking quietly to Davey, their heads bent close together. The wedding cake was very good—she'd been too panicked to enjoy it at her previous weddings.

Harald and Suhki went to their rooms later than Marit and Davey had at the first wedding, but earlier than at the second. A whole procession of people followed them, Marit and Davey swept up in it, and when the crowd cleared they found themselves alone in the hallway.

"I suppose we can go up to bed, then?" Marit said.

Davey shrugged. Well, if they were meant to go back to the

banquet, someone should have told them so. They went back to their own room.

♛

Harald did not come to breakfast the morning after the wedding, which Marit supposed she should have expected. But she hadn't, and she and Davey were seldom in the presence of the king and queen both without Harald as a buffer.

It was a bit awkward. The king talked to Davey a little; Marit didn't bother listening closely, as she found their conversations usually boring and difficult to follow. It was a relief to be done with it.

After breakfast they went out into the garden with their snowshoes, then spent some time in the library before going back to their room. They were not expected at dinner that night, and saw no one but Smilla after leaving the breakfast table. It was peaceful, but lonely.

"Do you think they had a good day?" Marit asked. Davey didn't have to ask who she meant. It was strange, going a whole day without seeing Harald.

"Better than we did after our weddings, I'm sure. One day spent miserable and terrified, and one spent climbing endless stairs."

"We did have rather terrible weddings, didn't we?"

"We did. But I think it's turned out well."

"Yes," Marit agreed. "Quite well."

Harald was back at breakfast the next morning, and Suhki with him. The translator didn't join them, so Marit supposed they must be communicating well enough. The king had said a few days ago that Harald would be spending an hour with the translator each day, working to learn Suhki's language.

For several days they saw Harald only at breakfast, and occasionally at dinner. Davey was lonely; Marit could see it. She was, too, but Harald wasn't her brother, just her friend.

"We could go to his room," she suggested. "Find him."

"No, he's busy. He—he needs time to get to know Suhki, on his own. When they've settled a little he'll be around again."

"All right," Marit agreed, a little reluctantly. Harald did love Davey; he was right that he'd be back when the excitement wore off.

♛

"Marit," the queen said.

Surprised, she took too long to respond. The king and queen rarely addressed Marit at breakfast, and she was no longer offended by it. She knew that they saw her and Davey as a unit, and they talked to him instead of her because they wanted to draw him out, to accustom him to interacting with them.

"Yes, Your Majesty?" she asked.

"David has been teaching you to read and write, has he not?"

"Yes."

"Is it going well?"

"I think so."

"Excellent. Would the two of you mind including Suhki in your lessons?"

♛

After that the four of them were often together. Harald sat in front of the fire, doing whatever Harald did, while Davey and the girls, spread in front of the window, poured over books and made messes with charcoal and ink. Suhki was quiet, but nice, Marit thought. She often distracted Davey from the task at hand with lessons in her own language, and pretended to be quite apologetic about it after.

The three of them were there without Harald, one evening just before dinner—he had gone to a meeting with the king, and would collect them for dinner when he was done.

Suhki was much more popular than Marit at things like court dinners, for all that Marit was said to have slain a dragon. Neither of them talked much. But when Suhki was not talking, she looked respectful and interested, and when she did talk it was still respectful and interesting. Marit was seldom happy to be with the court, and when she spoke often said things she should not. This was probably a contributing factor.

Marit had no particular desire to be liked by the court. Davey, they had all gotten used to, and that was what mattered.

Harald came in late and unhappy, clutching an unmarked envelope. Davey asked what it was, and he tried, absurdly, to hide it behind his back.

"Nothing," he said. "Politics. It's nothing."

Davey darted back to pluck the envelope from between his fingers, and he opened it, seeming to shrink as he read. Harald snatched it away, and Davey dropped down onto the rug.

"Davey?" Marit said. He didn't look up, and she turned to Harald.

"No." He refolded the letter and shoved it into his pocket, then bent down beside Davey. "Idiot," he said, angry and affectionate all at once, "I tried to warn you."

Davey nodded and said nothing.

"I suppose we won't be going to dinner now?" Marit asked. She was very good at reading Davey by then, and could see the misery and guilt in every line of his body.

"I'm sorry," Davey said. "I'm sorry. I just—I'm sorry."

She sat down beside him. "Do you want to tell me what was in the letter?"

"It was nothing. Like Harald said. Nothing important, just stupid political things about the—the lind—and if we go to—it was only a letter for the king from a baron in the east. It doesn't matter."

Marit thought he was near tears.

Suhki sat down at the edge of the hearth. "It will be all right," she said. "Hush now, and I will tell you a story. It has been hard to learn words for, so you must be quiet and listen."

Davey nodded.

"Once there was a great white dragon. This dragon began to love an ordinary man, and to be with him she made herself a woman. They were married, and for a long time they were happy together. But the dragon's husband was tricked by a wicked man, and he did what he should not have, and saw her true form. He did not know she was a dragon. He was afraid, and he died of it, and his wife was very sad. But she knew magic flowers to heal the sick and raise the dead, and she went on a long journey to find them. I don't know the words to tell all her journey. But she got the flowers, and came home to bring her husband back. He had only been surprised, but she was his wife, before anything else, and he loved her still when she brought him back, and they lived happily together, the man and his dragon bride."

It had been intended to calm him, and worked amazingly well. Marit did not know how many details of the lindworm Suhki knew, whether it was a coincidence or whether she understood exactly how meaningful he would find a story of a white dragon who undid death and found acceptance, and lived happily among normal men. He looked up at her and smiled, then turned to Marit.

"We should go to dinner; I'll be fine."

She took his arm and pulled him to his feet and to the door, and heard Harald behind them, voice full of awe and affection, saying "Su, you're a miracle."

Marit was glad to have another princess.

♛

They were in the library. Marit was supposed to be practicing her writing, but had lapsed into doodling.

Davey lay sprawled on the floor, graceful and undignified. She was trying to draw him, but she wasn't really an artist—not with charcoal and paper, at least—and it wasn't coming out right.

He looked up and met her eyes, holding her gaze for a moment before he ducked his head. "Don't look at me like that."

"Like what?"

"Like we're really—like you—never mind. Are you ready to go?" She nodded, and he stood easily, set his book down, and swept another one off the table. "I'm going to teach myself Greek. There are a lot of myths with people being turned into things."

"Any snakes?"

"Only one I know of. And he was pretty old when it happened. But still, it should be interesting. Ida never liked to turn the pages for me when I read mythology."

"Why not?"

"Well, she told me not to take the Lord's name in vain, so when I read about other gods I started taking their names in vain instead, and it annoyed her."

"You don't do that anymore."

Davey nodded, but she didn't think he'd actually heard; he was sorting through a stack of books. It made her rather sad sometimes, glimpses of his life before, when he was a lindworm who had not yet eaten anyone, when he was just a person in a body unlike her own, and not the mess of trauma and confusion and guilt he'd become in the first several months they'd known each other. She wondered how many little details of who he'd been were lost forever the night he changed.

"Davey?"

"Hm?"

"Are you happy?"

He dropped his book and looked slowly up at her, stricken. "I—"

"You should be happy."

"No. I shouldn't. I was until you asked me that."

"Why shouldn't you?"

"The war?"

"Forget the war. And tell me all the Greek myths when you've translated them."

"All right."

"Promise?"

"Of course."

♛

Marit was sitting with the queen at dinner, which was odd enough to make her uneasy. The royal family seldom sat together, to spread their attention between more people. Marit and Davey had sat together in the beginning, but as they both became used to the dinners, were separated more and more often. Suhki, too, was sometimes seated with Harald because of her newness to the court. But Marit had never sat near the king or queen.

"I have been wishing to speak to you," the queen said, justifying Marit's sense of uneasiness. She was growing to like the queen, but they seldom had things to talk about, and when they did, it happened at breakfast, with Suhki and all of their husbands present as well.

"About what?" she asked.

"I will soon begin training Suhki in her duties as future queen. I had wondered if you would be willing to join our lessons."

"Why would I need training in being a queen?"

"You don't need the training," the queen said, "and you are free to refuse it. But I believe that you and David both could be valuable assets to the throne. You, David, and Suhki all grew up in worlds very different from Harald's. You can offer a viewpoint he wouldn't normally have access to. This is one of the reasons it's important for the crown prince to marry a foreign princess. And Harald has the benefit of a brother and sister-in-law with their own unique perspectives as well."

"Davey helps Harald and the king with their work sometimes," Marit said. She still wasn't sure exactly what that work entailed.

"Yes," said the queen. "I am asking you to help Suhki the same way. She does not have the benefit of years of training in the roles of royalty, and you would be learning together. You would be able to help each other, and later Harald."

"All right. I can do that."

"Excellent. We'll begin next week."

♛

Whenever they could be, they were outside.

Suhki had lived somewhere far warmer before, and loved the snow nearly as much as Davey did. They danced in it and were delighted together. Harald watched them, and laughed, and wrapped his arms around Suhki when she was done to warm her.

When they could not be outside, it was because they were with the king or queen, or practicing their reading and writing, or, in Harald's case, continuing to learn Suhki's language. Marit thought seldom of the war, these days. She felt she had a family in her new home, finally, and was busy and happy.

♛

It was Greta's birthday, and Marit had not seen her in weeks, not since Christmas.

She left early in the morning, bundled up for the weather, and therefore unrecognizable as a princess. She'd told Davey the night before that she would be leaving, and trusted him to make her excuses for breakfast and the appointment she'd had with the queen.

(She was enjoying the princess lessons with Suhki and the queen. They involved a lot of math and even more memorizing the names and faces of various important people. But it was nice to spend time with Suhki without their respective husbands, and she liked the queen more as she got to know her better. Marit thought by now she was more familiar with the queen than Davey was, but wasn't sure what to do about it. Davey was bonding with the king, which Marit had not managed and didn't much care to, but he already had a mother in Ida, and the queen seemed distant and aloof when she was unsure of herself.)

Her visit home was a surprise, and she wanted to be there early enough to help with chores, but she had slept later than planned, and was behind schedule.

She thought she knew the palace well enough by now to take a shortcut, but it seemed she was wrong. She was not quite sure where she was, or how to get back to somewhere familiar, and few were awake at this time. Staff, but it seemed this was not an area of the palace in need of any work at this time of day.

Eventually she found herself, somehow, in the great hall, which certainly should have been empty at this time of day. Instead she found it occupied by several unfamiliar men, some wearing what was clearly a uniform, and not one that belonged to any soldier or guard here.

She turned to leave, not sure what was happening, but very sure she wanted no part of it, and one of the men caught her arm.

"Here's a girl," he said. "Perhaps she can help." His voice was slightly accented, and she was certain he didn't know who she was.

Marit tried to pull away, and his grip tightened painfully.

"If you could please unhand my wife," said a cold voice she didn't recognize immediately as Davey's.

The man released her, and Marit took a step away before turning to look at Davey, crossing the room toward them from the other door. He was wearing his crown, though it was crooked, and he looked a bit winded.

"Prince Harald?" asked the man who'd grabbed her.

"No, I'm the other one." He reached them, and wrapped an arm around Marit's waist almost absently.

"We had expected a warmer welcome."

"And we had expected that you would announce yourselves, rather than wandering unattended through our home in the earliest hours of the morning. If you wait here, I will see that my father the king comes to greet you at his earliest convenience."

Davey left the room without another word, tugging Marit along.

"Who were those people?" she asked when they were alone.

"Ambassadors. From the country whose princess—exchanging ambassadors to arrange some sort of deal is our last desperate attempt to avoid a war. They shouldn't have been here until tomorrow, and they should never have laid a hand on you."

"They didn't know I was a princess."

"Still," he said. "I saw them out the window and came down to warn the king they were here—I didn't expect to find them with you."

"I was on my way to see Greta. I got lost a little."

"I don't think you should leave today. Alone, in the woods—I don't—I don't trust them."

The king was in the study with Harald—they had an hour before family breakfast. Davey walked in without knocking, and dropped into an empty chair opposite the desk.

"Your guests are harassing my wife."

The king raised his eyebrows. "My guests?"

"The ones we were expecting."

"Oh. They—you're all right, Marit? They didn't—"

"I'm fine." She looked over at Davey; she didn't know what her place was when he took the lead.

"Father, they were—they're waiting in the throne room. I said I'd send you there."

The king stood up. "Harald, fetch your mother. And your wife."

Harald paused between Marit and Davey before going. "You're all right, though? You're both all right?"

Davey looked down, and Marit perched on the arm of the chair to take his hand. Harald nodded and left.

She was still in her peasant snow things when the official introductions were made. The rest of them had managed to look actually royal. Suhki was gorgeous in something foreign and blue, and Davey wore his crown well for once, and Marit was nothing at all like a princess.

She wouldn't see Greta and her father today. She didn't know when she would see them.

She didn't pay a terrible amount of attention to the introductions; their names and titles would hardly impact her. She stood in front of Davey and tried to forget that if anyone could still get him killed, it was these men. He was no longer as self-possessed as he'd been when he found her.

"And this is my younger son, David. And Marit, his wife. I believe you met them earlier?"

"We did." No one in the group mentioned the circumstances of their meeting. "Prince, Princess." The one in charge nodded at them. "It's a pleasure to see you again."

Marit edged back, closer to Davey, and since the absent-minded protectiveness hadn't made a reappearance, she carefully pulled his arms around her waist, then rested her head on his shoulder—a little awkward, since they were very nearly the same height, with the difference in her favor, but she managed. He was stiff at first, nervous about the visitors, but he relaxed slowly, and they leaned into each other, waiting to see what would happen next.

She was noticing how Davey was supporting most of her weight, and wondering when he'd become strong enough to do so, and therefore had no idea what they had all been talking about when he nudged her.

"I'm sorry, what?"

"Our guests look forward to seeing us at dinner."

"Oh. The feeling is mutual, I'm sure." She probably couldn't have sounded less sincere if she'd tried.

"You must forgive my son and daughter-in-law," said the king. "They are both rather new at this."

"Of course." The man bowed again, which put his face at a wonderful level for a knee to the chin—he was the one who'd grabbed her. Marit resisted temptation.

"I really am fine," Davey told her as they walked back to the room. Family breakfast had been cancelled, and a messenger was on his way to Greta with the present Marit had wanted to deliver herself.

"Of course." He wasn't fine. He was visibly distressed. She knew he was frightened of the ambassadors, of the coming war, and she knew he felt even more guilty than afraid.

"Father will handle it."

"Davey—"

"We shouldn't walk around the palace alone now. Just in case." He wouldn't say any more about it. That night he balked at going to dinner, and Marit had no inclination to argue. The queen could have a fit tomorrow; there were worse things in the world than her anger.

"I'm fine," he said. "I'm fine."

"Really."

"Marit..."

She pulled him to the bed to sit down, and tried to twine herself around him. He ran his hands through her hair and closed his eyes.

"Marit."

"Everything is going to be all right. We won't go to war. And if we do, we'll win. And none of it will be your fault, Davey."

♛

They skipped breakfast the next morning, as well, but returned to dinner that night. They were seated together, as they seldom were these days, and did their best to avoid any visitors. Marit looked around the room and noticed for the first time that it was emptier than it had once been; she had been focused lately on Suhki and Harald and Davey, and thought little of the people who were only her friends because they were Harald's.

"Where is everyone?" she asked Davey, quietly.

"Jon's family lives on an estate near the border, and he's gone to help his mother and little siblings move somewhere safer. Felix is leading one of the troops of soldiers moving into position. Trudy's father has sent her back to their home country."

"Oh."

"The war is coming."

She knew this, but somehow it seemed more real than it had.

Chapter Thirteen

Marit walked back into the room after her lessons with the queen to find Davey sitting on the floor, staring intently at the opposite wall.

"Davey? Are you all right?" He didn't react at all, and she knelt down. "What is it?" She started to wrap her arm around his shoulder, and he unfolded and pulled away.

"Nothing. I'm fine. It's nothing."

It was almost never nothing, with Davey, but she let it go, for the time being. "All right. If you're sure."

"I'm fine."

"We have to go, then. Harald and Suhki are waiting for us in the stables."

"The stables," he repeated.

"Yes. Didn't I tell you?"

"Tell me what?"

She beamed at him. "They're going to teach us to ride horses." Harald had promised to show her, with or without Davey, months ago now.

"He's—Marit, we—why would you do that to me?"

She stood and took his arm. "You're stronger now. It'll be fun."

♛

"I hate horses."

"We know this, Davey." It was the fifth time he'd said it in twenty minutes. Harald and Suhki both rode well—they had grown up with it, Marit supposed. She was doing well enough, she thought, all things considered. Getting on had been difficult, and she did not look forward to getting off, but it was not so hard to keep her seat, and she looked gleefully down at all the world, white beneath the horse's hooves.

But Davey, several times his horse's size a year ago, was absurdly small now on its back, and frightened and uncomfortable. He clung to the saddle, jostled about like a rag doll with each step, and he was beginning to look greenish.

"I wonder how they'd taste."

"Shut up, Davey," said Harald. "You all right, Marit?"

"Definitely."

They rode in silence after that, until Harald stopped abruptly, in a clearing in the woods, and jumped down. Suhki slipped carefully off of her horse, and turned to hold the reins for Davey's. "Careful."

Harald pulled him slowly down, Suhki keeping the horse steady. Marit waited. They would help her in a minute, but Harald was kissing Suhki first.

"Is this the part where we stop with the stupid horses and have private conversations where no one can overhear us?" Davey asked.

"What? You think I don't trust our visitors? Go help Marit."

She wrapped her arms around Davey's neck and dragged herself over the horse's back and onto the ground. "And here I thought you were just being a nice brother-in-law, teaching me to ride."

"I'm a very nice brother-in-law."

She moved her arms from Davey's neck to his chest and leaned in—it was cold. "How long do you think they'll stay?"

"Forever."

"Don't be pessimistic, Davey." Harald gathered all the reins and took a step forward. "Walk with me. I hate standing still in the cold."

"You could ride well," Suhki told Davey. "Too tense."

Marit nodded. "They weren't that bad, were they, Davey? They got you out of the palace. Snow and privacy—two of your favorite things."

"Legs. Legs are strange, but I don't think they're meant to be spread that far apart. Tails don't spread at all, you know."

"We'll get you a sidesaddle," said Harald. "Like the girls have sometimes."

"Wonderful."

"I'm tired." Marit plopped down abruptly, pulling Davey to the ground with her, putting herself almost in his lap. "It really is hard, isn't it? I can't believe you thought this was a good first thing to do, Harald." She rearranged herself carefully, pulling Davey's arms around her and leaning on his shoulder. "This is nice, though, isn't it? I can see why you'd sit out here all day. Not alone, though. Why would you want to be out here all alone?"

He didn't answer, and she leaned further into him. The riding, and the stress of the guests, had taken more out of her than she would like to admit, and she was exhausted, and rambling, and he'd hardly spoken to her today, except to complain about the horses, and he had been so distant lately. She'd hoped that having the horses to be angry about instead of the visitors would put him in a better mood overall, but it wasn't noticeably helpful so far. She removed her face from his coat to kiss him on the cheek. He stiffened, just slightly—if it were anyone else she wouldn't have noticed. "Davey? Sweetie? What's wrong?"

"I'm fine."

She suspected him of lying, and slid further into his lap, adjusting his arms around her waist again.

Harald looked at them both, frowning.

"Marit," he said, "can we talk for a minute?"

She stood and followed him a little further into the woods. "What's wrong?" she asked. He seemed suddenly quite serious.

"You've been...affectionate with him, lately."

"You kissed Suhki not five minutes ago."

"That's different."

"How?"

"Because Suhki and I both know exactly where we stand."

She frowned. "I don't understand. Am I not allowed to be affectionate with my husband?"

Harald sighed. "No, it's not—that's not it."

"Then what is it?"

"It's been nearly a year, Marit, and you haven't consummated your marriage. I know because I tried to talk to Davey about it the day before my wedding, and he didn't seem to know what I meant. And that's fine. No one is depending on you for an heir, and you don't have to do anything you don't want to."

Marit felt hot, despite the winter chill. "If it's fine, why are we talking about it?"

"Because your husband is in love with you."

"Davey's not—"

"Don't be stupid, Marit. He's loved you for months."

"Did he tell you?"

"He didn't have to. And I know you didn't ask for this, and you shouldn't have to—it's all right that you don't love him. But you can't be flirting with him."

"I'm not."

"You are. You were, just now."

"I was just—he's Davey."

"He's your husband. And you shouldn't be treating him like one unless you mean something by it."

They rejoined Davey and Suhki, getting pulled quickly into the snowball fight they'd started. Marit was thoroughly distracted, and didn't think of their conversation again until she was back on the horse. She was quiet for the rest of the afternoon, thinking, worrying—Davey didn't really, did he? Shouldn't she have noticed?

She accepted Harald's assistance in dismounting when they returned to the stables, and then drifted slowly back to their room, Davey trailing behind. It was nearly dark, and the outer layers of her clothing were soaked through.

She shed the hat, coat, scarf, and mittens on the floor, then went to the fireplace. She'd meant to stoke the fire, but was distracted, again, by anxious, confused thoughts.

"Are you all right?" Davey asked, frowning.

"Fine." Marit wrapped an arm absently around him, pulling back awkwardly as she remembered the conversation with Harald. "Just tired."

"Are you sure?"

"I'm fine, Davey. We should change for dinner."

Marit did not have nightmares as often as Davey, who still woke screaming at least once a week, despite his sleeping draught, and had many more dreams in silence, but she did have them. Two, in particular, came back to haunt her again and again. The first began with the lindworm looming over her at the altar, and ended when he had eaten her. Sometimes, he turned into Davey before eating her, and on those nights she had to slip out of bed and sit in front of the fire alone, away from him, until morning.

In the second dream, she was beating the lindworm with the whips dipped in lye, except he wasn't the lindworm; he was Davey, in his human form.

On that night it was the second dream.

She woke suddenly and in a panic, waking Davey with her. (She had long since ceased to be uncomfortable sharing a bed with him, and they often became tangled in each other as they slept, which made it nearly impossible to wake from even the quietest of nightmares alone.)

"Marit?"

"I'm all right."

"My fault or yours?" he asked, which was how they differentiated her two nightmares.

"Mine."

"I'll build up the fire," he said. She seldom slept again after this nightmare. The sky was just beginning to lighten, and the room was cold, the fire down to coals.

Marit followed Davey to the fireplace, sitting on the rug while he worked on it. She felt awkward, and couldn't remember why at first. Davey finished with the fire and came to sit beside her; he smiled, and she remembered her conversation with his brother.

She decided suddenly to be angry with Harald. Who was he to decide how she felt about her husband?

"Kiss me, Davey," she said, and he did.

She pulled away after a moment to look at him; the light of the fire cast strange shadows on his face, and she couldn't tell what he was thinking. Suddenly very tired, she turned to press her face into his chest. He wrapped an arm around her shoulders, and soon she was asleep.

Marit woke up in the morning tangled comfortably around Davey, on the floor in front of a still-burning fire. He was still asleep, which was good—it gave her some time to think about the fact that she had dramatically changed their relationship last night, in a way she could never take back. Not without hurting someone she loved, and that was—well, that was the issue, wasn't it?

She did love him. She had loved him, and had known she loved him, for a long time. She hadn't bothered to consider how she loved him—she had certainly not, from the beginning, loved him as a wife should love her husband, but he had become her best friend long ago.

She found she was not bothered at the thought of being a wife to him, as she certainly was in the beginning. (Not bothered beyond lingering concerns about his naivety, but that was another problem entirely, and one she maintained it was not her responsibility to solve, wife or not.)

She loved Davey. She was glad to have him, for all the things it had cost her. She would, given the choice, stay here with him over returning to her family and the life she should have had.

Davey had, somehow, gone from monster to burden to friend.

She was ready, she thought, for him to become her husband in more than name.

She separated herself from him slowly, trying not to disturb him, and went to use the chamber pot and wash her face. When she went back to the fireplace Davey was awake. Marit sat down beside him.

"Good morning," she said.

He smiled at her, a small, unsure thing, and she leaned forward to kiss him.

"All right?" she asked.

He nodded, exhaling shakily. "All right."

She kissed him again, and this time he kissed back.

"Davey," she said after a few minutes, "I think you should talk to Harald today. Alone. About marriage."

"All right," he said.

She kissed him once more, quickly, and stood. "We should get dressed—it's nearly time for breakfast."

After they ate, and after the king and queen left, Marit told Suhki she wanted to show her something, and led her down the hall, leaving the boys alone.

Marit then found herself alone with Suhki, and no plan.

"I didn't actually have anything to show you," she confessed. "I just wanted Davey to have a conversation alone with Harald."

"That is fine. We could go outside? Harald says the snow will be gone soon."

"Probably—it was mostly gone by this time last year. But that was an early spring."

They made their way downstairs and into the gardens, stopping at Suhki's rooms on the way to get her coat and a spare for Marit. They sat down on one of the stone benches near where the roses bloomed in the summer.

She wasn't often alone with Suhki. She spent time with Harald and Davey and Suhki, or with the queen and Suhki, but she thought this was the first time they'd been alone together since Harald had asked her to introduce herself before the wedding.

She was longing for and dreading, in equal measure, her return to Davey. They would have to talk more, she supposed, and it would be awkward, and they would—she didn't regret the kiss, but perhaps she should have spent more time thinking about it first.

"I kissed Davey," she said aloud. She really wasn't close enough to Suhki yet to be confiding in her, but there was no one else to confide in, except for Davey himself.

"Good," Suhki said. "You're late."

"Late?"

"Harald says it is almost a year."

"Since we got married?"

Suhki nodded.

Marit glanced around; it was a bitterly cold morning, and no one else was about. "I suppose it is. Only officially that's when I married the lindworm, not Davey, so don't go talking to anyone else about it."

She nodded again, frowning. "Strange secret. A thousand miles away we know the truth."

"A thousand miles away I guess they don't care if some prince they'll never meet ate some princess they also never would have met. It's more personal, closer to home."

"A dragon can't help being a dragon."

"But they didn't have to feed him foreign princesses." Marit stood. "We should go inside—I'm freezing. Do you think the boys are done talking yet?"

"What are they talking about?"

"Sex," Marit answered absently, forgetting for a moment that she was talking not to one of her own friends from home, but to a noblewoman, who probably had complicated rules about things you weren't supposed to talk about. She looked over; Suhki seemed a little scandalized, but she hadn't actually said anything yet, so Marit decided to explain further. "I'm not sure he actually knows what it is. Or how to do it. Or anything, really."

Suhki nodded. She was bright red, but that might have been

from the cold. "Let's talk about...not boys for a while," she suggested.

"All right. We'll have to talk about something else then. Tell me about your home? I'm so sick of being the one always telling stories about where I'm from. Most of Harald's friends have just lived the exact same lives, I think."

Davey was back by the time Marit returned to their room.

"Did you have a good talk with Harald?"

"Yes," he said, blushing.

"Good." She joined him in front of the fire, grabbing her current tangled bundle of yarn as she went.

She felt awkward, as she had not with Davey for many months. She picked at her yarn and made nothing with it. Davey was holding a book, but she didn't think he was reading; he hadn't turned a page in several minutes.

"I love you," Marit said, realizing suddenly that she hadn't said it before.

Davey's answering smile was bigger than she'd ever seen. "I love you too," he said.

They would be awkward until they'd dealt with this. She stood and pulled him toward the bed, hoping Harald had been thorough; she really only knew the mechanics as they applied to livestock.

"We'll—we'll have to try not to have any children. I don't think we'd make good parents. Certainly not yet."

Davey nodded. "I'm still learning how to take care of myself. Ida has a charm for that, I think—for the not-having-children. But I don't know how she makes it, and I think you need to have it on your person during any, um. Potential child-making activities?"

"We'll ask her someday. For now we'll have to make do." Marit had no intention of living half-married to her husband for however many months it took Ida to return. They'd made a decision, and they were going to see it through. Immediately, ideally.

♛

Marit woke the next morning as she always did, wrapped up in Davey. He was awake already.

"It's late," she said.

Davey shrugged. "Harald said he'd tell them not to expect us at breakfast. Since it is, in some ways, our wedding night."

"Please tell me Harald is not telling the king and queen we're having a wedding night right now."

"Oh. Um. I'm sure he knows better than to get into specifics."

"I hope so."

"It was a good wedding night."

"Third time's the charm," Marit agreed.

"Sometimes," he said quietly, as they got dressed, "it's the wedding night that turns a monster into a man."

"You're already a man, Davey."

"Near enough," he said, and kissed her again.

Chapter Fourteen

There was to be another ball. Marit felt they had more balls than was strictly necessary, but her opinion on the matter was not taken into consideration, despite the fact that this ball was, essentially, for her.

It had been a year since she'd married the lindworm. Since she had, supposedly, slain the lindworm and rescued Davey. It would be odd, the queen said, if they didn't celebrate. And they could not afford oddness at this time.

Marit thought that if they could not afford oddness at the edge of war, they could even less afford extravagances such as a ball. The queen had conceded, at least, that they needn't be involved in the wardrobe planning; their sizes had not changed, and she would commission them something appropriate.

(It had been fun, going to the tailor, but Marit couldn't bear the thought of pretending to one more person that this was something she wanted to celebrate. It was the anniversary of the worst night of her life, the night she'd been taken from her family, been betrayed by her king, been deliberately fed to a dragon, and unknowingly performed something resembling black magic, torturing, in the process, a man she had come to love. There was not a single moment of that day that she thought of fondly. It was the source of every nightmare she'd had in the last year. She was glad to be here now. She had built a new family that she loved, and her father and sister would be always provided for. But she would never want to celebrate the way it had happened.)

The ball was an extravagant affair, almost frantic in its elegance. They'd gone to Harald and Suhki's rooms to be dressed up by their maids and serving men. It was crowded, and Davey was quiet and unhappy during the preparations.

He roused himself a little to come and do up her laces; he knew the ladies always made them too tight.

"You know, we could still skip this," she suggested.

"It's in your honor, more or less."

"Yours too."

"No, it's celebrating my survival. Or death, depending. It's celebrating your heroism. It's for you."

"Except that my heroism is all a lie."

His hands stilled, and then his arms snaked around her waist, and his chin was on her shoulder. "You saved me, Marit. Never mind that you didn't stick a sword through a dragon to do it. You saved me."

"Mm. Am I all tied up?"

"You're set."

She turned to face him.

"And I'm fine. Really."

She wove through the crowd to find Suhki, who had promised to help with her hair, and soon the four of them stood ready outside the doors to the ballroom.

"I can't do it," Davey said. "I can't do it."

Suhki turned to him. "You are a dragon," she said. "You are strong."

Davey nodded, though he didn't look fully convinced, and Harald opened the doors.

There were streamers hung from the ceiling, and Marit's dress, white with lace and pearls, was far fancier than anything they'd made her wear before, even the dress with three sets of laces. Davey was stiff and uncomfortable, but holding her hand, and all the colors were too bright, and the skirts too big, and the room too crowded, and the music too loud.

Harald convinced Davey to dance with Suhki before he went to talk to important people, leaving Marit alone. "Kirsten and Helga are at the buffet table," he told her before he left. "You haven't talked to them in days."

She went over to see them, but was waylaid by one of the ambassador's men.

"Princess Marit."

She curtsied wordlessly and inclined her head; she never had bothered to learn all the names, and the queen seemed disinclined to press the issue, but her curtsies had gotten much more graceful.

"Isn't your husband with us tonight? I had been hoping to speak with him."

"I'm so sorry—he's just gone off with his sister-in-law." She'd strangle him with her bare hands before she'd let him speak with Davey.

"I see. And how is he coping? I understand the event commemorated tonight was quite traumatic for him."

"Oh, yes. Being saved from years of abuse takes such a toll."

The man nodded solemnly. "I can imagine. And of course it's a day of celebration, but surely it must dig up unpleasant memories of the days that came before."

It was a good point, really. She'd been trying not to think about that aspect of things. They weren't celebrating his death; they were celebrating his rebirth. Or something. But they never talked about his actual life. Or about the fact that he'd lost everything he knew just as surely as Marit had, for all that it had been necessary.

"Yes, well, he's handling it quite well. I know he'd be touched by your concern."

"And how different has life been for him, Princess, since the change?"

The change. He knew. Of course he knew; even Suhki's kingdom had known. And neither of them would say it. She was just a farm girl; she didn't know how to play these games. She was supposed to say something—something subtle and threatening and—she didn't know how to have the sort of conversation where you both pretended to be talking about something else.

Perhaps she could just be obtuse.

"Oh, it's been just wonderful. Living in the palace, everyone caring so much what happens to us. Did you know that Prince Harald once threatened to hang a man for asking a question he didn't like?" She was fairly certain he'd been joking.

"I did not." He did not appear as intimidated by this as she had hoped he would. "Tell me, is it true that he's been deteriorating again?"

"I—excuse me?"

"We've heard he was barely functional, even six months ago. There was some speculation that he would die, perhaps even by his own hand. Is it true that the pressures of war have drawn him back towards this state?"

Marit didn't know the rules anymore. This wasn't subtle court politics. There was no way to respond to that like a princess.

"Forgive my impertinence. You must understand how concerned we are about the wellbeing of our neighbors."

"Of course. And that would explain why we're nearly at war."

"It is, I admit, a complex matter."

She didn't know what to do. The music had gotten quieter, finally. Were none of Harald's friends nearby to overhear and save her?

He was going on, still, about the same things. Things he had no right to ask, or should have no right to ask, but he must know the official boundaries better than she did. He was probably counting on it, probably wanted to fluster her, to manipulate her into saying something stupid. And now he was waiting for a response.

She saw Davey coming from the corner of her eye, just in time, and turned to meet him, throwing her arms around his neck as he caught her waist. "Davey!" She kissed him, half aware, and wholly unconcerned, that the entire court must now be watching. She had said his name very loudly. "I'm so glad you're here. This man has been saying the most frightfully insensitive things."

"Oh? What kinds of things?" She knew that she was talking like one of Harald's fancy friends, or trying to, and that he must be puzzled by it, but if Davey was going to sound like a prince to these men, then she wanted to sound like a princess.

"About the lindworm, and your health."

"My health is excellent," Davey assured the man. "I appreciate your concern. If you'll excuse us, I've promised my wife a dance."

"I hate him," Marit whispered, when they were a safe distance away. "I hate him."

"He's only doing his job, I'm sure," Davey said. He sounded very tired, and Marit reached up gently to touch his face.

"I suppose we'd better dance, then."

"I suppose so."

They managed, for a few minutes, but were both more bothered by the encounter than they wanted to admit. Marit was mostly succeeding in burying her fear under a determined sort of anger, but Davey was shaking a little, and clumsier than he had been in some time.

Marit stopped abruptly in the middle of the dance floor the second time he stepped on her foot.

"Sorry," he said.

She shook her head. "Davey..."

She was so angry, and so afraid. She had been happy. She had a new brother and sister, and a husband she loved, and her life was not what she expected, but it was good. And now these men were here to take it all away, and she couldn't stop it; she couldn't fight them. She didn't know how to fight things like a princess, wasn't used to having to fight at all. She had spent so many months fighting to keep Davey alive, to keep him safe. And she had fought to remain herself in a new world that should have no place for someone like her, and succeeded, and now herself was a person who didn't know her role—or didn't have one—in this new fight.

She wanted to punch the ambassador. She wanted to spit in his face. She knew that would only make the situation worse, but oh, how she wanted it.

It wasn't fair. She had learned how to protect Davey from himself, how to protect him from Harald, from the king and queen. She didn't know how to protect him from whole nations; she didn't think she could.

"Davey," she said again, and she kissed him, in the center of the ballroom, in front of the whole court, because she wanted to, and if she couldn't punch the ambassador or spit on him, she would at least have one thing she wanted tonight.

She pulled away after a moment, and they tried again to dance.

"Ida would turn them into toads if she were here," Davey said. "Of course, that would only be a bigger political disaster."

"I would like it if they were toads, though," Marit said, a little wistfully.

"I used to spend quite a lot of time convincing her not to turn people into toads. I succeeded at least half the time."

It was the first time he'd mentioned Ida in a long time. Marit changed the subject, asking him about his dance with Suhki. She didn't much care to think about Ida.

♛

It was a week later that the long-expected blow was finally delivered.

They were at dinner.

Davey was facing her, laughing about nothing in particular, a wineglass in his right hand, when the messenger rushed into the dining room. Later Marit would wonder about that wineglass—Davey drank water, and could occasionally be coaxed into juice or something hot, but attempts at milk had not been successful, and she couldn't remember seeing him with wine before. He was outgoing that night, almost wildly so, and she'd been too busy assuming it was a good sign to worry about how unlike him it was. But maybe he'd known. Maybe he was wild and excited and drinking wine because he'd seen it coming, and hadn't wanted to.

She'd seen the king opening the letter, behind Davey, seen his face change, and then he had cleared his throat, and the entire room had gone quiet. Davey had swiveled around to look at him, the fingers of his left hand still on Marit's arm.

"We are at war."

The wineglass dropped and shattered, and the fingers slipped away. Marit grabbed his hands, which were shaking, almost instinctively, fixated on red wine seeping into the carpet. No one said anything. Finally a serving man ran forward to scrub it up, and Marit looked away in time to see the rest of the room doing the same. The ambassador was smiling.

"War?" Harald echoed hollowly. A choking sound came from Davey, and Marit pulled him closer. Harald seemed to come out of the stupor that enveloped the room. He stood and took the letter from the king's hand.

The king stood, too, and the letter passed to the queen. "If everyone will excuse us, I believe there are some family matters to attend to," the king said. "We will have an official council session tomorrow, at ten in the morning. I will see all of my ministers then."

Marit started pulling Davey away, the queen hovering anxiously behind them. If he was crying it wasn't audible; she couldn't see his face, but he was shaking as if he might be. Harald whispered something to Suhki, and she stood up. The six of them went into the hallway.

"Are you all right?" Harald asked before they separated.

"He's not," said Marit. Davey himself didn't react. The queen touched his shoulder, and he flinched away. She stepped back.

"It's not your fault," she said. The king said nothing, and Marit steered Davey back towards their room. She locked the door, and he sat shakily on the edge of the bed.

"I knew it was coming," he said. "I knew—I'm not—it's bad enough, killing two people. I don't want to be responsible for the deaths of hundreds, of thousands."

"You won't be."

"Wars kill. And it is my actions that caused this war.'

"It is your fault, for eating the princesses. And it is the king's fault, for providing them, and it is Ida's fault, for sending you here to eat them. You, at least, were only doing what a lindworm does; they had a choice, and they chose this."

Davey didn't argue, but Marit doubted he was convinced. They sat there quietly, each consumed with their own worries, until it was time to go to bed.

♛

In the morning, Davey sat down at the breakfast table and said, "You should tell them the truth. About me. You should tell them."

"David," the queen said.

"It would be better. For everyone. If you could blame it all on me. You could give me to them, and everyone else would be fine. You wouldn't have to send soldiers to die."

"We should send you to die instead?"

He shrugged.

"It wouldn't matter," said the king. "We would still be the people who fed you."

"Say you didn't understand, the first time. Obviously I was under a spell; humans parents don't generally produce dragon children. You thought it was like a fairy story, and marriage would break the curse. You didn't know what would happen. It wasn't your fault."

"And what of the second girl?" the queen asked.

"You were afraid. You'll remember I was significantly more intimidating, before Marit came. I threatened you. I threatened everyone. One dead girl every few months is better than the whole kingdom destroyed, isn't it?"

"A less convincing argument when the one dead girl comes from someone else's kingdom," the king said.

"The war is nothing to do with you," Harald said. "You needn't even be here. Erik and Kirsten are sailing out with their parents in a week; you can go along. All of you, Davey, Suhki, Marit. You'd be safe at their grandfather's estate until the war is over."

"You think I would leave?" Suhki asked, clearly outraged.

"We're not going anywhere," Marit agreed.

"Of course not," Davey said. "You think I would run and hide while the rest of you take responsibility for your parts in this?"

"No," the queen said. "We will stand or we will fall, together. As a family."

"I just want you to be safe," Harald said.

"I knew about—about the lindworm," Suhki said. "I didn't come here to be safe. I came here for a family, and for an adventure. I will not leave the family I sought for the safety I didn't."

Marit left them to sort it out, pulling Davey into the hall as soon as the king dismissed them.

"Are you really still trying to get yourself killed? After everything?"

"No," he said, catching her hands. "I'm sorry. I didn't mean—I don't want to die. And I want less to be locked up forever where their king can take out his revenge at his leisure. But I don't—I don't want other people to die, either, if there's a way to prevent it."

"All right," she said. "All right. I don't—I don't want that either."

The nightmares returned. He woke screaming every night, and cried until he fell asleep again, while Marit did what she could for him, which wasn't much. During the day, when he smiled and kissed her and did paperwork for the king, neither of them mentioned it. Marit knew she ought to. She also knew that he didn't want her to. Every morning, after he kissed her and before he got out of bed, he looked at her, eyebrows slightly raised, half daring her to say something, half begging her not to.

So she didn't.

But they were on edge, both of them, if quietly so, and she was hardly surprised when she walked into their room and found him on the floor, sitting in a pile of his own dead snake skin.

Somehow they had never moved it from under the bed.

"Davey? Sweetheart?"

He looked slowly up at her and said, almost dreamily, "I raised the dead once."

"Yes, you told me," she said, imagining how worried she would be if the story hadn't come up before. She was worried enough as it was. "Are you all right?"

"Fine," he said. "I used to think—if I hadn't eaten them whole, skin and bones and all—but that was stupid. The dead never come back right."

"Davey..."

"I'm fine," he said again. He shoved the skins back under the bed and stood, reaching out as if he would touch her. She stepped back.

"You're covered in little bits of your own dead skin and dried blood. You'll be washing before you touch me."

He nodded; she stepped into the hall to find someone who could run them a bath.

Marit would bathe too, as long as they had hot water prepared; she went first, as Davey was dirtier just now. The maids had brought up the tub and left again, so that they could have their privacy.

"We should talk about the nightmares," Marit said, as she stepped out of the tub and into the towel Davey had unfolded for her.

"I'm fine," he said, climbing into the tub.

"You're not."

He stared up at her, silent, for a very long time. Finally he said, "Every morning after breakfast, the king tells me how many people have died—how many people I've killed—it's not many, yet, but there will be more, and I—and every night I see their blood, not on my hands, because my dreams never made the transition to humanity, but dripping from my mouth. Because I've never stopped being a lindworm, Marit. I've only ever played at being human. And how long can it be before the game has to end?"

She reached out to touch his arm. "You think you'll turn back?"

He shook his head. "No. I don't know. I just—this still feels like a dream. Over a year, and when I'm asleep—that feels real. I never really got used to the idea of arms and legs. I can use them, but they don't—they don't feel right, Marit. Blood dripping from my mouth? That feels right. I wake screaming because I know I'm a monster. And I don't talk about it, because what is there to say?"

"You're not a monster. Not anymore. Ida said you never were."

"And you know she was wrong."

"I know," Marit agreed. "But you aren't a monster now."

He shrugged. "I never once felt like a human in a lindworm's body. I feel very much like a lindworm in the body of a man."

"I love you," she said. "I don't care what you are, or were, or think you are. I love you."

"I love you too," he said, stepping out of the tub. He added thoughtfully, a moment later, "I probably wouldn't have survived, without the skins. When I—when I was very ill. Sleeping on top of them likely kept me alive."

Later, as they prepared for bed, he told her softly, "I do feel more human when I'm with you."

♕

They returned from breakfast one morning to find their door slightly ajar.

Marit had one key, and Smilla had the other, to take care of tasks the queen had deemed beneath a prince and princess, while they were out. But this was not a time of day when Smilla would be in their room. And Marit had been very careful to keep their door locked since the ambassadors had arrived, and even more so since war had been declared.

She glanced over at Davey, who looked as concerned as she was. Shrugging, Marit pushed open the door; she didn't know what else to do. It would be embarrassing to go looking for help when they didn't even know whether anything was wrong.

There was something wrong. A guest, uninvited, standing in the center of their room.

"Hello, sweetheart," Ida said. "I hear you've started a war."

Chapter Fifteen

They stood frozen in the doorway for what felt like a very long time. Finally, Davey went forward to hug Ida, and Marit closed and locked their door.

"How did you know?" Davey asked. "How did you—there shouldn't even have been time for the news to reach you, never mind for you to get back."

"You know I have my own little messengers, dear. A sparrow brought me the news, and I rode the North Wind here as soon as I could track him down—you know how tricky the Winds can be, or I would have been here sooner."

Marit had thought they would have much more time, and maybe some warning, before Ida came back. She and Davey hadn't talked about this. They didn't have a plan, hadn't worked out how their relationship with Ida would need to change when they had both grown up and settled in a little.

"I'll call someone to prepare a room for you," she said, deciding to set down one boundary immediately, without consulting her husband. They would not be sharing a bedroom with his foster mother when there were other spaces available.

Davey nodded, and Marit found someone in the hall who could take a message to whoever handled assigning rooms to unexpected guests. Then she left Davey and Ida together to catch up, moving quickly away without being sure where she was going. Her safe space had been invaded.

She didn't want Ida here. Perhaps that was selfish. She was Davey's mother, and she had power, likely enough to make a difference in this war. But Marit didn't want to share Davey, didn't want to have to be nice to a woman she knew would have gladly let her die, a woman she knew had chosen her specifically, out of all the girls in the world, to be eaten by a monster.

They had come back to their room after breakfast because they had nowhere else to go. The king had a private meeting of some sort, and Harald and Suhki were asking any last-minute questions of their translator before he finally went back to his normal life tomorrow.

With no one else to talk to, and no desire to wander alone in a palace that now contained people they were at war with, Marit found herself in the queen's office.

"Ida is back," she told her.

The queen looked up and frowned. Marit sat down without being invited, comfortable enough with the queen now to do so.

"She will be a valuable asset in the war," the queen said after a too-long pause.

"Yes," Marit agreed with no enthusiasm.

"Would you like to help me with this project?"

"Yes, please," Marit said, accepting a few hours of distraction from the problem as all the queen had to offer her.

♛

When she got back to their room, Ida was gone, and Davey was sitting at the fire, reading. He set his book aside and stood when Marit came in.

"Where have you been?"

"With your mother," she said. "The other one."

"They know Ida's here, then," he said, and Marit nodded. "That's good. She's settled in her room, and said she might go to the cottage for some supplies—she came here straight away."

The days were still quite short at this time of year, but Marit supposed wise women were accustomed to walking through dark forests alone.

"I doubt we'll see her again before tomorrow. She'll want to talk to Father about the war in the morning; I'd rather not be there for that, to listen to her blame him for everything, and me and herself for nothing."

"I thought you'd be glad to have her back."

"I am," he said. "I am. But I find I've grown and changed in many ways since she was here last, and I'm not quite sure how to talk to her anymore."

Marit nodded. She had begun to feel that way, sometimes, when she was able to see Greta and her father, and was sure she'd changed far less than Davey.

♛

The king told them at breakfast that he would be meeting with Ida after. Marit was rather surprised that Ida had not invited herself to breakfast, but then she could hardly claim anymore that she needed to be there for Davey's sake, and she and the queen did not like each other.

The king and the queen would both be there, and Harald as well; the rest of them were excused. The queen said they needn't give Ida an over-inflated sense of importance by bringing the entire royal family to her. This may have been true, but the real reason they weren't attending the meeting was that no one wanted Davey in the middle of whatever argument was sure to break out, and neither Suhki nor Marit had enough experience or training yet to be much use when it came to strategy, which was probably what they would discuss—the most strategic use of Ida's power and influence to aid in the war effort.

The three of them went up to Suhki and Harald's rooms, settling in the area Suhki called her parlor, which had a small fireplace and several soft chairs, as well as nearly everything Suhki had brought from her old home—four lovely paintings and a beautiful, delicate tea set.

"She is your—" Suhki paused, frowning her searching-for-a-word frown. "Your stepmother?"

"More like his foster mother," Marit said, and explained, when Suhki frowned again, "She is the woman who took care of him as a child, when he was not living here."

Suhki nodded. "And she is magic?"

"Very magic," Davey said.

"What did she mean," Marit asked, "when she said she rode the wind to get here?"

"Just that. She called it by name and sat on its back, and she was here as quickly as the North Wind could carry her, which is very quickly indeed."

"Have you ridden the wind with her?"

"A few times, when I was very small and there was a far-off emergency to see to. She tries not to overuse the winds—they are not agreeable, most of them, and do not wait on the convenience of mortals, even mortals like Ida, who they have known from a child."

They sat in silenced for a few minutes, Marit struggling to imagine Ida as a child.

Suhki sighed. "Will we always be a little on the outside?"

This was not the first meeting that had been attended by the king and queen and their oldest son only. Indeed, most meetings were like that, although Davey got invited to more than the girls. And Marit didn't particularly want to be in a mini war council with Ida, but—well.

"No," Davey said decisively. "You're the queen-to-be; you'll have to be on the inside eventually."

"It'll just take time," Marit agreed. "The queen must have felt like an outsider too, once."

"I am so sick of the outside," Suhki said. "I have been here since my mother died."

"Tell us about it?" Marit suggested. Suhki had been here, and been their friend, for some time now, but they had still heard little of her past.

She nodded. "We were rich, but not—not important. It was me

and Mother and Grandfather. I knew who my father was, but I had never met him. We had a home in—in the south. The palace was farther north—maybe I would have seen snow if I'd stayed there long enough. But I never went farther than our own big city, when I was young. My mother didn't need or want to marry, and it was the two of us always together, while my grandfather worked. And then they were taken in the same week by a sickness that came through our city, and since there was no other family, my father sent for me."

Marit stood and went to squeeze herself into the seat beside Suhki, not quite large enough for two, and wrapped an arm around her shoulders. Suhki smiled at her, a little watery.

"I think he was fond of me, but the queen was not, and his other children weren't, either. I tried to avoid them all. My mother—she said that she and my father were sweethearts when they were young, and they met again for a time after he was married, and that is when I came. It was an arranged marriage with the queen, and I think she was afraid he loved my mother more than her, and maybe me more than her children. I do not think he did, but she was afraid, and it was—it was not a good place to be. But it is for the best, because now I have Harald."

"That was an arranged marriage too," Davey said.

"Yes, but I love him, and I know that he loves me, and he has no children to disrupt our lives in twenty years. Tell me about your mother, Davey? The Ida-mother."

Marit moved back into her own seat, as Suhki's sorrow had passed for now. She didn't care to hear much about Ida, except that any stories Davey had to tell of her would feature him as well, and she always appreciated baby lindworm stories. For all that he had been terrifying when they met, she was convinced he must have been adorable as a baby dragon.

Harald joined them before long, but had no real news to share. "They argued. They fought like children, Father and Ida, while Mother sat there glaring. Ida left in a huff, and we've got nowhere as far as actual planning. Give them all a few days to settle down, I suppose, and we'll try again. Come walk in the gardens with me? I need some air after that, and the trees are starting to bud."

♛

Marit had been doing her best to avoid Ida since her return, with good success. She knew that Davey spent time with her often, but she and Davey were no longer so joined at the hip, and when he wanted to be with Ida, she went to find Harald or Suhki or the queen. She thought the queen was becoming rather fond of her. She also thought the queen was rather desperately jealous of Ida, for which she couldn't blame her.

"I don't think he knows you love him," she said one day, as they sat in the queen's office together.

The queen looked up, surprised. "Of course I love him. He's my son."

"You've never told him. And you don't spend time with him like the king does. And every time you go to touch him you change your mind."

"I don't know that he'd want to be touched by me."

Marit shrugged. "He doesn't see the reaching out. He only sees the pulling back."

"He has a mother already. One who knows how to love him."

"Well, I prefer you," Marit said, and the queen smiled, blushing faintly.

♛

When she returned to her room it was empty; it was longer than Davey would usually spend with Ida, these days, but perhaps he'd met up with Harald or the king after. She was just trying to untangle a knitting project enough to see where she'd left off when there was a knock on the door.

She opened it to Ida. "Davey isn't here," she said.

"I know," Ida said, and let herself in, even though Marit hadn't opened the door wide enough to indicate an invitation. "I've hardly seen you since I've been back."

Sighing, Marit closed the door, and went to shove her knitting back onto the shelf. It was no good, trying to get the room into any semblance of order for their guest; she'd seen it all. Davey always went to her new room, wherever that was, but she'd let herself into theirs in the first place, and who knew how long she'd had to poke around before they got back.

"What do you want with me?"

Ida didn't answer right away, wandering to the window to look out for a minute first.

"I knew you would suit each other," she said at last.

"You knew we would suit each other if he didn't eat me first."

"You can't still be angry about that."

As if Ida had any right to decide the direction or duration of her feelings. "I'm not angry he nearly ate me. I'm angry you deliberately fed me to him—me, specifically. Is that why? You thought we'd like each other if I survived?"

"I saw you in the forest, and I knew you had the strength and the courage and the kindness to do what needed to be done."

"And what about the princesses? What did you know about them?"

"Nothing. That was Olaf's business; I stepped in when it became clear he couldn't handle it."

"It should have been clear from the beginning that he couldn't handle it! Handling the situation would have meant slaying the dragon; if you thought it was safe to send Davey to him, you already knew he wouldn't handle it."

"And you can be grateful he didn't, since it gave you a husband you love."

"I can be grateful for Davey and still hate you," Marit said, and left the room, deciding that would be easier than ousting Ida.

♕

She went down to dinner still in the clothes she'd worn all day, which the queen would not deem appropriate dinner wear, but she didn't know where Davey was, or whether Ida was still in their room, and she didn't want to face her alone again.

She wasn't seated near Davey that night, and didn't quite dare to cross the room to find him, with the ambassadors hanging about always ready to draw her into conversation, and so didn't really speak to him until they were on their way to the room later.

"I heard you had a row with Ida," Davey said, voice unreadable.

"I've had them before," she said, as lightly as she could manage, "and I'll have them again. Aren't disagreements with the mother-in-law rather traditional?"

"You like my mother better than I do," Davey countered, "which is just as well, since she likes you better than she likes me, as well."

"Your mother loves you."

"She's afraid to touch me."

"She's afraid you don't want to be touched," Marit said. She shook her head. That was the queen's conversation to have, if she ever worked out how. "We were talking about Ida."

"And I thought you didn't much want to be, and was offering a change of subject."

"Oh."

"We can certainly talk about her if you want to."

Marit didn't want to, but she supposed they'd have to eventually; it might as well be now. "I used to wonder why the king chose me of all girls to be your bride. The answer is he didn't—Ida did."

Davey stopped walking abruptly in the middle of the hall.

"The queen told me, months ago. It was after Ida left, and I didn't want to burden you with my anger at someone you loved."

"I can go yell at her for you," he offered, voice a little shaky. "If you like."

"I can yell well enough myself."

"I'm sorry," he said.

Marit shrugged. "It isn't your fault. She saw me in the forest and thought we'd get on if I lived long enough; she was right about that, at least."

"She won't be here long. I won't—I won't offer to tell her to go away, because I rather think we might need her, with the war. But she'll leave when it's done, and you shan't have to see her or think of her for a long, long time."

Marit took his hand, and they resumed the walk back to their room.

♛

She woke that night to Davey's hand on her arm.

"It is not morning," she said. They woke each other often in the midst of nightmares, but he was fully awake and not noticeably distraught; she thought he had woken her deliberately, and was annoyed.

"Shh."

They sat in silence for a full minute.

"Davey—"

"Don't you hear it?" he whispered. "Someone's trying to get in."

She didn't hear it, but trusted Davey. The fire had gone out completely, and the room was dark. She stood and made her way carefully over to the fireplace to pick up the poker. She didn't know who might be picking their lock in the dead of night, but doubted it was anyone with good intentions.

She met Davey at the door; he turned the lock.

The door swung open to reveal a man with a knife, his lock-picking tools scattered on the ground. It was too dark to see his face clearly.

A knife. She had a fire poker, which was at least as deadly handled right, but he was probably trained. The queen had not yet taught her how princesses were meant to handle assassins.

She screamed.

Davey's room had probably been chosen originally because it was remote enough to prevent anyone hearing screams, but surely, with a war on, there would be guards of some sort stationed nearby, for just this sort of emergency.

The man dropped his knife and fled. Davey caught her arm when she tried to follow, and pulled her to sit on the ground. Or maybe she sunk there herself. She couldn't tell.

"You'll only get yourself killed," he said. She dropped the poker, and screamed again, just to be certain. Davey wrapped his arms around her. It wasn't long before the guards appeared.

"Princess? Are you all right?" She shook her head. "What happened?"

"Man with a knife. He went that way." She pointed.

"No," Davey said, "you'll never catch him. Find the ambassador."

"Your Highness–"

"Arrest him."

"On what grounds?"

"On the grounds that there was an assassin outside my bedroom. I want all of his men in your custody. Now."

They only hesitated for a moment; whatever else they may have suspected he had been, Davey was their prince. He stood and grabbed the last man as they left.

"Go and get my brother. Send him to my father's chambers."

The man nodded and turned around, and Davey pulled Marit to her feet.

"Are you all right?"

She nodded shakily.

"We're all right," he said. "Everything is all right. Come on."

She trailed behind as he stormed down the halls, stopping finally at a door she'd never seen and pounding furiously. She thought vaguely that he didn't often storm.

A maid appeared, still half asleep.

"Prince David?"

"I need to see my parents."

"They're sleeping."

"Yes, well, so were we, until a man with a knife tried to break into our room." He pushed past her, stopping abruptly when he came face to face with the queen, still tying her robe.

"David? What on earth is going on?"

"There's been an assassination attempt."

"Who?"

"Us. Just now. Marit needs to sit down." He turned to face her for the first time since leaving their doorway. "Are you all right?

You're not all right. Everything is fine now, I promise." He maneuvered her into a chair. "Where's Father?"

The queen disappeared into the blackness, and returned with King Olaf and a candle. Harald was there by then, too, with Suhki.

"What happened?"

"I had the ambassador arrested. And all his men."

"You did what?"

Marit let Suhki fuss over her, murmuring things in her own language and checking for wounds, as he explained, yet again, about the assassination attempt.

Such a nasty word, assassination. Sibilant. Serpentine.

"It could have been anyone," the king said. It was not likely to be anyone else, when the ambassador represented a country that had recently declared war. But they would need proof.

Davey held out a knife with an elaborately carved blue handle. He must have picked it up outside their door—Marit had been too shocked to notice much. "It belongs to the ambassador. You must have seen him wear it. He may not have been the man outside the door, but he certainly armed him, at least."

The king took the knife, and turned it in his hands, and didn't say anything.

"They can kill me any time they want. I don't care. But do you think they'd break into our room and just kill me? He would have hurt Marit. So yes, I had them arrested. I feel I was within my rights."

"Why now?" the queen asked. "Why would they try something like that now?"

"They know who he—what he was," Marit said. "The one man all but told me so at the ball. I don't know why they'd wait until now to do something about it."

"I do," Davey said grimly. "Ida. She's here for—I know she knew you before, Father, but she's here for me. If I was dead, I doubt she'd apply the same effort to helping you with this war."

"I'll go see to it they're all in custody," the king said. "No one was hurt?"

"We're fine," Marit whispered.

"Good. Harald, take them to your rooms for the night. Just to be safe."

"I need to—"

"We'll talk in the morning, David. We'll have an official council in the afternoon. Now go take care of your wife."

Harald walked them to the rooms he shared with Suhki. The four of them went in, and Davey stoked the fire. Marit sat numb on the rug beside him. They could not sleep now.

"Nothing happened," he said.

"He tried to kill us. Just because we—because we're—I don't even know why. Davey, he tried to kill us."

She cried then, properly, in the open, as she had not allowed herself to cry since marrying the lindworm, because she could not show weakness then, because she had to be the grown up for Davey. She was only eighteen; she had never wanted to be a grown up or a princess, and now there were men in the world who wanted her dead.

Davey held her, and whispered things that were vaguely soothing, and Harald and Suhki sat beside them. At least she didn't have to be a grown up alone anymore.

Late, late, when the sun was the thinnest sliver of light on the horizon, they were all still awake. It was not a night for sleeping.

"I missed all the dragon things," Suhki said quietly. "I thought the excitement was mostly over."

"There is certainly excitement tonight," Davey said. "Ida is going to be furious."

Marit had forgotten Ida completely, but she was sure Davey had not. He had chosen to go to the king and queen instead. Marit wasn't sure if it was the assassination attempt or that choice that she would be furious about.

♛

Ida joined them at breakfast that morning, though Marit was certain she hadn't been invited. There were only six places set.

She had not slept since Davey woke her, and was too tired to pay much attention to her surroundings. She thought she would be able to sleep after breakfast, when they returned to their own room; perhaps she shouldn't feel safer to sleep there than in Harald's room, since it was there that they'd been attacked. But it was home, and she was certain everything would seem better when she was in her own bed.

She was vaguely aware that Ida was arguing with the king and queen, but didn't care what they were arguing about until Ida said, "Clearly they aren't safe alone," and she realized they were trying to take her room from her.

"I could move back in," Ida continued.

"No," the queen said, before Marit could say the same thing. "It's a single room; there's no space for a third person."

"Then move them."

"I don't want to be moved," Marit said.

"It will be safer," the king told her. "You shouldn't be so secluded at a time like this. You shouldn't have to go through half a dozen hallways and nearly as many stairways to find us. The royal rooms have always been near each other."

"It will be temporary," the queen said, making that all three authority figures in Marit's current life sided against her.

Harald and Suhki whispered back and forth for a moment, and then Harald said, more loudly, "Suhki and I have adjoining suites, but hers aren't in use; that's meant for arranged marriages where people don't get along. We share a space. Davey and Marit could move into her rooms. They'd be nearer to everything, and very near to me if anything happened."

"Just until the war ends?" Davey asked, and the king nodded. "Marit?"

"All right," she agreed. Wars could last for years, but it was the best offer she was likely to get. "Just us in the suite, though. We don't need Ida there if Harald is only a door away."

Harald and Suhki accompanied them to get their things. Marit thought Ida would have liked to be helping, too, but the king was talking to her, quiet and urgent.

They had few enough important items to be carried easily, just the contents of their little shelf. Harald said he'd send someone for the clothing later.

Suhki's unused suite consisted of several rooms. There was a bedchamber, a waiting area, an office, a closet, an entire separate room for the chamber pot, and two rooms meant to be occupied by servants.

Marit and Davey had no servants, and wanted no servants, and she doubted they would make much use of anything but the bedroom.

She asked, before Harald and Suhki left to let them settle in, "Did they catch the assassin?"

"I don't know." Harald said, and she remembered that he had been with them all night and all morning. "I'll find out. Soon."

And then they were alone. Marit felt small and awkward in what were clearly royal rooms—Harald had the royal heir's traditional chambers, which made this a room meant for the future queen or prince consort.

"It will only be for a little while," Davey said.

"You don't like it either, do you?"

"No," he admitted.

"I think we could fit five of my father's house in this space."

"We'll keep to the bedroom and the closet, and pretend the rest doesn't exist. Or we could move into the servants' chambers, if all the opulence gets too unnerving."

"The servants' chambers—do you think the queen will try to assign people to us again?"

He frowned. "Probably not, now. She should know us well enough to know we'd be uncomfortable."

"Because our comfort is always your mother's first priority."

"Well, she should also know we can't stop talking about secret things in our own bedroom, and I don't think she has the time now to thoroughly vet all potential candidates for people that can be trusted with snaky secrets. Besides, Harald and Suhki and all their servants are a door away; it'll be easier to get help for big events."

They set about organizing their few possessions, which took too little time. Marit felt adrift, her home stripped from her by the lindworm for a second time.

"I'll make a fire," Davey said after a few minutes.

He did, and they sat in front of it until they fell asleep, and slept until Harald came to tell them to dress for dinner.

♛

The king was very businesslike at breakfast the next morning. "We will have a council at three today. Our prisoners will have to be...questioned, first, of course."

"Of course," Davey echoed. Marit was not sure what the king's pause meant, but was afraid it mattered a great deal.

"Things have grown serious, David. Our country is in a bad position. We have had assassins in our halls. If they can get to you, it will not be much harder to attack Harald, or even myself. Our next in line, after Harald, cannot become king. He is a distant cousin, and too young, and too far from the city."

"Oh."

"Things have changed since you turned down your place in the succession, David. We're at war."

Davey looked over at Harald.

"Say yes, Davey. Second in line? It's still not likely. I don't plan on dying any time soon. But if it happened, you'd make a good king."

"If you die," he said. He looked down at his plate, then up again, seeming suddenly very young. "Please don't die."

The king nodded. "I'll announce it at the council. Would you like to be present for the first round of questioning?"

"No. No, I can't."

"Of course. It's all right, David."

No one had asked Marit. She couldn't think of many things worse than being a queen.

It didn't matter. They were at war. If Harald died life wasn't worth thinking about at all, never mind about ruling anything. Davey would be devastated. So would she. But she was a princess.

Sooner or later they'd have to be prepared to make sacrifices for the sake of the kingdom. Becoming a princess in the first place had seemed like sacrifice enough, but she should have known it would not be.

♛

A few days passed. Nothing happened, to speak of. Marit managed to avoid Ida, mostly. She spent long hours with Suhki, in one or the other of their adjoining rooms, while Davey was with Ida or with the king.

Whatever the king was telling Davey about the war now, he was keeping it to himself. Most of the men were in custody. A few had escaped, but they had the assassin, and the king had announced that it was safe for Marit and Davey to be in the hallways unsupervised, although going out alone to see her family was still absolutely forbidden.

Questioning them was going slowly. It didn't help that they had information about Davey they shouldn't. Everything had to be handled by Harald and King Olaf themselves, in case anyone else got answers to the wrong questions.

Davey was always invited, and never went. No one ever asked Marit if she wanted to help, which was just as well, since she had no particular desire to do so.

He was there with her, working, very quietly, probably on Greek, and she was bored. "I'm going out."

"Where?" He didn't look up.

"I don't know. To see if there is anyone still here that we care about?" Helga's family had sent her away a few days ago, and Katrina's family the week before; she thought that was everyone they knew a little, gone. "I'm bored. We've hardly left our room."

She opened the door to find Sir Tomas on the other side.

"Princess." He bowed slightly. "I've just been speaking with our prisoners. Tell me, is your husband here?"

She glanced back almost accidentally, just as Davey, who had been sprawled across the floor with his book, began to turn and sit up. Sir Tomas took a step forward, and she grabbed his arm. If he was here after seeing the prisoners, he knew the truth.

"Sir Tomas." He would kill Davey. He would kill him. "Sir Tomas, please. You don't understand."

He stopped abruptly, and she rushed to Davey, frozen in the center of the room, still clutching his book.

"Please."

"Good heavens, girl. You'd think I'd come here to kill someone."

"Haven't you? I—I mean, what did they tell you?"

Davey hadn't moved, but considering his reaction last time someone was near her with a knife, it seemed unlikely he was expecting a bloodbath.

"They told me my prince was trapped in the form of a monster for twenty years."

"Oh."

"That's a very nice way of putting it," Davey said.

"So you're not going to kill him?"

"I'm not going to kill him. Why would I kill him? Prince David, I am terribly sorry if anything in my conduct has suggested any inclination to—"

"No," said Davey.

"You kill monsters," Marit said, panicked despite having assured Davey a dozen times that Sir Tomas would surely not kill him.

"There is a difference between a monster and a boy under a spell. I am only glad, now, that I was never aware there was a lindworm in the kingdom to slay."

Davey nodded. The book dropped from his shaking fingers, landing on the floor with a thud.

"So what did you come for?" Marit was far too tired to be trusting. "How did you even get in? The king said only he and Harald were interrogating."

"I was curious. The door was unlocked." The door had not been unlocked. King Olaf would not be so careless. "I asked some questions. It's what I do."

"I thought what you did was hunting monsters."

"That too."

"But I'm not one?" Davey asked.

"Never." He bowed. "You are my prince. And things are getting unpleasant—I suspect for you especially so. I merely wished for you to know that when I say I am on your side, I am doing so under no false pretenses."

He bowed again, and left.

"That was strange," said Marit.

Davey nodded. He sat down again slowly, and Marit sat beside him, no longer interested in going out.

Chapter Sixteen

The assassins had delayed the king's planning with Ida; the next time they met to discuss the war, Marit and Davey and Suhki came too. They met in a room unfamiliar to Marit, wood paneled and windowless. Marit sat at a small table between Davey and the queen, holding Davey's hand beneath the table, listening. She had not seen the king much outside of breakfast, and didn't pay much attention to him then; the king was the one who had come to collect her for the wedding, and she would never be close to him like she was to the rest of the family.

He seemed old now, and tired. The lindworm had cost him so much. "We cannot win this war," he said. "We have no allies; this business with the princesses has used up all the goodwill we've ever had, and even if they're not fighting us outright, no one is willing to come to our aid."

Ida hummed thoughtfully. "I haven't enough magic to turn an army, but if I could get to key leaders—the king, perhaps, the crown prince, the best general—a few strategically placed frogs would not go amiss."

"I have had quite enough of transformation magic, I think," said the queen.

"You have—"

"Their grievance is legitimate," Davey said, interrupting Ida.

Marit nodded, suddenly glad they'd come to this meeting. "Turning people to frogs is for—is for troublemakers in the forest, thieves and predators and bullies who need to learn a bit of respect. To do that now would—it would cheapen things. It would say that the pain we caused them was nothing, that we are the ones with no respect for the consequences of our actions."

"And slaughtering them on the battlefield doesn't say that?" Ida asked.

"No," the king said. "Wars are how it is done, how these conflicts are settled in this world, and war is how they, not we, have chosen to move forward with this; we will respect that. Magic and trickery would be one more thing for them to be rightfully angry at."

Ida left, muttering something about stubborn children. She returned the next day with a solution, no dragons and heroes and enchantments, but only one ordinary thing, the best she could offer.

"The old queen, the mother of this king, was a friend of mine. She is long since dead, and her son does not much care for me. But there is a debt to be paid, and I think if I ask he will come here now to talk with Olaf face to face. Little blood has been shed so far, and we may yet reach a treaty with no more. There is hope, Davey," she said, because she addressed herself almost always to Davey, ignoring the rest of them when she could. Marit thought she would throw them all over for Davey, not just their family but their kingdom, if only Davey would allow it.

She was glad that he would not allow it, glad that he, as a human, had more sense and compassion than the people who loved him.

♛

For months Marit's world had been stagnant, an eternal summer locked behind stone walls with Davey destroyed by guilt and fear. The winter had been life again, a wonderful relief. And now spring was fading into summer again, the movement would not stop, and she could not catch her breath. She would take even the lindworm again for just a moment of calm. It was only a few more days before the debt was paid.

The king arrived, elegant and intimidating with a large entourage of ministers and officers and whatever else a king needed to travel with, all dressed in blue. Most of his army was posted a few miles outside the city, with his second son to lead them. Introductions were made, and Marit managed a decent curtsey, and Davey a decent bow.

But he had gone white and still when the king walked in, and she thought he was very afraid. He had been standing a few steps away when things began, and she did not dare now to go and take his hand, in case it might alert the strangers to his distress. There was no reason for him to be so distressed, and they could not begin this visit with suspicion.

The queen was polite and dignified, and made a long speech welcoming everyone. Marit didn't really listen. As the queen wrapped up, a young soldier she knew a little came in through the back, standing anxiously behind her. Marit turned around. No one ever stood anxiously behind her. Especially not in important meetings where she was mostly ornamental.

"Yes?" she asked him quietly.

"Excuse me, Princess, but your sister is here at the gate. She would not leave until you were sent for."

Greta? Now? Marit looked over at Davey, then at the stranger king in his velvet robe, and shook her head. "Not now. Tell her to go home."

She turned back to the conversation in time to hear her own king say, "We will have to discuss ransom, of course." They were talking about the ambassadors.

"You say he ordered an assassination on your son?"

King Olaf nodded.

"You may keep them, then, and do as you please. There is no place for murderers in my court."

There was not much talking after that. There would be official discussions in the coming days; for now the visitors would unpack and rest.

"Is he mad?" Marit asked as soon as they were safely away. "They would have given everything away if they'd been released."

"The word of an assassin is worth very little," Davey said.

Harald nodded. "Anyway, they would have been found dead before their release. Father would have returned the ransom, of course, very apologetic about whatever zealots fill his court, but what other fate could assassins deserve?"

Marit felt sick. Davey looked about the same. She asked, for something to say, "And who would the zealot be?"

Harald shrugged. "Maybe Sir Tomas. Since he knows the truth and knows how to get his hands dirty."

"We don't need more dirt," Davey said.

He was angry. They split from Harald and Suhki at their door, retreating to the little space they had carved out for themselves in all the grandness of the new rooms.

"His daughter had his nose. Before I ate her."

"Davey..."

He didn't answer, just turned to look out the window again, and she squeezed into the chair beside him, thinking of Greta. She hadn't seen her in weeks and weeks, and there was no knowing when she might see her again. With a war on, she might never see her again. But she was a princess now, and she couldn't up and leave halfway through a meeting with a foreign king. Nor could she, with his ambassador assassins in their prison and his soldiers likely in their forest, go to find Greta and apologize.

For a long time they sat in silence. Finally she looked over at his pile of Greek books in front of the fireplace, and asked, for something to say, "Have you found any serpent stories?"

He nodded.

"Tell me one."

He told her, his voice flat and uninterested, "Once there was a woman who angered the greatest goddess. She was cursed and became a snake below the waist, and could not sleep. This drove her mad, and so she devoured her own children."

Not a good distraction, then. She tried not to sound upset. "Oh, Davey. Tell me a happy story."

"Once a man and a woman were in love, but the woman was sentenced to die. To save her, the man found another woman with snakes for hair, and he chopped off her head. She was so hideous that her head turned their enemies to stone."

"Davey."

"The man and the woman were quite happy in the end."

"Davey," she said again.

"I'm sorry. Nothing ends happily for serpents."

"Decapitation is not the solution to all problems."

"I know." He continued to stare out the window, and she was not sure he knew at all.

Chapter Seventeen

War was strange. It was not at all what Marit had thought, not from here in the palace. There were endless meetings full of fancy people being polite and friendly while their subjects killed each other on a battlefield far away.

She hated it. She had seldom felt so little like she belonged in this place. There were—Smilla was her friend, though she saw her seldom enough now. Smilla was her friend, and the boy she loved was fighting and perhaps dying for a cause that meant nothing to him, while Marit sat across the table from the enemy king eating delicacies.

Their guests had been there a week. Marit was on the outskirts again—meetings and meetings and meetings, decisions never made, manners never wavering, while Marit sat in her too-large room alone. Davey went to the meetings when he could, and told her about them, though there was nothing really to tell, no progress ever made.

There were meetings he couldn't attend. Meetings the king had banned him from for his own sake, and meetings on mornings when he woke still shaking from interrupted nightmares, mornings when he could think of nothing but how this was all his fault, and couldn't trust himself to sit across the room from their enemies and not confess his sins.

Marit liked those mornings, though she felt guilty for it. She didn't want her husband to be unhappy and afraid. But she wanted him to be hers. She was so lonely, lately. She dreamed often of going home, of sitting down between Greta and her father at their small, splintered table, of doing the chores she used to find so tedious.

Suhki was invited to more meetings than Marit, though mostly to sit prettily by Harald's side; she did not know, yet, how to do all the things she would need to do someday as queen. But she was still foreign and new, and sometimes her presence was not required. During those meetings, she sat with Marit in some little corner of one of their rooms, and they tried to find things to talk about that weren't the war.

They went to church together on Sunday, the king and all his men filling the pews of their palace chapel, another step in this strange dance of pretending they weren't out to kill each other, all of them sitting peacefully to listen to Father Gregor.

They couldn't afford any oddities, now. Marit and Davey sat with the rest of the family, as they had not since the first week. Communion was passed throughout the pews, as it had not been since the first week. When the Communion elements came by, Davey took his share and passed them on, silent and steady, but Marit, sitting too close, could feel his leg shaking.

"Always the blood," he murmured when she leaned in to kiss his cheek, and she saw the wine spilling out the day war was declared, the lindworm's blood staining her white shifts.

"Yes," she agreed softly, "always the blood."

After the service the congregation dispersed; Marit sat waiting as Davey went to speak with Father Gregor. She watched as a man in enemy blue talked for a moment with Harald before he and Suhki left the room. When they were gone he came to the queen, and said something to her too softly for Marit to hear, though she was standing only a few feet away.

The queen answered more loudly, in a language Marit didn't

recognize; there was a heated exchange, and then the man said, softly, "Lizzie," and she stepped back, shaking her head.

Marit and Davey reached the queen at the same time, and the man left without acknowledging either of them.

"Are you all right, Mother?"

"I'm fine."

It occurred to Marit suddenly that she had no idea where the queen had come from originally; she had been the queen since long before Marit was born. "We're not—we're not at war with your homeland, are we?"

"No," the queen said. "That was my cousin; he's married to their queen's sister."

"What did he want?" Davey asked.

"He was advising us to surrender and agree to all of his king's terms." She looked around the chapel; the only other person still there was Father Gregor, quietly sorting through his sermon notes. "I had wanted to speak with you both; my cousin is right that we likely cannot win this war, and I would not have—tomorrow. Tomorrow the two of you will dress in whatever of your clothing you think I would hate the most, and go to Marit's family. Sir Tomas will accompany you. You will give any livestock they keep to neighbors, pack up their possessions, and bring them here. I will not have the family of my family harmed in this war, and I will not have them recognized and ransomed, or tortured for information. They will stay in the palace for as long as we have enemies in the forest."

Her father wouldn't like it. But the queen was right, and it would be for the best.

♛

It was a quiet day, spent mostly in their room. Davey had found an interesting book earlier in the week, and was reading it aloud to her. The door between the two sets of rooms was open, as it often was, and Suhki came through to listen for a while as well. Harald came by after yet another meeting with foreign ministers, and offered to take them all out riding the next day, if the king could spare them for an hour or two.

"Can't," Davey said.

"Can't, or don't want to?" Harald asked. Davey was still not fond of horses.

"Can't," Marit told him. "We're going to collect my family in the morning."

"Good. They'll be safer here. I've got to go; more meetings." He bent down to kiss Suhki, and then he was gone, as quickly as he'd come.

Suhki sighed. "Always busy. He said Sunday was for resting."

"I don't think kings get resting days," Davey said. "Or future kings. Not when there's a war on."

"It will be good to have your family here," Davey said as they dressed for dinner. "You've missed them."

Marit nodded. "Just as long as they don't meet your family."

He frowned. "They've already met my family. We all went shopping with the queen."

"I meant Ida."

"Oh. Yes, I suppose we should avoid that."

"I don't know how many times Father has told Greta to watch her attitude or some old woman in the woods would curse her; I don't need a baby sister to de-frog on top of all this."

"Well, for girls, Ida's more likely to make frogs come out of their mouths when they talk than to actually turn them into frogs."

"That's not better. You realize that's not better, right?"

"I realize. But she'll know that cursing the in-laws is unacceptable."

"They still shouldn't meet. I told them about—about Ida picking me, long before I told you. My father will want to yell at her—they'll both want to yell at her. They'd have liked to yell at your father, but you can't—you can't just yell at your king, so—I just don't want to spend any more time listening to any of our families fighting."

"It'll be fine," Davey said. "I'll make sure Mother puts them in an entirely different wing from Ida. And we'll only be all here together until the war is over."

Marit tried not to think about when the war was over; no one seemed convinced it would end in their victory.

♛

At dinner that night, Marit saw Suhki not quite backed into a corner by one of their guests; she ran over to check on her.

"Suhki? Are you all right?"

She nodded. "He was just showing me his knife. Isn't it pretty?"

Marit glanced down. It was a lovely knife, much like the knife an assassin had nearly used on her and Davey, with a delicate blue and white carved handle. She wondered whether showing your knife to the princess of a country you were at war with was some kind of subtle threat.

"Have you seen Harald?" she asked.

Suhki gestured vaguely toward the door, knife still in her hand. "Talking to Sir Tomas, I think."

The queen called Marit then, and she left Suhki, a little reluctantly.

When they all sat down for dinner Suhki was where she was meant to be, sitting beside Davey at the other end of the table. That was all right, then; she had known it was silly to worry. A man would hardly stab a princess with his pretty knife in the middle of a crowded hall. But she felt she was made of worry, lately.

♛

In the morning, as they were getting dressed, there was a knock on the door connecting their space to Harald and Suhki's. Marit went to open it, straightening her favorite red bell skirt as she went. It was good to be in her own clothing; it was even better that she would be with her own family soon.

"Almost ready?" Harald asked when she opened the door.

"Almost," she said. Davey came to stand beside her, still buttoning his vest.

"I've just spoken to Father," Harald said. "Sir Tomas is needed here. But you shouldn't—don't tell Mother, but I think you should go without him. You won't be easily recognizable dressed like that, and your family—they need to be here, where they'll be safe, as soon as possible."

"The queen wouldn't like it," Marit said. But she wanted, so badly, to go home today.

"It's fine," Davey said. "It's fine. We'll go anyway."

"Be careful," Harald told them. "I'll see you tonight."

It would be the first time Davey had seen her childhood home. He had grown so much stronger since he first became a man, and it was not a difficult walk, though it was a rather long one.

Whatever enemy soldiers might be camped in their woods, they were not nearby. The sun was shining, and flowers and leaves were by now fully open. It was a beautiful day, and for once the war seemed distant and unimportant, though it was because of the war they were making this trip.

Marit walked barefoot in the cool dirt, shoes in one hand, Davey's hand in the other. He paused to pick a few small flowers for her; she paused to kiss him for a while. There was no sense in rushing; that would only look suspicious, if there were soldiers about that they hadn't seen. They were young lovers on a stroll in the forest, and for the time it would take them to reach their destination, for just this short time, she wanted to pretend that was all they were.

She didn't have to explain herself to Davey. He was as stressed and tired and grateful for this reprieve as she was.

Even taking their time, they arrived in not much more than an hour. Marit left Davey out in the yard for a few minutes, wanting a private reunion with her father and sister before she demanded that they uproot their entire lives for a war her husband had caused.

It was easier to convince her father than she'd expected. They split up, to take the animals to their three nearest neighbors; Marit and Davey took the goats to Annette's family.

Annette was long since gone, shipped away to live with distant relatives in the same week Marit was married to the lindworm. That made things easier. It was hard enough to speak to her mother, after a year in the palace, to make halting, awkward introductions to her husband the prince and explain that the goats were a gift from her father, that he and Greta were leaving home. She couldn't begin to imagine facing Annette again.

They had played together as children. Marit had helped Annette and her mother roll lefse every winter until she was married, and now the woman was a stranger.

She was suddenly angry—mostly with herself, she thought, though she wasn't quite sure why. For growing, for changing, for adapting to her new environment? For being happily married to Davey, who was the reason Annette was far away, and her mother living all alone?

They left the goats and returned to the house. Marit's good mood was spoiled, all the sun and trees and dirt in the world unable to return it, and Davey followed her silently, jogging a little to keep up.

Marit helped Greta to pack her things, while Davey helped her father, and they had lunch before leaving. She would not have taken food from her family, who needed it more, usually. She always brought food when she visited. But there was no sense in leaving food here, where it would go bad, or where animals would break in to eat it.

Greta talked the whole way back, telling stories from the last few months and asking what it would be like to live in the palace. Would she get new dresses, like Marit?

Marit thought she was nervous, talking to fill the silence; she seemed cheerful, but Greta had always been good at seeming happy when she wasn't.

When they reached the palace gate there were twice as many guards posted as usual. The four of them were rushed through the gates as soon as Davey was recognized; no one spoke to them. Marit glanced over at Davey, who looked as puzzled as she was. They'd have to ask Harald if something had happened—why double the guard at the gate when the enemy was already in the palace?

Their new rooms shared a hallway with the king and queen's, and as they walked past their door the queen came out.

"David,"' she said, and came forward to hug him.

Marit watched; he stood frozen for only a moment before cautiously returning the embrace.

The queen pulled away quickly, but kept her hands on his shoulders. "Clean up, change into something nice, and come back to me, as quickly as you can. Do you understand?"

Davey nodded sharply. The queen went back into her rooms, and they went to theirs.

"Something is wrong," Greta said quietly. "Isn't it?"

Marit nodded; this had been obvious since they approached the gate, but she had no idea what it was. She and Davey changed quickly, too worried to bother much about modesty. She picked a few twigs out of his hair; he braided hers and did up the laces on her dress. Her feet were filthy; there was nothing to be done about that now. She pulled on her stockings over the dirt, thinking guiltily of the people who would have to clean them.

"We'll be back soon," Marit said. "That door, there, leads to Harald and Suhki's room. If there's an emergency they won't be there, but someone is always in the room, and you can go there if anything—if anything happens."

Davey and Marit went back to the queen's door, where they were ushered in quickly and quietly.

"The king's second son," the queen said, "the one left with his army, has been stabbed. He's being transported here, but he's not expected to survive the night. The knife—he was stabbed with one of their knives, and it was left in the wound, but no one in the vicinity was missing theirs. They think—"

"They think Father ordered it." Davey said.

The queen nodded. "No one can know you were out of the palace today. Marit, your family must not leave your quarters. I meant to give them their own space, but—every servant Harald and

Suhki have will swear that the adjoining doors were open and the four of you were together all day."

"Where are Harald and Suhki?" Marit asked.

"In the throne room with Olaf, waiting for the prince to arrive. I'm needed there now; I was waiting for you. The two of you will join us when you've spoken to Marit's family."

She swept out, leaving them in her sitting room alone.

"Lindworm skin has healing powers." Davey said softly.

"You don't think—"

"Ida," he said.

"Yes," Marit agreed after a moment of thought. Ida had caused nearly every bad thing in the last year of her life—why not this?

"Ida works in the background; she wouldn't do her own stabbing. Who else?"

Marit looked back over the last two days, a few strange things falling into place—the knife, Sir Tomas being suddenly unavailable this morning. "Suhki. Harald. Sir Tomas." She frowned. "Should I be offended they didn't ask me for help?"

"No. You should be glad. I love you the most, which means I would find you hardest to forgive for doing something like that for my sake."

"I wouldn't have agreed to it."

"Which is why I love you the most."

Marit remembered the queen saying, once, that Ida loved Davey beyond reason. Marit did not. She loved Davey dearly, but well within the bounds of reason. She knew what would make her stop loving him, though she knew just as well that he would never do any of those things—if he struck her, if he laid with another woman, if he demanded more princesses to eat.

There were things she would not do for him no matter how much she loved him. She did not think that made her love smaller or worth less than Ida's.

"I can see it's the sort of thing Ida would do," she said, "and Sir Tomas doesn't surprise me. Perhaps Suhki does not know you well enough yet to know how you would hate it. But Harald—he must have been involved. Suhki wouldn't have been without him, and I saw her. Why would Harald—he should know it would be a betrayal to kill someone in your name."

"I'm his little brother," Davey said, as if that was all that needed saying.

It was true, for all that Davey was a few insignificant minutes older; he was Harald's little brother as surely as Greta was Marit's little sister. Harald had taught him to dance and ride a horse and snowshoe. He'd given him the undoubtably awkward talk about consummating his marriage, he teased him and babied him in turns, and he was fiercely protective.

Marit would stab a man for Greta, of course. She would stab a man for Davey, too. But a man who was standing there, threatening them. Not one she had to seek out, miles away.

"What will we do now?" she asked him.

"I don't know."

They sat in silence for a few minutes.

"I can't—I can't see her," Davey said.

Marit nodded. "I'll find her. You explain the situation to my family. We'll meet in the throne room."

She turned to go; Davey grabbed her hand and pulled her back. He kissed her. "Be careful."

"Everything will be fine," she told him, not believing it at all. Sir Tomas has stabbed a man for them. Suhki had given him the knife. Nothing was fine.

She knew where to find Ida. She walked down familiar halls, silent and empty, until she reached their abandoned bedroom. As she expected, the door was open. Ida was sitting on the floor, pulling piles of skin out from under the bed.

"You're going to use his skin to heal the prince you had stabbed. He won't thank you for this."

Ida looked up; she didn't seem surprised to see her. "I don't need his gratitude. I just need his survival."

"You aren't doing this for him; you know he would rather die than cause more death. You're—this is selfish."

Ida sighed. "I am far older than I look, Marit. And yes, I'm aware I look quite old. I was far younger than you the last time I had a family of my own. I have spent lifetimes caring for other people's children, lost or cast aside. I had the care of Olaf for a year when he was a boy. Other people's children, and I always have to give them back, no matter how little their parents deserve them.

"But Davey is mine. Conceived by my magic, raised from infancy. Olaf and Elizabeth had their child, and Davey was a monster—why shouldn't I keep him? He is my son, and I will allow no harm to come to him, no matter how much he may hate me for it.

"The deed's already been done; the prince will die without my interference. Surely neither of you wants that."

"No," Marit agreed. "It's too late to stop this now."

"Good."

"You'll leave when this is done. You'll leave and you won't come back until he sends for you, not if it takes years, not if it never happens at all. This—you know what a betrayal this is, and the least you can do to amend it is to never look in his eyes and make him remember it."

Ida nodded, stiffly. "This forest will be empty a wise woman for many years before he forgives me, but he will. Perhaps when he has children of his own he will understand." Ida stood, a bundle of skins in her arms. "Take the rest, won't you, dear? I'm afraid it's too much for me to carry."

Marit bent, reluctantly, to gather what remained on the floor, and Ida hummed thoughtfully.

"I knew the moment I saw you, six years old and chasing a butterfly, you were never meant for forests and farmers. It's a shame; I'd have taken you as my apprentice if you hadn't been meant for Davey."

Marit stiffened, nearly dropping the skins. "You watched me as a child?"

"Well, of course I did. You lived in my forest."

"Not your forest anymore. Not your kingdom, until Davey calls for you. And thank God for him—better a monster's bride than a witch like you."

She left the room quickly, confident that Ida would follow her, insulted or not.

She knew Ida loved Davey, but it wasn't her kind of love, wasn't the kind of person she'd have wanted to become, alone in a forest for decades, casting curses on impolite children and granting gifts to crying girls as it struck her fancy. Ida was no more human than Davey had been when she met them, she thought, older than she looked and a hundred years removed from real things.

They reached the throne room at the same time as the foreign prince, carried in on a stretcher.

"Marit," Ida said softly, just before she stepped into the room.

Marit paused, turning back toward her.

"It was not all dark, the magic that saved him."

"The last step," Marit guessed—embracing a dying thing did not seem dark.

Ida nodded. "If you had not felt something, some...kindness for him, in that moment, he would not have changed. And if he had not changed, he would not have survived the night. I put his life in your hands, and you did not disappoint me. I am glad he will have you when I am gone."

Marit nodded before turning away, slipping quietly into her place beside Davey. She glanced back at Ida, making her way to the king, before she turned her attention to the current situation.

The other king was there, along with what must have been every man he'd brought here, and a couple dozen soldiers Marit was quite sure hadn't been with him before. The prince's stretcher had been placed on the ground, and there was a crowd around him; Marit recognized Father Gregor and the doctor who had helped Davey, months ago.

Davey reached out to touch Marit's pile of snake skin.

"All right?" Marit whispered.

"As long as he's still alive. I won't raise the dead again."

The queen was standing on Davey's other side; she looked over at them, eyebrows raised.

"Ida," Marit mouthed, and she nodded, frowning.

The rest of the family was several feet away. Harald and Ida were both talking to the king, and Marit couldn't see his face. It took her a moment to spot Suhki, but she was there, behind the king—good. Marit was angry, though not as angry as Davey, but Suhki and Harald were her family. She wanted everyone accounted for; they were in a room full of enemies, and they'd just attempted an assassination.

Not an assassination, exactly. What did you call it when the assassin only aimed to wound?

Finally, the crowd dispersed a little, and word spread through the room that the prince was not dead yet, though he may be soon. Marit stood on her toes, straining for a view of the prince.

He looked young, though older than her. Perhaps Suhki's age. And he was only here because his sister was dead; it would be so cruel, if they cost his father a second child today.

The two kings came together; Davey hurried forward, and Marit and the queen followed.

"We have a great healing magic here," King Olaf said. "End this war, and we will save your son."

"We will save your son regardless," Davey said.

"We will save him if you end the war," Harald said, shooting an exasperated look at Davey. Davey looked away.

The king nodded. "If he lives. If he lives we will set this all aside and go home."

Ida stepped forward.

"No," Davey said sharply, pale and brilliant and angry. "No. I'll do it."

"Your new son is a sorcerer?" the king asked.

"I know this spell," said Davey. "Only this one."

It was suspicious. But what did it matter if they guessed he was the lindworm, when they'd already agreed to end the war?

Ida melted back into the crowd, looking older than she ever had; Marit thought they would not see her for a long, long time. She held out the skins, and Davey took the piece on top.

He handled it gently, almost reverently. The last piece he had of the life he'd lived for twenty years, and now he would give it up to fix his mistakes, and everyone else's.

"Help me?" he asked. Marit thrust the remaining skin into the queen's arms and followed him to kneel beside the dying prince.

She took a rag from someone standing nearby, and did her best to wipe away the blood. Davey took the skin, ripped now into smaller pieces, and began pressing it into the wound, murmuring words Marit didn't know.

She thought of his stories, in the early days, of enchanted men and women who became whole when their animal skins were destroyed. She thought of him telling her, not long ago, that he still felt like a lindworm, and she wondered—if they used his skins to heal others, would that make him whole too?

The prince made a soft, pained sound.

"Davey, he's barely breathing."

Davey looked up at her, eyes huge and blue and frightened, and pressed more skin into the wound. He held them there and whispered while she waited, praying that this was enough. And she imagined a future where all the skins had been shredded, where Davey was healed completely and had healed others, where he could be human in his dreams.

Then he removed his hands from the wound, and nothing had changed. The future crashed down around her and all the world was frozen, and she could not hear the prince's breathing.

She took Davey's bloody hands in her own, and they stared at each other over the body until they heard him gasp, and looked down to see his wound slowly closing, Davey's fingerprints still bloody on the skin of his back.

He would live.

Epilogue

She had tried to send the children all back to Harald's rooms, when it was clear the prince would live. But David had shaken his head, and Marit, holding his bloody hand, had glared. Their own room was far too unsafe to return to.

"My rooms, then," the queen offered. "But I won't have Ida there."

"Thank you, Mother," David said, and the two of them went quietly with the guards she called to escort them. Harald took a step, as if to follow them, but Suhki put a hand on his arm, and he stopped. She retreated to their shared rooms not long after, with another escort; Harald stayed.

Physicians of both courts confirmed the prince was healing well, and he was sent to a guest suite with several attendants and a squad of soldiers to recover, while the rest of them worked out the details of the treaty David had made. Messengers were sent to both armies, with orders not to engage.

The queen stayed focused on the task at hand, and did not let her eyes drift to the floor, where the body and the lindworm skins and her son had been. He had taken the remaining skins with him when he left the room.

At last, the foreign king agreed to spend the night in peace, and finalize anything remaining in the morning.

Harald went to join his wife. He was troubled, and David was avoiding him, and she had to set her own family's problems aside until she had resolved the kingdom's.

Olaf sent for Ida, who could not be found. As she was not allowed in their bedchamber, he resolved to wait in the throne room until she turned up. The queen went to bed alone, and was half surprised to find Marit and David both still there, and Ida absent.

Marit was asleep, not on any of the soft furniture about the suite, but on a rug in front of the fire, her head resting on David's boot. David looked up at her, and smiled, small and strained and tired.

At least it was a smile. She had not yet received enough from him to take them for granted.

His skins, she noted, were piled not on the same rug as Marit, which was meant to collect sparks and soot and the other detritus of a fireplace, but on a rather expensive one a few feet away. She decided, with some effort, not to be annoyed. The rug could be cleaned, or if necessary replaced. She found a pillow of the right size that it could be exchanged for his foot beneath Marit's head.

"Thank you," he whispered, and stood, and stretched. He had cleaned, but not well; there were a few thin streaks of blood on his arms, and the untucked hem of his shirt was stained with it. "Where's Father?"

"Waiting for Ida."

"I don't think she'll come. Marit sent her away."

She raised one careful eyebrow as she sat on the couch across from the fire, and motioned for him to join her. "Marit has that authority?"

"She sent her away on my behalf," he clarified as he sat, nearer to her than she expected, and described, slowly and shakily, the way Ida had colluded with her son—with the son Ida had not raised—to attempt an assassination.

So much blood, so much blood, on her family's hands, and all of it had started with her.

"There should never have been two of you," she murmured, half forgetting, until David went stiff and still beside her, that she wasn't alone. She turned and took his hands, despite the not-insignificant risk that they still held traces of another man's blood. "I'm glad there are. I am so glad to have you here at last. I wish that I could have been—that I had known how to—but I disobeyed the wise woman's instructions, and I made of you a monster, and all that has followed is my fault."

She had been so afraid. There had been four miscarriages in the first four years of her marriage, followed by nine years of barrenness. If she went a decade without conceiving, with no heir yet produced, Olaf could request an annulment, and the pope would grant it. She'd known Olaf wouldn't want to; he had grown to love her by then. But they had agreed on their wedding night to put their kingdom before themselves, and he needed an heir badly. His nearest cousin was a vile man who could not be trusted with the throne.

She had eaten the flower Ida told her would grant a daughter first, because she had thought a daughter would best stave off the loneliness she still felt in her husband's court, any time he was not at her side. And then she had remembered that her husband's court was not as modern as her own, and may object to a daughter inheriting. A daughter would render an annulment impossible, but would not necessarily give them an heir. So she had eaten the second flower, despite Ida's warning to choose only one. She had expected the punishment for disobedience to fall on her, not the child. And she had needed to have a son.

Somehow, she had gotten two.

"I was first," David said quietly. "If you'd done it right, you wouldn't have Harald."

"How lucky I am, then, to have you both."

As soon as the lindworm appeared, she had known that it was hers, though she had convinced herself long since that she had only imagined birthing it. It had spoken, and she would have given it anything it asked for. It had eaten a bride, and she had hated herself, because if it was intelligent, it could presumably have been raised not to eat young women, if only she had been there for the raising of it.

She had forbidden Olaf and Harald from killing it. She had known it would end only in disaster, and so she had not let herself love it, had not let herself get to know it, had not let herself be a mother. She couldn't bear it. But she couldn't bear to see it dead, either, and so she had let it cause death, instead.

"Lucky?" David repeated doubtfully.

"Lucky." She looked at his pale, tired face, at the nose and eyes and cheekbones he'd inherited from her, at his curls, deeper gold than usual in the light of the fire. There was a drop of blood on his cheek. They had started and ended this with blood, and yet she couldn't regret it.

They sat in peaceful silence for a few minutes. It was late; she should get them both to bed.

Soon.

"I would have tried," she told him. She had wanted children badly enough to accept any she bore, if he hadn't slithered away. And David had proven himself very lovable, when she allowed herself to love him. "I probably would have failed; I don't have Ida's experience with bloodlust and curses. But it would have been my honor to try."

He shifted closer, close enough to touch. She risked an arm around his shoulders, and he didn't stiffen beneath her. She allowed herself a few precious minutes to hold him.

"All right. Wake your wife; she can't be comfortable there on the floor. You'll sleep in my bed, and in the morning you'll both bathe, and dress as befits your station. There's plenty of work to be done yet, before we send our visitors home."

David nodded, and stood, and went to shake Marit awake.

Tomorrow there would be political matters to address, and questions to ask about the lindworm skins, and Harald to lecture about consulting his parents before having foreign princes stabbed. But for now, she would watch over her son while he slept.

King Lindorm

Translated from Svend Gruntdvig's *Gamle Dansk Minder i Folkemunde*

Note:

This is my translation; it is by no means an excellent translation, but it is a project I've enjoyed working on, and there are too few versions of this story available, so I thought I would add mine to the mix.

This is not the version of the story that mine is most directly based on, which was a later and more widely available version, often misattributed to Norwegian folklorists Asbjørnsen and Moe. This is the earliest version of the story I have been able to find.

I have only translated the first half of this story, as that is the part relevant to my retelling. The second half is often excluded from translations, and I did not know it existed before reading my source material for this translation. The second half belongs to another fairy tale type, one you may recognize from "The Maiden with No Hands," "Our Lady's Child," or "The Seven Swans."

In the second half, the Lindworm—now a human king—goes to war, leaving his pregnant wife at home. A wicked knight is tasked with delivering letters between the Lindworm and his wife; he changes out the letters to cause trouble, leading the king to believe that his wife has given birth to dogs, and leading the wife to believe that the king wants her banished or killed. Eventually they sort out all the misunderstandings and live happily ever after.

I am not fluent in Danish, but I have done my best with this story. While working on it, I found that my priority in translation was maintaining the unique rhythm and turns of phrase. There are sentences I could have tidied up, after my initial rough translation, to sound more "correct." I chose not to because I found the tone and rhythm of my rough translations more appealing.

This project was complicated not only by my imperfect understanding of Danish, but also by the fact that my primary source material was a book printed some time ago; publication dates are not always as clear on older works, but the only date mentioned on the title page is 1854, and frankly it looks like a book printed in 1854. The typeface is an older style that is in many places unclear to readers of today; many letters look very similar to each other, and I often had to copy out five or six possible spellings for a word and then work out which one of them was a real Danish word. Additionally, it seems that the spellings of some words have changed over time.

I was determined to translate this particular work, rather that tracking down a later, and clearer, one, for multiple reasons. Firstly, I'm quite sure this one is in the public domain. Secondly, it is, to the best of my knowledge, the first recorded version of the story. Finally, I have a particular fondness for Svend Grundtvig, the collector of this story, and too few of his works have been translated directly. My favorite thing about Grundtvig is that he will tell you the details of who/when/where he got a story from, as you will see below.

There is one word I was utterly unable to find a translation for: Bensnøfel. Based on the context I suspect it is a location, but I was unable to find any other references to a place by that name.

Old Danish Memories from the Mouths of the People:
Folktales, Ballads, Folksongs
And Other Remnants of Ancient Poetry and Belief,
Which Live Yet in the Remembrance of the Danish People,
Gathered and Published
By
Svend Grundtvig

King Lindorm

(Told in 1854 by Maren Mathisdatter, 67 years old, in Tureby by Løtten in Bensnøfel; recorded by Adjunct A. Levisen.)
(Translated from the Danish by Jenny Prater)

Once there was a King, who had so lovely a Queen. At last they had a wedding and when they went to bed the first night, there was nothing written on their wedding sheets; but when they stood up, it stood there written, that they should have no children together. The King hereover was highly grieved, but the Queen more: she shook, it was so hard that they should have no heir to their Kingdom. One day she went out in deep thought and came then to a remote place. There she met an old woman, who asked if she would tell her what was wrong; the Queen looked up and answered: "Now, it cannot help anything to tell you: this is a thing you cannot help me in."

"Now, it might even happen that I could," said the old woman, and asked if she would only say what was wrong.

Yes, she could easily say it: and she told her, how it stood written on the bed of their wedding night, that they should have no children, and it was for that she was now so sad.

She could give her counsel enough, said the old woman: then she might have children. In the evening, as the sun went down, she should take a Rovs (a drinking cup with two handles) and leave it in the northwest corner of the garden; in the morning, when the sun rose up, she should take it up again. Then there would stand two roses under it, one red and one white. Should she take the red and eat it, then it would be a boy; should she take the white, then it would be a girl; but she must not take them both.

The Queen came home and did as the old woman had said. In the morning, the sun rose up, and so she went into the garden and took the Rovs up, and there stood two roses: one red and one white. Now she knew not which one she should take and eat: if she took the red, and it was a boy, then he might go to war and be defeated, and so she might as well have had no children. She thought she would take the white, so it would be a girl, and she could stay home with them until she was married and went to another Kingdom. So she took the white and ate it. It tasted so very good that she took the red and ate it too. She thought to herself: so she would have twins, and did not think any farther.

Now it came to pass that the King was at war, and when the Queen noticed that she was with child, she wrote to him and let him know, whereover he was much pleased. And now it was in the fullness of time that she should give birth to a Lindorm. As soon as he was born, he dug himself under the bed in her chamber, and there he had his home. There he stayed, and a letter came from the King, saying that he would be home in a short time. And the time came for the King to come home and he was driving his carriage up to the Palace, and the Queen went out to receive him, and the Lindorm also went out to greet the King. He jumped up beside the coach and said, "Welcome home, Father!"

"What!" said the King, "am I your father?"

"Yes, if you do not wish to be my father, I shall split both you and the castle apart."

So he had to accept it after all. They went in, and the Queen had to make her explanation of what had come to pass with the old woman and herself.

A few days later, the whole council and all the nobles were summoned, and welcomed the King home and celebrated his victory over all his enemies. The Lindorm came also and said: "Now I will be married, Father!"

"Yes, and who do you think will have you?" said the King.

"If you do not get me a wife, whether young or old, whether big or small, whether rich or poor; then I shall split both you and the castle apart."

The King wrote out to all the kingdoms, if any would have the King's son. So there came so very lovely a princess; it seemed so strange to her that she should never look to see who she would have, until she should enter the hall they would be married in. Then came the Lindorm and stood at her side. The wedding day was over, and they went into the room with each other. As soon as he came in with her, he split her apart.

There it was, and it was the King's birthday some time after. Then when they all sat at the table, the Lindorm came again and said, "Now I will be married, Father!"

The King said: "Who do you think will have you now?"

"If you do not get me a wife, whether young or old, whether big or small, whether rich or poor: I shall split both you and the castle apart."

The King wrote to many kingdoms, to ask if any would have the King's son. There came again so very lovely a princess from afar. She did not see the groom until she came into the hall they were married in. Then came the Lindorm and stood at her side. But when the wedding day was over, and they came into the room with each other, the Lindorm split her apart also.

Some time after that, it was the Queen's birthday. Then the Lindorm came in; he came to sit at the table and again he said: "Now I will be married, Father!"

"Now I cannot give you more wives," said the King, "now two mighty Kings make war against me, whose daughters I have given you for wives, and what shall I do with them?"

"Let them come! So long as you have me, they must come, even if there are ten, but if you do not get me a wife, whether young or old, whether big or small, whether rich or poor: so shall I split both you and the castle apart."

The King was made to promise it, but he was much distressed.

There was now an old man, who was a shepherd for the King. He had a small house in the woods, and he also had a daughter. The

King went out to him and said: "Listen, good man! Will you not let me wed your daughter to my son?"

"Oh no, that I cannot do, for I have only one child, to support me in my old age. For another thing, if he will not spare so lovely a princess, so he will not spare my daughter, and so I think it is a sin."

But the King would have her, and the old man was made to give his consent.

The old shepherd went home and told this to his daughter. She was very sad and went through the woods in deep thought. As she went, there came an old woman also through the forest, and she would pluck berries and apples. She was in a blue skirt and a red vest.

"What is it that you are so sad for?" she said.

"I can easily have reason to be sad, but it cannot help to tell you this, for it is not something you can help me in."

"Oh, it might even happen," said the old woman, "if only you will tell me!"

"Yes, it is such: I must have the King's son, and it is a Lindorm; he has split two princesses apart, and now I know that he will also split me apart."

"Oh, there could well be a solution to this, if you will obey me," said the old woman.

Yes, she would obey her.

"Now when you have stood before the priest with him, and you know you will enter the chamber, then you shall wear ten gowns; and if you do not have them, then you must borrow them. Then you must demand a tub full of lye and a tub full of sweet milk, and as many whips as a fellow can carry in his arms, and these must be put into the chamber. As soon as the Lindorm gets there, he will say: Fair Maiden, cast off a gown! Then you shall say: King Lindorm, cast off a skin! So he shall say such to you and you to him, until you get to the ninth gown and him to the ninth skin: then he will have no more, but you shall be in one gown. Then you must take hold of him, when he is nothing but a hunk of bloody flesh; then you shall dip the whips in the lye and whip him as long as you think he can bear it; then you shall put him in the sweet milk after, and then you shall wrap him in the nine gowns and lay him in your arms; and then you shall go to sleep, if only for a little while."

She thanked her for the good advice, but she was afraid nonetheless: it was a great risk to take with so cruel a beast.

The wedding day came, and there came a coach so big and so magnificent; there were two ladies in it who were to dress her as the most beautiful bride. She came up through the King's Guard and into the hall, the Lindorm came in and stood behind her, and they were married. It was drawing to night, and they were going to the bridal bed. So she demanded a tub full of lye and a tub full of sweet milk and whips there. The men did laugh at it; it was peasant nonsense and fancies, but the King said what she asked for she should have, and so she did. Before she went into the chamber, she put on the nine gowns, as well as the one she was in. Then they came into the chamber, and the Lindorm said: "Fair maiden, cast off a gown!"

So she said, "King Lindorm, cast off a skin!"

And so it was, until she came to the ninth gown, and he to the ninth skin; and then she grasped the whips, for by then he lay on the ground, and could hardly move, and the blood ran from him. So she took the whips and dipped them in lye and whipped him, as strongly as she could, and for so long, so there were bits and pieces stuck to the whips; so she bathed him in the sweet milk, and she wrapped him in the nine gowns. And so she went to the bed and took him in her arms. At last she fell asleep, but it was late. When she woke again, she lay in the arms of a beautiful prince.

Morning came, and no one dared to look in the bridal door, for they were afraid it was with her as with the others. Then the King wanted to go and look inside. This time as he opened the bridal door she said, "Come right in! All is well here."

He came in and was so glad, he fetched the Queen and all the others; and there was such a celebration over the wedding bed. They got up and came into another chamber and got dressed; for their chamber looked bad. Then the wedding was held again with joy and pleasure, and the King and Queen held her so dear: they never knew the good they would do her, because she had saved their son.

Essays

This is a series of casual essays I originally wrote for my blog, Halfway to Fairyland, back in 2017. All are on the topic of the fairy tale Prince Lindworm—history, analysis, and information on various versions. They have been edited for clarity, flow, and updated information.

The Allegory of the Lindworm

I don't remember the first time I read "Prince Lindworm," but I do remember the first time I understood it. It was the spring semester of my freshman year of college, and I was sitting in the left front corner of my British Literature class. As usual, I had two notebooks open—one for class notes, and one for anything actually interesting that I thought of while paying slightly less attention to class than I should have been.

On this particular day, I was neglecting Byron in favor of speculating on why, when the Lindworm's spell was broken, we just forgot about the dead girls and everything was hunky dory. Then I thought about his mom eating the flowers, and suddenly, the whole ridiculous thing made sense. It's a Christian allegory.

You start out with a woman eating something she was specifically told not to eat. Hello, Eve. Nice to see you—it's been a while.

Because of the mother's dietary choices, the child is born cursed. Fall of man.

Then along comes our girl, and she's willing to give her life for the sake of her kingdom, because she rocks. And because of her sacrifice (see: Crucifixion), our fallen man is redeemed, i.e. returned to humanity. And when this happens, when he is purified by her sacrifice, all of his sins are forgiven. He is embraced by the father and immediately welcomed home.

The basic structure of this story is drawn directly from the basic structure of the Bible.

And of course, it's not that simple. There's more, much more, because this story is just a little crazy. There are definitely Prodigal Son elements in the versions where the queen gives birth to a prince as well as a monster, but I'll let you think about that on your own time, because I'm much more interested in the spell-breaking.

What I consider the really big revelation here happened a few weeks after that day in British Literature, though it was also related to the class. I was writing an in-depth analysis of Tennyson's "The Journey of the Magi." The Catholic sacrament of penance ended up being a major theme. And that got me thinking more about the specifics of the transformation, which had previously struck me as baffling, creepy, and just this side of suggestive.

So let's review the transformation, step by step.

Step one: molting. We cast off the old self, the sins. It's really hard and it kind of hurts.

Step two: whips soaked in lye. The lye is purifying, right? That's soap. The whips are a little...we can call that penance or something. I promised Biblical connections, but not necessarily theological soundness. Think hair shirts. He's paying for his sins and being made clean.

Step three: dunk in a tub of milk. The reason behind use of milk is not completely clear; it could be a color-related connotation with purity. Alternately, Francis James Child of the Child Ballads does reference in his notes on "Tam Lin" a few instances of a dunk in milk being a necessary step for transformation and vitalization, in Russian and German sources. And in Corinthians and Hebrews, milk is symbolic of basic doctrine. Regardless of the significance of milk specifically, this third step is obviously a baptism.

Step four is the embrace. We're going to call this acceptance into the body of Christ, and ignore any sexual undertones we might be picking up.

And then the fallen son is welcomed home with opens arms,

easily and fully forgiven, and everyone lives happily ever after.

Our last mystery to solve in this story falls well before the transformation scene, with the flowers. We've got the scene in general down as representing the fall of man, but let's get into the specifics. Eat this one if you want a girl, that one if you want a boy. So the mom eats the girl flower, and then she eats the boy flower. She winds up with a boy lindworm, and in some versions also a boy human.

Note the lack of girl here, despite the initial intake of the girl flower. I'm completely down with the lindworm as punishment for disobedient flower-consumption, but why is it a boy? Just further punishment? Logically, if she's going to have two kids, the first born should be a human daughter, in line with the first flower, and the second should be a male lindworm due to the forbidden flower. If there's only one kid, why is it a boy? Did the entire request for a girl get nullified by the second flower?

Why isn't the lindworm a girl? If the lindworm is a boy, why doesn't he have a sister? Specifically, an older sister? I don't have an answer. It's been years and years of intermittent research, and I don't have an answer.

Sources, and the Citing Thereof

I first encountered "Prince Lindworm," long ago, in a collection of Scandinavian fairy tales called *East of the Sun and West of the Moon*, illustrated by Kay Nielsen. This book was allegedly an Asbjørnsen and Moe collection. This book belonged to my grandparents. I later acquired my own Asbjørnsen and Moe collection. And then two more. I kind of kept buying these books because I wanted my own copy of "Prince Lindworm." But it wasn't there. So I googled the complete works of Asbjornsen and Moe. It wasn't there.

I took advantage of my university's interlibrary loan system to request every single book in the country that mentioned lindworms. Or lindorms. Or lindwyrms, or a variety of other spellings.

Several other books and authors and random people on the internet attributed the story to Asbjornsen and Moe. Who definitely didn't record it. The reason for this, as far as I can tell? This book my grandparents had, really nice hardcover, fancy publisher, gorgeous illustrations—it was kind of a big deal. All sorts of people had read the story in this book, and only this book, and assumed the information provided was reliable.

And here's where the publishers went wrong. There's an editor's note in the front. It explains that all but two of the stories in the volume are from one particular translation of the works of Asbjorsen and Moe. What they neglected to mention is that one of those two stories was not only from a different translator, but a different source entirely.

So "Prince Lindworm" didn't come from Norway. That's settled. I also quickly learned that it didn't come from Sweden, as Andrew Lang claimed when he included it in his *Pink Fairy Book*. (The *Pink Fairy Book*, alas, is a mess of incorrect citations and third-hand translations, some following an absolute baffling path to the English language.)

It took me a very long time to track down the origin. I believe it's much better documented now in various places, but at the time, ten years ago, no one seemed to know where this story came from.

This story was originally recorded in Danish by Svend Grundtvig. If you have reached this section of the book, you've already either read or chosen to skip my translation.

It should not have taken the time and effort that it did to learn this information.

Folk stories don't belong to anyone, because they're so mutable, because a story is really a community, a conversation. But that doesn't mean I don't want to know where the conversation started. This is only one of many, many cases of a fairy tale being published without correct attribution. Since these stories are in the public domain, people think the source doesn't matter. But it absolutely does. It may have happened long enough ago that copyright laws don't apply, but someone still worked hard on this story, whether that means actually writing it, or collecting and analyzing various versions of it from their community, editing it, and publishing it to share as a part of their culture. These people deserve credit, especially if you're profiting financially off of their work.

How hard can it possibly be to say, "hey, this historically and culturally significant story that I'm making a profit on because it's been in the public domain for a hundred years originally came from Denmark"?

There is no excuse not to give fairy tales the correct attribution. Anthology and picture book-based fairy tales have got to be the easiest writing to make a profit on. The story has been marinating in your brain forever, right? Do you even remember a time before you knew "Cinderella"? Just tell it in your own words, and someone else will come along and slap some beautiful illustrations on, and you're good to go. It costs five minutes and zero dollars to add in a little note saying, "This adaptation was inspired by the French version of the story as recorded by Charles Perrault."

So. For the record. The novel you just read was inspired by a folktale first recorded in Danish by Svend Grundtvig. And because Grundtvig did know how to cite his sources, I can also tell you that it was told in 1854 by Maren Mathisdatter, age 67, in Fureby. It was recorded by Adjunct A. Levisen. Thank you to all three of them for the work they did to bring this story to the wider world.

Version Comparison

Over the years, I have managed to find three different versions of King Lindorm—the one that appears in Svend Grundtvig's *Gamle Dansk Minder i Folkemunde*, the one that appears in Andrew Lang's *Pink Fairy Book*, and the one that appears in the Folio Society's *East of the Sun and West of the Moon*. (There is no indication of where this story came from originally or who translated it, so we're just going to call it the Folio version here.)

All three stories start the same way. The queen wants baby, the queen can't have baby, and an old woman tells her how to make it happen. Lang's version deviates most from the others in the beginning. In the other two versions, the queen encounters the old woman while out on a walk; in Lang's, the old woman comes to the palace and seeks out the queen specifically to impart her wisdom.

In both Gruntvig's version and the Folio version, the queen is to eat only one of two differently-colored roses that will grow up overnight under a two-handled cup left in the garden. Very specific, perfectly identical. The lindworm comes because the queen eats both roses.

In Lang's version, the queen is to take a bath in her room. Two red onions will appear under the bathtub afterwards, and she is to peel and eat both. Her mistake is that she eats the onions without peeling them. (Note that in this version the queen is not given the option to choose the gender of her child.)

Another little deviation in Lang's version is that the queen apparently doesn't know she's given birth to a lindworm. Her waiting woman tosses the lindworm out of the window as soon as it's born, and the queen doesn't notice it at all.

Lang and Folio both feature a normal, human prince born after the lindworm. In Gruntvig's version the lindworm is an only child. Since Gruntvig's version has no siblings, he approaches the king directly to ask for a bride. In the other two, he waits until the prince goes out to find a bride, and then goes up to him and says, "Hey, I'm your secret brother, and since I'm older, I get to get married first."

Here, again, Lang's version deviates significantly. The other lindworms both marry two foreign princesses, who they eat, and then a local shepherd's daughter selected by the king. Lang's lindworm marries and then eats an unspecified number of slave women before a wicked stepmother offers up her stepdaughter as a bride. Specifically, she tells the king that her stepdaughter would like to marry the lindworm, and the king apparently doesn't question this. He for some reason finds it believable that a young woman would volunteer to marry a monster who's already eaten multiple previous wives, without asking for any kind of compensation for her family or anything.

After this girl's marriage is arranged, she goes to her mother's grave, where she's given three nuts. This is what happens in the place of her meeting an old woman and getting instructions in the other two versions.

Lang's main girl goes through similar basic wedding prep steps to the others, with no indication of where she got the idea from; while the other girls have a tub of lye, tub of milk, whips, and ten gowns/shifts, Lang's girl has the tube of lye, only seven shifts, and three scrubbing brushes. After they go through the whole take-off-your-shift-take-off-your-skin situation, Lang's girl just scrubs him until he turns into a man.

The other two versions, of course, have the much more

complex and disgusting transformation sequence of dip whips in lye, whip lindworm, dunk lindworm in milk, take lindworm to the bed, embrace.

The Folio version ends immediately after this, with the girl and the transformed prince living happily ever after. The other two stories continue.

In the second half of Lang's version, the old king dies, the lindworm becomes king, the lindworm goes to fight in a war, and the girl's stepmother steals a bunch of letters and tells a bunch of lies that result in the girl and her two young sons fleeing the palace until the lindworm comes to find them. During this time, the girl uses her magic nuts to save a man named Peter.

In the second half of Gruntvig's version, the old king and the lindworm both go off to war, it's a character called the Red Knight who switches the letters, and while she and the babies are away, our girl helps two other men who've also been transformed into animals.

Lang's version definitely deviates significantly from the others; it has no points in common with Grundtvig's aside from the most basic plot: barren queen, ignoring food instructions =lindworm, brides eaten, transformation involving shedding/undressing and lye, heroine flees into the woods with children due to mail-tampering, saving someone else before reunion with lindworm.

The Folio version deviates from Grundtvig's only in that it ends halfway through and includes a second prince.

Somehow, despite its differences from the others, Lang's version feels the least unique. I was definitely first drawn to "Prince Lindworm," as a child because despite falling into my much-beloved Enchanted Bridegroom category, it felt very different from any other story I'd read. The beast as a snake-like creature, the brides being eaten, the unsettling transformation sequence—it was all just great. This was the Folio version, that I was reading as a child. But when I first encountered the second half of the story in Grundtvig's version, it was also delightfully unique and bizarre. The lindworm's mother—the girl's mother-in-law, often a villainous figure—is 100% on her side, and the main person to try to help her through what happens next. And the milk situation is just—well, it's something.

Lang's version, despite being the same basic story, feels bland and unoriginal. There's an evil stepmother, which is just sort of cliché. The transformation sequence has been cut down and seriously sanitized. And then the situation where he marries an unspecified number of slave women in the place of two princesses—well, I have a number of issues with that.

Firstly, the number three is so often symbolic in fairy tales, and to replace the three total marriages with an unspecified number is lame, but that's a dumb, nitpicky issue. The marriages to slave women indicate that this is a country that holds slaves, which I don't love. But my big issue with this is that a significant part of the charm of the other versions is just the absolute, idiotic absurdity of marrying your monster son to a second princess after he eats the first. You know what's going to happen now—the same thing that happened last time. He's going to eat the princess, and another powerful king is going to be rightfully angry with you. Marrying him instead to someone who won't be missed lowers the stakes and raises the rationality in a way that bores me, and also implies that some potential brides are worth less. With the first couple brides as princesses, we know they matter even though we never properly meet them, because their deaths put the threat of war over our heads—which is probably why the king and the lindworm go off to war shortly after the spell is broken in Grundtvig's version. "A whole bunch of random slave girls died with no consequences and then we met our main character" just seems sort of...cheap.

While I did enjoy reading Lang's version, I don't think I would have fallen in love with this story if it was the first I encountered. I think the other versions are both more absurd and more meaningful.

Born a Monster/Growing Up Beastly

While animal bridegrooms are an extremely popular folktale motif, it's fairly rare to encounter bridegrooms who were originally born non-human. (This is particularly interesting as it is much more common for brides to be born nonhuman—see "The Little Mermaid," anything about selkies, "Undine," "Melusine"—there's also a distinct aquatic theme here, but I'm getting off-topic.)

There are only two other stories like this that come to mind: "The Pig King" (Italian and French) and "Hans My Hedgehog" (German). (I am sure there are other stories out there that fit into this category, but there are hundreds of thousands of fairy tales in the world, and I can only read a small percentage of them, and can remember even less.)

"Prince Lindworm" differs from these other two born-a-monster stories in that his reason for being a monster is slightly more traditional. Monster bridegrooms are generally turned into monsters as a punishment—usually for a fairly minor offense, such as general rudeness or turning down romantic advances. The lindworm is a lindworm because of his mother's minor offense of eating too many flowers. There's no punishment involved in Hans' or the Pig King's monstrousness; their parents wanted desperately to have children, and someone magical heard their pleas and said yeah, okay, sure—but with a fun little twist. (Although Hans' dad did bring it on himself by saying "I want a kid so bad I wouldn't even care if he was a hedgehog.")

All three stories involve the beast marrying before his transformation. But while Hans and both versions of the Pig King remain beasts at least part-time for some time after their marriage (months, at least), the lindworm is transformed on their wedding night. Hans and the French pig are the types of characters that can only be permanently freed from their animal forms when the animal skins are destroyed. Which their wives handle, having become extremely fed up with this whole bestiality situation. The terms of transformation for the Italian pig are just that he be married three times. (Which, by the way, no one actually knew about, including the pig. The terms and conditions of this curse were a complete mystery, and he was marrying multiple times because his wives kept trying to kill him. Personally, if I didn't know about the three weddings ending my curse, I probably wouldn't have kept getting married after multiple spouses attempted to kill me.)

"Prince Lindworm" just feels more like an enchanted bridegroom story than the others—partly because of the consequences-for-your-actions element of his lindworm-iness, but mostly I think because of the transformation sequence, and the role the main girl plays.

Hans' bride comes off more like a Brave Little Tailor girl than an enchanted bridegroom girl; you don't really get the sense that she's saving him from enchantment. He won the right to marry her through tailor-typical feats, and their relationship is something that she endures until she figures out she can make it a little more bearable by trashing his hedgehog skin.

The pig king's bride lying with him every night when he's not wearing an animal skin is actually pretty common in folklore, with the best example being "East of the Sun, West of the Moon"—and of course there's "Cupid and Psyche," too. But I do feel that a fundamental part of those stories is the journey that the girl goes on after seeing his face, which "The Pig King" lacks.

I think an important part of enchanted bridegroom stories is the step where the girl does something to save the beast—whether that's going on a journey to find him, initiating a bizarre transformation sequence, or searching frantically through the palace to find him and marry him before he dies of sorrow. And it's a part that ever other born-a-monster story I've encountered lacks.

The thing that really makes "Prince Lindworm" stand out from other stories of this type, however, is that his actual behavior is much more monstrous. I believe this is primarily due to his upbringing, or rather lack thereof; the others were raised by human parents, but we have no idea how the lindworm was raised.

Before the lindworm gets transformed into a man, he eats two princesses. Which is...not great. However. He is a lindworm. Which is a kind of dragon. Presumably they have dietary needs that differ from a human's?

While I have many questions about this story that are not addressed in the original text, the main one is what on earth did the lindworm think was going on here? So. Several points.

Firstly, there is a distinct possibility that he's sort of a baby lindworm. (At least in the early Danish version. In the later version incorrectly attributed to Asbjorsen and Moe, we have a clearer timeline.) The queen gives birth while the king is at war. The lindworm slithers away, and reappears as the king is coming home from war.

Is this a war that's lasted fifteen to twenty years? Did the king come home from the first war, stay home for several years, then go fight in another war that he's returning from when the lindworm approaches him? Did the queen give birth to a fully grown lindworm that met the king a few months later? Did the queen give birth to a baby lindworm that was an adult by the time the king got home, either because lindworms grow faster than humans or because magic? Did she give birth to a baby lindworm that's still a baby? How old is this lindworm?

Secondly, how did the lindworm know the king was his dad? Because he clearly did. He just slithered up one day and said "Hey,

I'm your son. I want to get married."

Who raised this lindworm? Who told him who his bio parents were? The text says he burrows under the bedchamber as soon as he's born, and doesn't mention him having any further contact with the queen or with anyone else.

Thirdly, did the lindworm even know he was under a spell? He's been a lindworm for his entire life. He knew his parents were human, but do lindworms have access to comprehensive sex education? For all he knows, all lindworms might have human parents. Was he aware that he wasn't supposed to be a lindworm? Even if he was, did that necessarily mean he wanted to stop being a lindworm?

Fourthly, what was his ultimate goal here? He demands brides. He eats them. He demands more. Why?

Personally, I know nothing about lindworm culture and tradition. Maybe they're like reverse black widows or praying mantises, and eating their wives is just what they do. Or maybe he was just really hungry—though surely there would be people other than his new wives available to eat.

Why did he want to get married? Did he ever intend for a wife to survive past the wedding night?

Fifthly, the transformation. Did he see this coming? Again, did he even realize it was a possibility? When his final wife started demanding that he molt out of season, and then whipped him and bathed him in milk, what did he think was happening? Did he realize it was a transformation spell? Was he expecting it or hoping for it? Did he think it was just a bizarre human wedding tradition? Did the other two girls try to break the spell too, and do it wrong?

Shedding ten layers of skin in a row is going to be pretty incapacitating for any sort of reptile. Once he's done that, there's no defending himself from things like the whipping. If the other girls tried to break the spell too, but skipped the shedding step and went right to whipping, he might have eaten them in self-defense.

Sixthly, the aftermath. So our lindworm is now a handsome prince. Okay, now what? What does that even mean? He's literally always been a lindworm, with, as far as we can tell, lindworm behaviors and a lindworm palate. You aren't turning him back into a prince—you're turning him into a prince. Even if he always knew he was under a spell and it would someday be broken, that doesn't change the fact that he's inherently, fundamentally, a lindworm. He grew up as a lindworm, doing lindworm things.

He has no idea how to be a person, much less a prince. Walking, gesturing, chewing food—all exciting new experiences.

On the bright side, the king and queen didn't actually miss out on their possibly-only child's babyhood, after all—they still get to have all those fun experiences, just with an adult man who's on his third wife and ate the first two.

Th circumstances are wildly different from most enchanted bridegroom stories, but ultimately I think he's a victim, too. Brides for lunch and all.

It's not his fault he's a lindworm, and while he was a lindworm, he did, presumably, what lindworms do. And now he's a man, whether he wants to be or not. So he's lost everything he's ever known and been, and now he has to learn how to be a different kind of creature, from scratch, twenty years too late. (And depending on that whole king-at-war timeline, he may have just transitioned over night from a baby dragon to an adult man, which....yikes.)

What is the learning curve going to be like here? Let's assume he's not going to try to eat any more people, because of the sizing issue if nothing else—lindworms are probably a lot bigger than men. (How does he feel about the bride eating, looking back? Does he feel guilty? Does he shrug it off as a lindworm thing that he did when he was a lindworm? Is it all just kind of awkward?) Is he going to eat—or try to eat—a few cats or rats or lap dogs? How many months or years will it take him to remember he has to step out of bed in the mornings, instead of trying to slither and falling in a heap on the floor? When molting season comes around, is he going to try it and sprain something? (Or will molting forever be associated with terrible, terrible trauma after that bizarre transformation sequence?)

This guy has been totally screwed over since literally the moment of his conception, and for the stupidest reason. He didn't insult someone, didn't turn down their advances or refuse to share or help. His mom ate too many flowers. That's it. That's the whole reason he's a monster, the whole reason two innocent girls are dead. And he will never be able to fully move on from his time as a beast, because it was his entire life.

Transformation Through Violence, Transformation Through Love

There are a lot of enchanted bridegroom stories out there. And there are a lot of different ways for the spells to be broken. Although a lot of them are at least...subtly sexual in nature. Sometimes, as in the case of the original French novel "Beauty and the Beast," it's literally sex that breaks the spell, although this often gets sanitized in translation to an agreement to marry. In stories like "East of the Sun, West of the Moon," it's sharing a bed for a full year without seeing the enchanted bridegroom's face.

In fact, this is also an element in "Prince Lindworm"—she embraces him, and when they wake in the morning he's a man. More about that later.

But before that part, she makes him shed more layers of skin than can possibly be healthy, then whips him. With lye.

So here we're going to talk about the transformations that are about violence instead of sex or love. There are stories like "Hans My Hedgehog," where no harm is actually inflicted on the enchanted bridegroom, only on whatever facilitates his transformation—in most of these variants, it's an animal skin, which is burned by the bride figure in the story. Also, in most of these stories, the bridegroom has the ability to go back and forth between forms, and it's the bride who gets fed up and puts a stop to the transformations. It's probably no surprise that transformation-through-violence stories feature brides who are a little less friendly and sympathetic than most.

But the only other story type I know of that features such explicit violence as a catalyst for transformation (though I'm sure there are others out there; I can only know so many stories) is what we're going to call the Frogged Bridegroom. (There are a surprising number of frog-based enchanted bridegroom stories. Which, for the record, should not be confused with frog bride stories.) We have the German "The Frog King" and the Scottish "The Well of the World's End," among several others, but we're going to focus on those two.

In "The Frog King," the frog tries to get in bed with the princess, and she responds by picking him up and flinging him into the wall. Which, for a frog, is pretty much a death sentence. But instead of going splat, he turns into a handsome prince who, inexplicably, decides to marry her. (I suppose his eagerness to get in her bed while still a frog indicates a certain romantic interest, but for me, a crush would not survive attempted murder. Although, does it count as murder when the victim is a pervy amphibian?)

In "The Well of the World's End," a girl agrees to do whatever a frog asks for one night in exchange for a favor. This frog also gets in bed with the girl, but her subsequent violence isn't an understandable reaction to that skeeviness—the last thing the frog asks her to do before the night is over is chop off his head. Which she does, and, bam! Handsome prince.

So there's a significant difference, obviously, between these two stories—one girl is attacking her enchanted bridegroom, and one is doing something she's been asked to do to help him. And "Prince Lindworm" exists, weirdly, in the middle.

Is our girl's initial attack a response to unwanted sexual advances? No, because she was given instructions on what to do before she even met the lindworm. But also, sort of, maybe? I mean, she knew she was going to be marrying the lindworm, so unwanted sexual advances are likely a given. And the fact that he was willing to shed several layers of skin—certainly more than his body seems able to handle—just to get her naked is...well, that's a little worrying.

But does the lindworm want to be attacked because he knows it's an avenue for transformation? Maybe. We don't know. Probably not? As far as we can tell his plan is just to spend the rest of his life marrying and eating a girl every few months. Which doesn't seem really sustainable. The thing is, he knows his parents are the king and queen. So presumably he knows that he should be a human. Is he attempting to provoke the girls by threatening to eat them, knowing that a sufficiently violent response is going to restore his true form? Again, probably not. But maybe.

The question, I think, is why does violence trigger a transformation? Love, I understand. And sex, as an indication of love, sure. But why violence?

I don't know. I just don't know.

So, as nonsensical as "Prince Lindworm" seems to me at times, I think it actually makes more sense than the frog stories—it combines the violence with these other elements in a way that makes the whole thing more complex and meaningful, in its final step: the embrace.

There are a few things to keep in mind here. Firstly, hugging a dragon-thing that wants to eat you? Really gross and unpleasant. Secondly, hugging any sort of creature that has, through various abuses, become a quivering mass of exposed muscle and veins, likely bleeding profusely? Really, really gross and unpleasant. Thirdly, is "embrace" a euphemism? Maybe. Let's not dwell on the logistics of that. Fourthly, this girl is the lindworm's third bride, which probably means she's the third shot at transformation. An old woman in the forest told her what to do; there's no reason to believe she didn't give the same instructions to the two brides the lindworm ate, even if the text doesn't spell this out; there's a strong tradition in folklore of three people speaking to a mysterious old woman, and the first two ignoring her and dying.

So, my theory: the first two girls may have ignored the instructions entirely, but even if they didn't, they wouldn't have been able to complete the last step. Because it's the last step that makes our heroine remarkable. The last step is a kindness. To take up in your arms a disgusting, suffering thing, which would have destroyed you given the chance, to provide comfort—that takes a special kind of person.

A lot of weird, creepy things went into making the lindworm a man. But ultimately, the thing that changed him was one moment of kindness.

Deleted Scenes:

This book has, as I think most books have, been through many iterations. Things changed. Here you will find seven scenes that didn't survive to the final version. They may be familiar if you followed my Patreon back in 2017, though I have edited them a little. Some scenes don't appear in the final version at all; others may have some overlap with existing scenes, but deviate enough to count as something different. In earlier drafts, our characters visited Ida's home on multiple occasions, the North Wind that Ida rides in the final version appeared earlier, and Davey spent some time imprisoned after an identity reveal toward the end of the story.

These scenes were changed largely because Davey was changed—some of his behaviors, and consequently the way other characters interacted with him, weren't really working in earlier drafts, and I think both Davey and his family became more sympathetic characters in the final draft. If you are interested in the earlier edition from which these scenes were taken, it is still available for paid Patrons at patreon.com/konglindorm, though you may have to dig a little to find it.

I hope you enjoy these deleted scenes; it was the right decision for the story, but these were the pieces that were hardest to cut, so I'm glad to have them in the book again, even if they're in a different section.

First Deleted Scene: Davey and the Queen Disagree

She was not listening to the conversation between the king and queen. Davey was refusing to eat. Again. He never touched meat, but usually she had some luck with fruit. Smilla, muttering things about protein, could often coax him into handfuls of nuts, and occasionally bits of dried meat, which he had not seen before, and seemed not to recognize as meat.

It was easier when they were in their room alone, where she could pester him and where he would not be embarrassed by continued trouble with muscle control. She was wishing to be back there, and did not realize until the queen raised her voice that they were talking about Davey.

"It's all that woman Ida's fault."

Davey's fork dropped—not an uncommon occurrence, but it probably meant something this time.

"You mean the way you gave birth to a hideous monster who ate the daughters of two of the most powerful kings in the area?" he asked. "That's all Ida's fault?"

Davey never spoke without prodding at breakfast.

Hadn't the encounter with Harald been bad enough?

"Well, yes," the queen said. "All of that strange magic. And letting the monster roam free when she knew what it was capable of. Of course, the case could also be made that—"

Davey stood, fingers white as he clutched the table to maintain his balance. Marit stood too. They might have to run soon.

The queen referred to Davey and the lindworm as two separate entities, too.

Probably it was only in case of servants listening.

"Who ate the two flowers, Mother?"

There was a long, uncomfortable silence, then: "Who ate the two princesses, son?"

Marit stepped forward. He was starting to sway; tears would be happening in a moment. When she touched his arm, he said, "Not Ida," then swept out of the room, more or less stable, and Marit jogged to keep up with him.

She was noticing a pattern. Insults to Ida produced results.

Halfway to their room he stopped abruptly and leaned against the wall, staring down at his feet as if they were something completely foreign to him.

"Davey?"

"It's not Ida's fault."

"Of course not." Well, not all of it. Not the flowers, whatever they were. But she had set him loose on the world with his lindworm instincts.

"Ida took care of me."

"I know. Ida loves you. And I'm sure she'll be back soon."

He tore himself from the fascinating sight of his own feet to smile unhappily at her. It had been the wrong thing to say. "She won't. When I was little—when I was safe—we used to go off for months at a time. She hasn't been able to really leave for years now. Not since I started to get really bad, and she couldn't leave me alone for too long, and it was too risky to have me out and about, around other people. She left me for a month once, because she had to, and that was—that was bad. There were a lot of things she should have been doing, during those years—ending wars and turning people to frogs and helping people release enchanted princesses and such.

And she couldn't. Because of me. And now that she can leave me here with you, she's going to have to deal with all those things. It's going to take a long time."

♛

He was better after that. She couldn't think why. Tears happened less. She was woken by screaming nightmares less often, and if he was very withdrawn, it only meant peace for her. She pestered him less about food, and he only threw up occasionally. He spent hours at a time reading, and Marit hoped the priest wouldn't be wanting his Bible back.

When he was there on Sundays he always spoke to Davey. Marit thought it helped. He seemed to be in a slightly better mood after, even on the especially bad days.

It was all right. They could get through this. Just another forty years or so.

Second Deleted Scene: Davey's Health

Breakfasts had become worse. They spent most mornings in icy silence, after the queen's standard "Good morning, David."

Marit had almost forgotten what the king's voice sounded like when he addressed Davey. "The court is very concerned about your health. Should we be concerned about your health, David?"

She waited for him to cringe and whisper "no." Instead he looked straight up at the king and said, "I'm sure I'd feel better if I could eat a few more princesses." Before Marit had recovered enough to react, he added, "They tasted wonderful, you know."

The king's expression was moving from shock to fury. Davey looked...resolute, and suddenly Marit understood.

"Davey, shut up." She didn't bother to be subtle; she was too worried. He'd finally found a way to kill himself.

"I wonder how much better a king would taste." He smiled, insincere and vaguely alarming.

Marit kicked him under the table, hard. "Davey!"

"Maybe I could find a way to get changed back."

The royal family still hadn't said anything, but if he kept this up, he might actually succeed. How far could the king be pushed?

She needed him to cry. She needed him to cry now. For once, the fact that he was constantly on the brink of tears could work to her advantage. She leaned forward and whispered, "You didn't even know their names. Think of the blood in your mouth, the crunch of their bones in your throat. The way their flesh stuck between your fangs. Imagine how their fathers mourned."

It worked well enough. He could make light of it, a little, but she knew how to break him. She wrapped her arms around him protectively as he cried, and stared steadily across the table, waiting for a response.

Finally the queen said, with surprising gentleness, "David, perhaps you should return to your room until you can...compose yourself."

Marit stood, pulling him to his feet in the process.

"Just David," the queen clarified. "Marit, we'd like to talk to you. In private."

How many of Ida's secrets would she have to reveal to get them out of this mess? How many of Ida's secrets could she afford to reveal before they were looking, once again, at death for Davey?

"He's not going anywhere alone. Not like this."

"Fine. Harald, would you escort your brother back up to his room, please?"

"Absolutely not," said Marit. Harald would kill him. "We can talk with David here. You're the one who always wants him to participate in conversation."

The king sighed and looked at the queen. Marit watched their silent conversation and wondered if they loved each other. Finally he said, "Harald, I have that meeting with the count soon. I'd like you to go and fill in for me."

It was an obvious attempt to get rid of him, but Harald left without a word, and Marit tried without success to calm Davey in the silence that ensued. It wasn't fair to be annoyed now. She'd made him cry deliberately.

After a few minutes of this, the queen asked, very quietly, "Could he do it?"

"Change back?" Marit shook her head, although she had no idea. "Even if there were a way, he never would. He's—"

"He's just finished expressing a desire to do so," the king

pointed out. "Not ten minutes ago."

There was a pause, the silence interrupted only by Davey's gasps and sobs, while Marit tried to decide what she could afford to tell them. Triggering the tears had been bad enough—a violation of some unspoken promise to Ida—don't let them see him cry—but it had been better to let them see him broken than as a threat.

"We were talking about his health. He's—" This was hopeless. Ida could lie her way out of this, maybe. Or at least dance carefully around the truth. But Marit couldn't pull off anything less than complete honesty. "He's suicidal. He has been since he changed. The last few days, he's been quiet, and calm, and I thought that maybe he was getting better. Now I think he was planning." She stopped for a minute to try again to calm him, but it was only getting worse. "Davey—Davey, sweetie, I'm sorry. You're all right, now. You're all right. I need you stay with me here. Davey. Davey, please." She turned back to the king. "He was trying to provoke you, Your Majesty. He was trying to make you angry enough to have him killed."

"David?" the queen asked. "Is that true?"

He was crying too hard to even think of answering.

"Why do you always do that? Can't you just leave him alone?"

"David is twenty years old. He is fully capable of speaking for himself, and I fail to see how we will ever get past this if we persist in treating him like a small child. David, do you want to be treated like a small child?"

He looked up then, very slowly, and took a few deep breaths before he could answer. "I just want to have my head chopped off."

This statement was followed by a long and agonizing silence. Davey was done crying for the moment, and stared at the king again, waiting. But it was the queen who recovered first.

"Well, I'm afraid that's not an option. If you want to atone for your sins, David, you can start by coming to dinner, and by coming to the ball next week, and by being the prince we've told the kingdom you are."

"I am very sorry."

Marit wasn't sure what he was apologizing for, but apparently the queen understood. She sighed. "It's not entirely your fault. Olaf, why don't you take David off for some bonding time? I'm sure that would be beneficial, and I would like to speak with my daughter-in-law alone."

The king hauled Davey to his feet, and Marit didn't have the energy left to object. She was more concerned about herself alone with the queen than she was about him with the king. He had an arm around Davey's waist, helping him as he stumbled reluctantly forward. They'd be all right.

"How do you feel about your husband, Marit?" the queen asked when they were gone.

"We are desperately and passionately in love," she answered flatly.

The queen raised her eyebrows, and Marit went back to the truth.

"He's pathetic. He's lonely, and he's afraid, and no one else will take care of him, so I have to do it. I have to protect him."

"From me." The queen paused, maybe waiting for a confirmation that Marit didn't want to give her. "I know that you think I hate him. And it is true that I don't have the same motherly affection for him that I do for Harald. But I am very much aware that he exists only because of the foolishness of my youth. So I do care. I have a responsibility to David, and more importantly, I have a responsibility to this kingdom. You must understand, Marit, that if I am hard on him, it is only because no one else will be, and if we are to survive this someone has to."

There was another pause, for another response that Marit didn't have.

"I don't like Ida. She has a long and complicated history with my husband's family, and she made Harald possible, so I can hardly announce my dislike to the world. I know that she is a good witch, and I am grateful for what she has done. But I don't like her. She has put me—she has put all of us—into an impossible situation. I can't be a mother to him, partly because I am too busy being a queen, but also because that role has already been filled by someone else. And I cannot help but think that if she had handled things differently, we would not be in such an impossible position now. As you may have noticed, she is not here as we suffer in this position. I was very young, when David was born, and I was afraid, but mostly I was surprised. And Marit, I swear, if she had brought him back here right away, I would have taken care of him. I would give anything to have been his mother for the past twenty years, to have saved him, to have learned to love him the way I have seen that Ida loves him. But too much has happened since then, and the best thing I can do for him, now, is to treat him as I would treat Harald if he were acting like this, and hope that he gets the message."

Marit finally found her voice. "But he isn't Harald. He doesn't have the—he can't—"

"He can. He has to. Things are bad, Marit. Two princesses are dead. Their fathers—their very powerful fathers—are not happy. Half the court suspects the truth, and the only way to convince them is to convince ourselves. We have to present a unified front. We have to be a family. I need him to be a prince. I need him to be an adult, and to be a human. If we fail in this, I will probably be deposed. But David will be killed. Do you understand?"

Marit nodded.

"Good. Go back upstairs. David will come when the king is done with him. I wish...you should have told us how unstable he's been. There are too many people invested in this. If he dies—well, they all think he's unhealthy. If it looked natural, the rest of us could come out unscathed. Honestly, it would make things easier. But if he dies of suspicious causes now, everything is over."

The queen stood, and Marit left quickly, trying to work out how far she could trust her. Because, all right, maybe Davey did need someone to be a little hard on him. But even if she could believe that the queen could have loved a lindworm son, twenty years ago, well, that had been twenty years ago. And she had said that her responsibility to her kingdom was more important than her responsibility to Davey, and she had said that things would be easier if he was dead.

♛

Davey showed up not long after she returned to the room, in an eerie repetition of a few weeks before—a knock, Davey at the door with a book, and a companion with a firm hold on his elbow, although this time it was the king.

"I'll see you in the morning," he said. "Tell me what you think of the book."

"Thank you, Your Majesty." There was a pause. "Thank you, Father," he corrected himself, finally, and the king left, closing the door behind him. Davey sunk into a chair, clutching the book with an odd air of desperation.

"So? What was it like?"

"He patted my back a lot and talked about the sanctity of life."

"And what did you say?"

"I told him that sanctity of life is why we have the death penalty."

"Of course you did." He probably hadn't meant it to sound like he was talking back. Not in the state he'd been when they walked out. "And then what?"

"He got really quiet and patted my back some more."

"Davey..." Marit sighed. They'd have to have this conversation eventually; now was as good a time as any. "We were talking about your health. Do you—you stare at knives and hesitate on stairs, and you've just tried to get an execution. That's not healthy. Do you understand that? There's something wrong with you. And someday you're going to get better, and you're going to be glad I didn't let you die."

"No." He looked up at her for the first time in the conversation. "I don't understand that. If you think I'm sick, Marit, then you'd better just put me out of my misery, because it's the sort of wasting disease you're never going to find a cure for. They are dead, Marit. They are dead, and they are somewhere inside of me now, and I don't even know their names. If everyone knew the truth, they would be lining up to kill me. And here's the part you're really going to love—none of them are going to get the chance. I'm trapped in a body I don't understand, and I don't like it, and I'm fairly certain it's not working properly. I get less than half the sleep I should—and don't tell me you don't resent my trouble sleeping—and if I weighed any less I'd be a ghost. They weren't talking about my mental health, and they weren't wrong. This body is dying. This body is killing me. There is a limit to the number of things you can fix. You cannot save me. Can you understand that, Marit?"

"You're dying," she murmured. "You're not dying. Are you? Really? You can't—"

"Marit." He stood up and dropped the book. "All of the nights I haven't woken you in the last three weeks—every single night—I haven't slept. At all."

"That's three or four nights a week."

"I know." He pulled off his shirt, slowly and painfully, and Marit counted his ribs, and tried to process the fact that he'd actually lost more weight. She hadn't seen him without a shirt on since Ida's departure.

"But you've been eating. I've been watching you eating. And you've held it all down. Haven't you? I thought—" She hadn't really been paying so much attention, not since he'd stopped being so reluctant about it. Another way to get himself killed?

"I can't, Marit, I've tried—I swear to God I've tried. I eat as much as I can before I remember and I'm sick again, but it's never enough. If I tried to eat more I'd only throw it up."

"But—"

"I think the human body knows I don't belong in it. Knows I'm corrupt. It's rebelling. Trying to get rid of me, even if it has to destroy itself in the process."

"So it's sentient and independent? There's your body and your soul, and they both have a mind of their own?"

"I don't know. It doesn't matter. You can't save me. I am dying, Marit."

"But you don't want to."

"What?" He tilted his head, and Marit pushed on, very carefully not thinking about how much like the lindworm he looked whenever he was puzzled about something.

"You told me. I had no idea that things were this bad, physically. You could have kept on hiding it. You could have wasted slowly away with no interference, and left me thinking the queen had found some subtle way to assassinate you."

More puzzlement. "The queen..."

"Never mind. The point is, you keep on telling me I can't save you. But now I have to try. And I wouldn't have, if you hadn't—so you don't really want to die, do you, Davey?"

He sat back down, twisting the shirt in his hands. "I deserve to die. The world would be so much better off without me. If I could get out of it, that would be the one worthwhile thing I ever did with my life."

"But you don't want to."

"I suppose it depends on how noble I'm feeling at any given moment."

"How stupid you're feeling." He opened his mouth, but never had the chance to speak. "No. Shut up. Shut up. Davey, you don't—you can't—if you could get out of it, it would be the most cowardly, idiotic thing you ever did with your life. The princesses aren't coming back to life, and you're not planning on eating any more of them, so what harm do you think your existence is doing right now? The lies the king and queen are telling to save your life—they're too far into this to back out now, and they need your help to pull it off. If you kill yourself, you're dragging this whole kingdom down with you." She didn't mention what the queen had said about natural deaths, and fortunately he didn't bring up what she'd said about assassinations.

"You still can't save me, Marit. And even if you could, you still can't fix me. Wasting disease. No cure."

"I can. Both of them. I can. Watch me."

"How, Marit? What can you possibly—"

"Well, first of all, I'm going to track down Ida and bring her back here."

"No. You can't. Where she went—she wouldn't have left me. Not unless it was important enough that—they need her where she is right now."

"More than you need her?"

"Yes."

"Fine. Then we'll—we'll go to her house. We'll see if we can find anything she left there."

"I don't think I can do it. It's through the woods a few miles. Not too far, but farther than I can—" He stopped; she understood, anyway.

"Then I'll go. You can tell me how, and tell me what to look for, and I'll go find it. We'll be fine." He didn't answer, and after waiting in vain to hear more objections from Davey, Marit came up with one herself. "I can't leave you here alone, can I?"

"I'll be fine."

"I'd be gone all day. Plenty of time for you to get yourself killed."

"I wouldn't—"

"I'm not taking any chances. Not after what you tried today. Ida would never—"

"Ida's left me alone for weeks at a time."

"Ida left you alone." He'd mentioned it before, but she still couldn't picture it.

"Wise women have to travel. A lot. Especially when they're looking for cures for being a lindworm. And giant man eating snake monsters aren't portable. So yes, she left me alone, when she had to. Not for long, but a whole lot longer than one afternoon. And I spent some six months without her in the end. From when I went to the palace to when you came."

"Right. And look how well that turned out."

"I—" He stopped and squeezed his eyes shut.

Marit sighed and knelt down beside his chair. "Davey, I'm sorry. Of course you're not going to—I mean, not now. I shouldn't have—I shouldn't—would you look at me?"

He opened his eyes and raised his head, very slightly. "No. You're right. Don't leave me. Marit, I—gods. This is—don't leave, please."

"I won't. Promise. We'll figure something out." She was silent for a minute, thinking, and Davey lowered his head again. "You know, I haven't seen my family since the wedding."

"I'm sorry," he mumbled.

"No. I mean, we can—I can have someone go get them, like they did for the wedding. Bring them back here. Someone can stay with you, and two of us can go to Ida's house. It'll be perfect."

"Will either of them be willing to stay alone with me?"

"You're really not that intimidating anymore."

"I was thinking more about how I tore apart your entire family and you haven't seen them in weeks now. I'm sure they're not afraid of me, but they're on a long list of people who have every right to want me dead, so why should they help you help me?"

"They don't want you dead, Davey. No one wants you dead. I think they sort of like you. Or at least feel bad for you. I suppose we couldn't leave you alone with Greta, if only because she's extremely insensitive, but bonding time with your father-in-law could be a good idea. Or we could send them out to Ida's, and I could stay here with you. Whatever you want, Davey. However you're comfortable. We need to get this done."

He nodded slowly. "All right. When do you—when should we do it?"

"I'll ask the king to contact them at breakfast tomorrow. I can't take more royal interaction now."

He nodded again.

"I will save you, Davey." She picked up the book from the floor, set it in his lap, and stood up. It was time to change the subject. "Tell me about your new book."

"We were in his—I think he said it was his study. And I didn't want to hear any more about the sanctity of life, so I started pulling down books. History and records, things like that. Extremely detailed. The older ones were printed and bound, like this, but there was some hand written stuff—I think it was more recent. He wouldn't let me look at that. I wanted to see if I was there. I think he thought it was morbid."

"Well, it is, a little."

"I was just curious. I know what I did. Seeing what he said wasn't going to hurt my feelings." It may, however, have launched him into another series of pleas to be executed. "Anyway, he was surprised I could read, but then he said of course Ida would have taught me, and then he wanted to know how much I knew about the history of the kingdom, and I said not much. And he said that I was a prince; I should know where I came from. And besides, I must get bored. This would take my mind off things. So he gave me this one to read. Said it was the most interesting. Wars, I think."

"He gave you a book on wars to take your mind off of the way you killed people?" It was a valid point, but not one she should have made. She could see the tears coming. "Davey. Davey, sweetie, I didn't mean to—I didn't mean it. You're fine."

He blinked a couple times and recovered. "I'm fine. I'm—it's fine. He meant well. All those people killing each other—maybe he thought I could relate."

"Slightly morbid."

"Sorry. But it's fine. Really. People kill each other all the time. I can't—it'll be interesting. I've missed reading."

"You aren't going to get upset about it?"

"Promise."

"All right. Tell me if anything interesting happens."

Third Deleted Scene: Ida's House and Failed Spells

Greta and her father came early the next morning, and it was Davey who stumbled over to open the door.

There had been no screaming nightmares, and she remembered that probably meant he hadn't slept.

He didn't say anything, just closed the door after them and sunk into the armchair.

"Everything all right?" her father asked.

"No," Marit said. "I need to find something. I need you to watch Davey while I'm gone."

"Of course. What's the problem?"

"Nothing. I just—"

She had been responsible and independent since the king came to her door. She had handled the king, and she had handled the lindworm, and she was so tired of handling things.

"I just don't know how to help him, and I am so afraid."

Her father nodded, and hugged her, and Davey stared at her like a toddler who's just learned his mother cries too.

She'd never been vulnerable in any way near Davey. Even when he was the lindworm, she had only been angry.

"Go on, then," said her father. "Take Greta along. The prince will be fine here with me."

"Davey?"

He nodded, still staring, and she followed Greta to the door.

"Marit?" he said as she stepped into the hall.

"Yes, Davey?"

"I'm sorry."

"It's all right, Davey."

She didn't know what she was forgiving him for.

The king had come for her in early spring. Summer was well underway by now, grass long and moss green and wildflowers blooming, and all the world smelling alive, and as soon as they were away from the palace gates, Marit kicked off her boots and went running through the woods. It was some time before Greta caught up to her, carrying the abandoned shoes.

"I haven't been outside since they came for me."

"Don't go back."

"I can't go home. They'd find me."

"Run."

"Father's there still. And there's Davey."

Greta nodded. "What's wrong with him?"

She kicked a stump, staring at the ground. "He's dying."

"Let him."

Marit looked up. "You don't mean that."

"No. But Marit—never mind. Ask me what it's like, having a princess for a sister."

"What's it like?"

"The king's gold is good. We brag about you when we go to market. People ask questions about the lindworm and the prince and the war, and we don't have answers."

"I'm sorry."

"I have to do all of your chores, too."

"And that must be so hard for you. Anything else?"

"I think Sven likes me. Oh, and Shortshanks is limping—something to do with her hoof. But she should be fine."

"Of all the absurd things to name a cow—I mean maybe if it had been a bull."

"You told me it was cute."

"You were in pigtails and hand me downs that didn't fit yet. And you were still losing teeth. Everything you did was cute."

♛

Davey had given her clear directions. It didn't take long to find Ida's cottage, although it took longer than it could have. Marit was going to spend every moment she could here—Davey was not dying quickly, and he could give her this one day. Smilla had packed lunches for her and Greta.

It was quite large for a cottage in the woods—it would have to be, to hold Davey—with a thatched roof, in a clearing with small hills behind. The back wall was knocked out, as if it had come in contact with a rampaging snake monster.

Marit tried to picture Davey rampaging. Maybe, maybe the way he had been just after Ida left. And maybe with the lindworm instincts she'd never really seen.

"What do we need?" Greta asked. She didn't seem much bothered by the missing wall.

"I don't know. He said anything—anything that could be put in a potion. I don't know what you would—those jars on the shelf, maybe? We'll take those. He mentioned something about dried plants, wrapped in packets of brown paper. Check the drawers. I'm going to see if I can find a bag for everything."

There were iron bars splitting the house in two, and a thick door hanging open. Marit stared at the door for a long time, and at the splintered wood behind it, and the grassy hills behind that, and she did not go through. There was a large sack beneath an overturned table, and she started filling it with jars. Ida had not left behind as much as she hoped for, and despite clear labels, she didn't know what any of it was. Maybe Davey would have to teach her to read, after all.

If he was in a bad mood by the time she got back, he might not read the labels for her, or tell her what any of it could do.

♛

It was nearly nightfall when they returned to the palace, and Marit sent her family away and went to Davey. She could not talk about home and the farm, or think of how the sun felt on her hair, or what it was like to see daisies again. There was work to do.

Davey set everything out on the floor.

"Can you use this?"

"I can. Some of it."

"What do you need?"

"I need to mix things. A bowl, a spoon? Something to crush with?"

"I'll talk to Smilla in the morning—she already brought your dinner?"

He nodded. "She left something for you. It's on the table by the bed."

While she ate, she watched him sort through what she'd brought. "Was everything all right? With my father?"

Davey nodded. "He's nice. He told me stories about your chickens."

She smiled. "He would." The food had gotten cold. "Davey?"

"Yes?"

"Did Ida keep you in a cage?"

He looked up, dropping a handful of purple flowers. "I helped her build it."

"Davey..."

"It used to be only at night. Just in case. And when I got worse—we couldn't take chances, Marit."

"Did you—did you kill anyone before you came here?"

"No. I came close." He stood abruptly, scattering everything he'd laid out. "I—why are we—I should just—"

"Absolutely not. Not again. If things haven't gotten better by this ball I'll tell the queen everything and make her find a proper doctor. I will."

"I don't want to see any doctors."

"You won't have a choice. We cannot afford another royal

death in this palace."

He sighed. 'I'll work on it tomorrow."

"Good. Anyway, I'd miss you. Who else would care about chicken stories in a place like this?"

He was sick three times the next day, and she was half afraid he'd lied and sent her to collect his poison. An hour after the third time he looked up and said, "I think you should go into the hallway."

"Why?"

"Please, Marit?"

"You've been sick three times, and you tried to get executed earlier this week. I'm not leaving you alone."

"What would I do? It's not as if there are knives or staircases here."

"There's a window, more than high enough. And there was no knife on the plate Smilla left last night. Was there one before I came?"

"No. Gods, Marit. I'm going to start a fire."

"And that's better?"

"I'm not going to stand in it. But I need to do something serious. It's a spell—I watched Ida do it once, and I think I remember how it goes. But if I'm wrong—if I'm right it will smell bad. If I'm wrong the fire will spread, quickly, and you'll need to go for help."

"While you burn."

"I won't get it wrong on purpose. You could trust me."

"What would I trust you for? I gave up my whole life for you, after you tried to eat me, and then you went and tried to kill yourself."

"I was never going to eat you."

"Not right then, but Davey, you told me you would have."

"I'm sorry," he said. "I'm sorry."

"All right, don't cry now. I'm sorry. Tell me what this spell will do."

"I don't know."

"And I should trust you?"

He sighed, rubbing his eyes. "Get the doctor, then. After this dinner. We can—I'm sorry you gave up your whole life. You could still leave. You should."

"I really couldn't. Not now."

Davey shoved Ida's things under the bed, and drew his hand back as if he'd been burned. "The skins."

"I'd forgotten," Marit said. Amazing, that so much blood and pain could slip anyone's mind. "I should have—today, when we were out, and with bags to carry, I should have—I'll get rid of them when next we have the chance."

"No," he said, almost panicked and a bit too quickly. "No, don't, we—" He stopped.

"We what? Davey?"

He shook his head, and there was a long pause before he spoke again, dreamily. "Once there was a woman who was a frog, and every night she shed her skin and became a woman again. Once there was a cat who shed her fur at night. Once there was a man who could cast off his hedgehog prickles in the darkness, and a white bear, and once there was even a snake."

"Davey—"

"Ida told me. Ida used to tell me things, before she had to protect me. And they were married, all of them, and cast off their skins on their wedding nights, and I suppose I thought that was what Ida had intended for me, if I thought of it at all, but I did not know how to cast off my skin. I did not know that losing it would be so painful."

"Davey," Marit said again, but he was not listening.

"And then their husbands and wives, carefully prepared by women like Ida—maybe by Ida herself—their husbands and wives would find the animal skins and burn them, and then they would be free."

"Shall I burn your skins, Davey?"

He did not answer.

"Was that your dangerous spell? Would you have burned them

yourself?"

"It would not have worked," he said. "It will work no better if you do it. The spells are different, and I need my skins."

"Davey, you don't—"

"It was a stupid plan. Nothing is so simple, and I think if you took my skins away I would die."

"Davey."

"I do not know how to be a human. And I know that I cannot slip back into my old self with the sunrise, like the bears and the cats and hedgehogs, but I am too afraid to live without what is left of me, and the skins may be useful someday."

"How?'

He didn't answer.

"I'll get the doctor, then."

"Fine."

Fourth Deleted Scene: Marit and Davey Get Ready

There was something eerie about him that night, white and thin in a shirt of white and gold. The crown melted into his hair, the same gold as the shirt. They had tried to cut it this morning. He had refused. His eyes were almost as jarring as they had been when he was a lindworm, sunken deep into a face they were much too large for, and he stood silent and very still. Marit thought of pictures she'd seen in the margins of his Bible, fanatic saints, severe and devoted and always fasting.

She didn't know what he was devoted to.

There had been a flock of maids in their room earlier, calmer than the others but still too much, and the doctor hovering angrily. Davey had sat limp in a chair as they fussed with his clothing. They had done something absurd to her hair—she could feel it, pulling and hanging loose in all the strangest places, but focused on Davey, she had not even looked in the mirror offered.

He had spoken only once all day, when one of the women had something about Marit's lovely red curls.

"Her hair isn't red," he had said from across the room, and everything had frozen as he continued. "Red is brighter. Harsher. Yours is soft and golden-orange."

"All right," Marit said. Red was the color of blood, and blood still upset him. He had refused to wear red vests before.

Now in the crowded ballroom, wishing he would say something, she tried to count the people in red, and wished she had looked in the mirror.

No one else would notice her hair, anyway, or the dress she wore, gold to match Davey, and the finest thing she'd ever seen. Davey was much more interesting. It was useless to hope that the entire court wouldn't notice he was wasting away. If they were lucky, maybe no one but her would see how terrified he was to be there.

Fifth Deleted Scene: Back to Ida's

Marit and Davey went, with Sir Tomas to guard them, since people still worried about Davey. Harald stayed behind, attending a meeting he wouldn't tell them about.

It was the farthest from the palace Davey had ever gone, and he was slower than Marit had expected. She had planned to visit home, but did not think there would be time now. The weather was cooling, the grass losing color and the flowers mostly gone, and Davey was quiet and unhappy. He knew what she had agreed to, and why. Sir Tomas hung back, out of the way. Marit worried about the secrets he would see if he tried to enter the house. But he had been right there when the king had told them he would come, and she had not been able to explain why he should not. Davey glanced anxiously back at him, often stumbling when he did.

"Are you all right?"

"Fine," he said.

"You seem tired."

"I'm fine. We're nearly there, aren't we?"

In front of the house he froze.

It was much the same, except that it needed to be rethatched. The door hung open, though Marit was sure they had closed it carefully. Davey clutched the door frame, pale and shaking as he had not been in many weeks.

"You've been here before, haven't you?" he asked.

She nodded. "When you were sick."

He straightened and let go of the frame, but paused a moment longer on the threshold. Then he walked across the room and into the cage. Marit followed him in, and left Sir Tomas waiting in the trees outside.

"Davey?"

"This is where I lived for—well, I started sleeping in the cage when I was maybe fourteen? Full time for three years, at least."

"Davey."

"Ida wanted to give me a window, but I told her I'd find a way out of it on a bad day. The pigeons roosted up there." He pointed. "To send messages when she left me, but I kept eating them. And I had cushions in the back corner. They're gone now. I don't know what happened to them."

"Davey," she said again. He turned to look at her.

"Anything we need will be in that drawer behind you. I'm going to see if I can find—if I can find something."

"Are you all right?"

"Check the drawers. I'll be right out."

It was in no way an answer to the question she'd asked. But she did not think she could push him further without panic and tears.

He spoke from within the cage: "She planned this, you know."

"Planned what?"

"Leaving us how she did. So you'd be stuck with me, so you'd have to learn to like me. And so I'd have to cope and grow up."

"Did it work?" There was a bundle of papers in the drawer; she took it and went to the door of the cage.

"Do you like me?"

"Don't be stupid." She sat beside him in the corner. "Of course I like you."

"Am I growing up?"

"Are you coping?"

"Not so well today. But generally—I'm sorry. This isn't—did you find anything?" She handed him the bundle. He loosened the string around it and flipped through, plucking one sheet out and casting the others aside. "This one. We'll need some things. I suppose they're still under the bed. I'll just—I'll—gods. I'm sitting with my wife in my cage. Can we just—can we go home, Marit?"

"Of course. You're all right, Davey. Everything is all right."

"It's a nice cage, as far as cages go. Did I tell you I helped to build it?"

"It's a very nice cage. Let's go home then, yes? We'll just go home."

"Right." He stood up slowly, unsteadily. "Home. No cage at home. Should there be a cage?"

"Davey." She took his arm. "You're all right, sweetie. You're fine. You don't need a cage. You're fine."

"I'm fine," he repeated. "I'm fine."

"Let's go." She took the slip of paper from him and led him out of the cage, then out of the cottage. He stopped in the doorway, gripping the frame to hold himself up. "I never asked her to unlock that door. I didn't want to leave. I never—and I wouldn't fit anymore, so she made me burst through the back. That was poorly done. I could have burst out sooner. If I'd tried."

"Davey—"

Marit caught him as he collapsed, and called for Sir Tomas.

He emerged from the woods. "Is there a problem, Princess?"

"Davey. He just—" She knelt down beside him. "Sweetie, what's wrong? Can you walk? Can you tell me what happened?"

"I'm fine. I'm just—I'm sorry. I'm fine. I—why do I even have to have legs? Was it some kind of trade? We'll take the bloodlust away, but you have to have the legs instead? What kind of a deal is that?"

"Davey, please."

"I'm sorry. Let's just go."

Sir Tomas hovered behind them for the trip back, and Marit worried about what he must have overheard. Davey didn't speak again, and seemed not to have much more trouble than usual walking. He was a little wobbly, perhaps. Back in the room he pulled things from beneath the bed and looked over Ida's paper, taking careful notes. Sometimes he looked up at Marit and smiled. He seemed fine.

Sixth Deleted Scene: The North Wind

Harald's engagement was announced a few days later. Within the week he would be married.

They would have a small wedding. There had been enough of this, Harald had said, in the last year. He did not want a grand ceremony, with the preparation and waiting that would be required. He only wanted to be married. Let the people wonder how he had produced a bride from a world away so quickly. Let them assume she was travelling already when the announcement was made, and wonder that they did not see her ship in the port. He would ride the wind to Suhki, who would be waiting with her bags packed to meet him. She would meet his family when the wind entered through the same large windowed room it had before, and they would have their small ceremony in the chapel, then go upstairs, where she could rest and recover from her journey.

She had been invited to bring members of her own court along, but had wanted only her translator, who had been tutoring her since the arrangements began, so that soon he would not be necessary. The wind had offered to take her family to the wedding, and she had refused. Marit remembered her own refusal, and wondered if it was true that they had not heard, so far south, of the lindworm.

The king and queen had been there to send him off, and now

stood waiting before the open windows, while Marit and Davey sat against the wall, talking in whispers about inconsequential things. Davey had warned them it would be hours, and they should at least sit down if they would not leave. But they had seen their son ride away on the back of the wind, had seen him climb up onto nothing and assure them it was quite solid, and they would not move until they saw him safe on the ground again.

When they finally felt the rush of heat, Davey jumped up and went to the window, Marit close behind. The queen took a step forward, and then Harald was there again, suspended in the sky, a girl and an older man behind him, and a small mountain of boxes and bags. The wind blew into the room, and Harald was laughing.

"How was it?" Davey asked.

Harald jumped down, then lifted Suhki by the waist and brought her to the ground.

She was shorter than Marit, in a dress like nothing she'd ever seen, narrow patterned silk and beautiful, her hair disheveled from riding the wind.

"Wonderful," he said. "Everything was wonderful." He turned to help the other man as well, releasing Suhki reluctantly. "Although having a translator along doesn't do much for romance."

The wind shifted, and Suhki's luggage came tumbling down. Davey went forward to whisper something into it, and then it was gone.

Harald made all of the introductions, and Suhki, smiling, managed their language very well, turning to the interpreter only once or twice. It was a simpler language than most, and she had been practicing for months. Harald tried once to say something in her language, and she laughed at him, and then they went down the hall to be married. Someone would come and deliver their luggage to Harald's rooms.

There were only a few of Harald's friends there, and a few more important members of the court. Trudy came, and called him Harry again, and kissed him on the cheek and congratulated him. Father Gregor performed the ceremony, and it occurred to Marit that she had not seen the other priest in many weeks.

He had almost certainly known the truth about Davey, and he had not been agreeable and kind. He had been a threat.

He had forgiven her hatred on the night of her wedding, and she did not want to know what the king and queen might do to threats.

Harald took Suhki and the translator straight to his rooms when the vows were said, and they did not see them until breakfast the next morning. There were six chairs at the table again, and they came in late. They did not bring the translator. There was no place for him at the table.

Marit tried to imagine being taken from everything she knew, then going down to breakfast in the morning with strangers who had become her family, and no one to speak her language. At least her own new family had been the alternative to something worse. And Ida had come with them to breakfast.

"Good morning Harald," said the queen. "Suhki. Did you sleep well?" Harald told her that they had, and she did not comment on their lateness.

The arrangement of chairs had changed some since the beginning. Marit could not remember when—sometime after Harald had become their friend. They were not divided, three and three, to make sides in some silent battle, but spread evenly about the round table, and Marit was sitting beside the king, and did not mind.

The queen asked Suhki many questions about her journey, many of which Harald answered for her, but she did not seem unhappy. Marit thought the queen was glad to have a real princess there.

They did not see Harald for many days, outside of breakfast and the occasional dinner. He talked to Davey over breakfast, but mostly he was focused on his bride.

He had waited over a year for this.

Seventh Deleted Scene: The Confession

The war council was held in a large room with tables arranged in a circle, the two kings directly across from each other, their people scattered between. Harald sat at his father's right hand, and on his left was the queen, then Davey and Marit, then Suhki and finally Ida, who had no business sitting between the royal family and their ministers. But Ida did as she pleased. Marit stared at the rosemåling on the opposite wall, trying to memorize the details of the pattern.

It was mostly black, with spurts of red that were meant to be flowers.

They were talking about—well, about something. She had not been listening. She had been thinking of milking her cow, with Greta in two braids standing by. She had been thinking of home, which was no longer home. She did not know whether she would go back there, if she lost Davey, or stay here and try to be a princess alone. It was not something they had thought to discuss.

Davey touched her wrist beneath the table, and she looked over at him. He nodded and started to stand.

"Davey..." she whispered.

The queen reached up, her fingers brushing his arm. Marit did not think he had told her what he intended to do. But she must know him well enough now to guess. "David, you don't have to do this."

"Yes. I do." He bent down to kiss Marit, and then he was in the center of the room, the center of attention, and their lives were over.

"My name is David. I am the elder son of King Olaf, and I am the lindworm. I ate your daughter. My family was only foolish enough to love me unconditionally, and the rest of the kingdom has no part in this. Take me and end it."

The room exploded. Everyone was yelling—the enemies demanding immediate action, the court enraged as if they hadn't known all along. Ida and Harald were on their feet, trying to explain, and Marit realized that Davey had never told Ida his plan. The king tried to bring the room to order, deceptively impassive, while the queen stared steadily at Davey, swaying slightly in the center of the room. He didn't turn back. Suhki reached over to grab Marit's hand, and suddenly missing Greta, she squeezed back without looking away from Davey.

He was wearing his new crown, the one set with emeralds. He still didn't look like a prince.

He didn't look like a monster, either.

When the room was calm, it was the queen who stood to speak. "He is our son. I will not pretend that he is innocent in what happened, but it was not his fault alone. We love him as you loved your daughter, and we would ask for your mercy."

Marit heard nothing after that. She was fixed on Davey, on the back of his golden head as he stood still facing the enemy king, and it was only the pressure of Suhki's hand that kept her from running to him.

And then the pressure was gone, and she turned to see Suhki speaking to the queen, who looked small and pale and too much like Davey. She turned back and saw that men had come to stand beside him, and she asked, her voice shrill and too loud in the room gone suddenly silent, "What is happening?"

Harald was beside her in a moment, explaining, "They are

taking him down to the dungeon until something has been decided. There will be several days of negotiations."

"And what will be decided?"

His voice was toneless and steady, and he would not meet her eyes. She thought he was very afraid. "They may take him away with them. He may be beheaded. He may be released. The war may continue. It may end. We may have to pay dearly for the end. We will try to pay with gold, and not with Davey and more blood."

Marit nodded and went to Ida, who stood in front of Davey and three stiff soldiers, talking quickly and in another language. Davey seemed not to be listening, and Ida turned around.

"Marit. I have a plan."

"No plans," Davey said. He started out of the room with the soldiers, and Marit followed, jogging to keep up. She did not know who else might come to the dungeon behind her. She did not care. There would be two guards at all times, one of the men explained—one from each kingdom, to see that the prince was neither harmed nor released.

It was this man who stepped forward to unlock the cell, and Davey stepped calmly into it and dropped to the floor. Marit slipped in at the last minute to sit down beside him.

"Princess," the guard said. She glared up at him, silent, and he locked the door and left. One thing she'd learned about being royalty, at least.

"You're just going to stay with me, then?" Davey put his arm around her waist, smiling slightly, and she leaned into his shoulder. "Perfect. Get someone to poison me, and we could be Loki and Sigyn."

She pulled away.

"What?"

"You're—I think you're enjoying this. Do you really still—How can you—Davey, they could kill you any moment, and you're happy."

He was quiet for a while. Finally he told her, "I thought they would kill me. Immediately. I never thought, when I stood up, that

I would see your face again. And now you're sitting beside me. So yes. I'm happy. They probably will kill me any moment, but I'll be grateful for this extra time with you."

Marit kissed him. "I don't want you to die."

"I never wanted anyone to die."

"You are much kinder than Loki," she said. Loki had wanted death of innocents, or had not minded it. Comparisons to the old gods would get them nowhere, and she wished he could find himself in better stories.

The floor was stone, cold and hard, as were the walls, and there was nothing there worth seeing. She closed her eyes and leaned into him, and they sat together for many hours.

She did not know how long it had been when Suhki came down—only that the guards had changed.

"Come upstairs," she said. "People to talk to."

Marit shook her head. "I can't leave Davey."

"I'll be fine, Marit."

"I will stay with him."

A guard came forward to let her out of the cell, and she kissed Davey before she went. "I'll be back."

Suhki knelt down beside the bars. "I will tell you about the Dragon King of the North Sea," she said.

He would be fine.

♛

She went to dinner, where the king and all his men were waiting to interrogate her about Davey. She saw Ida across the room, and realized that everyone had probably heard her version by now, and that it had probably been a lie.

She told the truth. Let them sort out the conflicting stories for themselves—it might buy Davey more time.

Davey, she thought, would rather they told the truth. He had been trying from the beginning to tell the truth, although perhaps his reasons had changed.

She went back to the prison when dinner was done, and sent Suhki away. Davey sent her away not long after.

"You cannot sleep in a prison cell. We'll gain nothing by both of us suffering."

♕

Marit could not bear to go back to her room alone, and after some wandering found herself outside Harald's door. Suhki let her in, and the three of them sat silent in front of the fire for a long time. Ida appeared, as if by magic, late in the night when they should all have been asleep.

"Davey is all right," she said. "He's sleeping now."

"What will we do?" Harald asked. It was the first time any of them had spoken since Marit entered the room.

"We will be fine," Suhki said. "My father will come with his army and kill them all."

Ida shook her head. "It's too far. The winds cannot transport so many, and Davey will be long dead by the time they have sailed here."

"Davey doesn't want anyone else dead," Marit said.

They didn't listen.

"This is what Davey chose," she said. She did not approve of his choice, any more than the rest of them, but she thought he had the right to make it.

♕

She went back to Davey in the morning, when Harald and Suhki were finally asleep, and Ida had disappeared as Ida did. His two guards stood stoic, and she slipped past them to kneel beside the bars.

"Davey?"

He sat up and smiled at her. He had taken off his jacket—it lay crumpled in the corner, with the crown on top, and his shirt was not tucked in. He looked even less like a prince than he had the day before, and she reached through the bars to grab his hands.

"You must have somewhere else to be," he said.

"Not really."

"You're wearing the same clothes as yesterday, and I don't think you've slept."

"I couldn't."

"I really am fine, Marit."

"I'm not."

"I'm sorry. But we will be fine. Both of us. You should change clothes, and go to breakfast, and come back later with clean clothes for me, yes?"

She nodded slowly. "Yes."

"And don't let Ida hurt anyone on my behalf."

"Yes," she said again, and stood, wondering when Davey had become able to handle what she couldn't.

Acknowledgements:

I would like to take this opportunity to thank all of my supporters on Patreon—Jeff and Sue Prater, Lynn and Lowell Nystrom, Beth and Steve Cragle, sharp_chedder, mushki, DSC, Animone, and Margeling. I would also like to thank Angela Shannon and my entire interim writing workshop class, who edited and critiqued the three drafts of this story I produced in January 2015. We've come a long way since then. I would like to thank my therapist, for pushing me to finally finish the final draft, and Ingram Spark, for the NaNoWriMo winner coupon that made printing the first edition a little more affordable. Finally, thank you to Mark Bruce and Joey Horsman, whose college literature classes helped me to better understand all the weird intricacies of my source material, allowing for a better and more complex adaptation.

www.ingramcontent.com/pod-product-compliance
Lightning Source LLC
Chambersburg PA
CBHW020458310726
48979CB00016B/2700/J